HANGOVER SQUARE

Patrick Hamilton

HANGOVER SQUARE

A story of darkest Earl's Court

Europa
editions

Europa Editions
116 East 16th Street
New York, N.Y. 10003
www.europaeditions.com
info@europaeditions.com

Hamilton, Patrick
Hangover Square

Library of Congress Cataloging in Publication Data is available
ISBN 978-1-933372-06-8

First Edition 2006

Book design by Emanuele Ragnisco
www.mekkanografici.com

Printed in Canada

HANGOVER SQUARE

CONTENTS

NOTE: The quotations from *Roget's Thesaurus* are made by permission of Messrs. Longmans, Green & Co., to whom the author and publishers make grateful acknowledgement.

SCHIZOPHRENIA: . . . a cleavage of the mental functions, associated with assumption by the affected person of a second personality.

Black's Medical Dictionary

THE FIRST PART

CHRISTMAS TRAVEL

Why so pale and wan, fond lover,
  Prythee, why so pale?
Will, if looking well can't move her,
  Looking ill prevail?
  Prythee, why so pale?

Why so dull and mute, young sinner?
Prythee, why so mute?
Will, when speaking well can't win her,
  Saying nothing do't?
Prythee, why so mute?

SIR J. SUCKLING

C *lick!* . . . Here it was again! He was walking along the cliff at Hunstanton and it had come again . . . *Click!* . . . Or would the word "snap" or "crack" describe it better?

It was a noise inside his head, and yet it was not a noise. It was the sound which a noise makes when it abruptly ceases: it had a temporarily deafening effect. It was as though one had blown one's nose too hard and the outer world had suddenly become dim and dead. And yet he was not physically deaf: it was merely that in this physical way alone could he think of what had happened in his head.

It was as though a shutter had fallen. It had fallen noiselessly, but the thing had been so quick that he could only think of it as a crack or a snap. It had come over his brain as a sudden film, induced by a foreign body, might come over the eye. He felt that if only he could "blink" his brain it would at once be dispelled. A film. Yes, it was like the other sort of film, too—a "talkie." It was as though he had been watching a talking film, and all at once the soundtrack had failed. The figures on the screen continued to move, to behave more or less logically; but they were figures in a new, silent, indescribably eerie world. Life, in fact, which had been for him a moment ago a "talkie," had all at once become a silent film. And there was no music.

He was not frightened, because by now he was used to it. This had been happening for the last year, the last two years— in fact he could trace it back as far as his early boyhood. Then it had been nothing so sharply defined, but how well he could remember what he called his "dead" moods, in which he could do nothing ordinarily, think of nothing ordinarily, could not attend to his lessons, could not play, could not even listen to his rowdy companions. They used to rag him until it at last became an accepted thing. "Old Bone" was said to be in one of his "dotty" moods. Mr. Thorne used to be sarcastic. "Or is this one of your—ah—delightfully convenient periods of amnesia, my dear Bone?" But even Mr. Thorne came to accept it. "Extra ordinary boy," he once heard Mr. Thorne say (not knowing that he was overheard), "I really believe it's perfectly genuine." And often, instead of making him look a fool in front of the class, he would stop, give him a curious, sympathetic look, and, telling him to sit down, would without any ironic comment ask the next boy to do what he had failed to do.

"Dead" moods—yes, all his life he had had "dead" moods, but in those days he had slowly slipped into and out of them— they had not been so frequent, so sudden, so dead, so completely dividing him from his other life. They did not arrive with this extraordinary "snap"—that had only been happening in the last year or so. At first he had been somewhat disturbed about it; had thought at moments of consulting a doctor even. But he had never done so, and now he knew he never would. He was well enough; the thing did not seriously inconvenience him; and there were too many other things to worry about— my God, there were too many other things to worry about!

And now he was walking along the cliff at Hunstanton, on Christmas afternoon, and the thing had happened again. He had had Christmas dinner with his aunt, and he had gone out, as he had told her, to "walk it off." He wore a light raincoat. He was thirty-four, and had a tall, strong, beefy, ungainly figure. He had a fresh, red complexion and a small moustache. His eyes were big and blue and sad and slightly bloodshot with beer and smoke. He looked as though he had been to an inferior public school and would be pleased to sell you a secondhand car. Just as certain people look unmistakably "horsey," bear the stamp of Newmarket, he bore the stamp of Great Portland Street. He made you think of road houses, and there are thousands of his sort frequenting the saloon bars of public-houses all over England. His full mouth was weak, however, rather than cruel. His name was George Harvey Bone.

It was, actually, only in the few moments following the sudden transition—the breaking down of the sound track, the change from the talkie to the silent film—that he now ever thought about, or indeed was conscious of—this extraordinary change which took place in his mind. Soon enough he was watching the silent film—the silent film without music—as though there had never been any talkie—as though what he saw had always been like this.

A silent film without music—he could have found no better way of describing the weird world in which he now moved. He looked at passing objects and people, but they had no colour, vivacity, meaning—he was mentally deaf to them. They moved like automatons, without motive, without volition of their own. He could hear what they said, he could understand their words, he could answer them, even; but he did this automatically, without having to think of what they had said or what he was saying in return. Therefore, though they spoke it was as though they had not spoken, as though they had moved their lips but remained silent. They had no valid existence; they were not creatures experiencing pleasure or pain. There was, in fact, no sensation, no pleasure or pain at all in this world: there was only himself—his dreary, numbed, dead self.

There was no sensation, but there was something to be done. Emphatically, most emphatically there was something to be done. So soon as he had recovered from the surprise—but nowadays it was hardly a surprise—of that snap in his head, that break in the sound track, that sudden burst into a new, silent world—so soon as he had recovered from this he was aware that something had to be done. He could not think what it was at first, but this did not worry him. He could never think of it at first, but it would come: if he didn't nag at it, but relaxed mentally, it would come.

For two or three minutes he walked along in a dream, barely conscious of anything. The motion of his body caused his raincoat to make a small thundering noise: his big sports shoes creaked and rustled on the grass of the cliff-top. On his left, down below, lay the vast grey sweep of the Wash under the sombre sky of Christmas afternoon; on his right the scrappy villas in the unfinished muddy roads. A few couples were about, cold, despairing, bowed down by the hopeless emptiness and misery of the season and time of day. He passed a shelter, around which some children were running, firing toy pistols at each other. Then he remembered, without any difficulty, what it was he had to do: he had to kill Netta Longdon.

He was going to kill her, and then he was going to Maidenhead, where he would be happy.

It was a relief to him to have remembered, for now he could think it all out. He liked thinking it out: the opportunity to do so was like lighting up a pipe, something to get at, to get his teeth into.

Why must he kill Netta? Because things had been going on too long, and he must get to Maidenhead and be peaceful and contented again. And why Maidenhead? Because he had been happy there with his sister, Ellen. They had had a splendid fortnight, and she had died a year or so later. He would go on the river again, and be at peace. He liked the High Street, too. He would not drink any more—or only an occasional beer. But first of all he had to kill Netta.

This Netta business had been going on too long. When was he going to kill her? Soon—this year certainly. At once would be best—as soon as he got back to London—he was going back tomorrow, Boxing Day. But these things had to be planned: he had so many plans: too many. The thing was so incredibly, absurdly easy. That was why it was so difficult to choose the right plan. You had only to hit her over the head when she was not looking. You had only to ask her to turn her back to you because you had a surprise for her, and then strike her down. You had only to invite her to a window, to ask her to look down at something, and then throw her out. You had only to put a scarf playfully round her neck, and fondle it admiringly, and then strangle her. You had only to surprise her in her bath, lift up her legs and hold her head down. All so easy; all so silent. Only there would be meddling from the police—"questions asked"—that had to be remembered: he wasn't going to have any questioning or meddling. But then of course the police couldn't find him in Maidenhead, or if they did they couldn't touch him there. No, there was no difficulty anywhere—it was a "cinch," as they said—but it had got to be planned, and he must do the planning now. It had all been going on too long.

When was it to be then? Tomorrow—Boxing Day—as soon as he saw her again. If he could get her alone—why not? No, there was something wrong with that. What was it? What on earth was it? . . . Oh yes—of course—the ten pounds. His aunt had given him ten pounds. She had given him a cheque this morning as a Christmas present. He must wait till he had spent the ten pounds—get the benefit of the ten pounds—before killing Netta. Obviously. What about the New Year, then—January the first? That seemed a good idea—starting the New Year—1939. The New Year—the turn of the year—that meant spring before long. Then it would be warmer, Maidenhead would be warmer. He didn't want to have to go to Maidenhead in the cold. He wanted to go on the river. Then he must wait for the spring. It was too cold to kill Netta yet. That sounded silly, but it was a fact.

Or was all this shilly-shallying on his part? Was he putting it off again? He was always putting it off. In some mysterious way it seemed to go right out of his head, and it had all been going on too long. Perhaps he ought to take himself in hand, and kill her while it was cold. Perhaps he ought not even to wait until he had had the benefit of his ten pounds. He had put it off such a long while now, and if he went on like this would it ever get done?

By now he had reached the edge of the Town Golf Course and he turned round and retraced his steps. A light wind struck him in the face and roared in his ears, and he looked at the feeble sun, in the nacreous sky, declining behind the bleak little winter resort of an aunt who had come up to scratch. Strange aunts, strange Hunstantons!—how did they stand it? He had had three days of it, and he'd have a fit if he didn't get back tomorrow. And yet Aunt Mary was a good sort, trying to do her duty by him as his nearest of kin, trying to be "modern," a "sport" as she called it, pretending that she liked "cocktails" though she was nearly seventy. My God—"cocktails!"— if she only knew! But she was a good sort. She would be cheerful at tea, and then when she saw he didn't want to talk she would leave him alone and let him sit in his chair and read *The Bar 20 Rides Again*, by Clarence Mulford. But of course he wouldn't be reading—he would be thinking of Netta and how and when he was going to kill her.

The Christmas Day children were still playing with their Christmas Day toy pistols around the Christmas Day shelter. The wet grass glowed in the diffused afternoon light. The little pier, completely deserted, jutted out into the sea, its silhouette shaking against the grey waves, as though it trembled with cold but intended to stay where it was to demonstrate some principle. On his left he passed the Boys' School, and then the row of boarding-houses, one after another, with their mad names; on his right the putting course and tennis courts. But no boys, and no boarders, and no putters, and no tennis players in the seaside town of his aunt on Christmas Day.

He turned left, and went upwards and away from the sea—the Wash in which King John had lost his jewels—towards the street which contained the semi-detached villa in which tea, with Christmas cake and cold turkey (in front of an electric fire at eight o'clock), awaited him.

CHAPTER TWO

Click! . . .

Hullo, hullo—here we are!—here we are again!

He was on Hunstanton Station and it had happened again. Click, snap, pop—whatever you like—and it all came flooding back!

The sound track had been resumed with a sudden switch; the grim, dreary, mysterious silent film had vanished utterly away, and all things were bright, clear, vivacious, sane, colourful and logical around him, as he carried his bag, at three o'clock on Boxing Day, along the platform of the little seaside terminus.

It had happened at the barrier, as he offered his ticket to be clipped by the man. You might have thought that the click of the man's implement as he punctured the ticket had been the click inside his head, but actually it had happened a fraction of a second later—a fraction of a fraction of a second, for the man still held his ticket, and he was still looking into the man's grey eyes, when he heard the shutter go up in his head, and everything came flooding back.

It was like bursting up into fresh air after swimming gravely for a long time in silent, green depths: the first thing of which he was aware was the terrific sustained hissing noise coming from the engine which was to take him back to London. While he yet looked into the man's eyes he was aware of this noise. He knew, too, perfectly well, that this noise had been going on ever since he had entered the station, while he was buying his ticket, while he was dragging his bag to the barrier. But it was only now, now that his brain had clicked back again, that he heard it. And with it every other sort of noise which had been going on before—the rolling of a station trolley, the clanking of milkcans, the slamming of compartment doors—was heard by him for the first time. And all this in the brief moment while he still looked into the eyes of the man who had punctured his ticket. Perhaps, because of his surprise at what had happened, he had looked into the eyes of the man too long. Perhaps the man had only caught his eye, had only looked at him because he had subconsciously wondered why this passenger was not getting a "move on." However that might be, he had only betrayed himself for a fraction of a second, and now he was walking up the platform.

What a noise that engine made! And yet it exhilarated him. He always had these few moments of exhilaration after his brain had "blinked" and he found himself hearing and understanding sounds and sights once again. After that first tremendous rush of noise and comprehension—exactly like the roar of clarification which would accompany the snatching away, from a man's two ears, of two oily blobs of cotton wool which he had worn for twenty-four hours—he took a simple elated pleasure in hearing and looking at everything he passed.

Then there was the pleasure of knowing exactly what he was doing. He knew where he was, and he knew what he was doing. It was Boxing Day, and he was taking the train back to London. He had spent the Christmas holiday with his aunt who had given him ten pounds. This was a station— Hunstanton station where he had arrived. Only it had been night when he arrived. Now he was catching the 3.4 in the afternoon. He must find a third-class compartment. Other people were going back to London, too. The engine was letting out steam, as engines will, as engines presumably have to before they start. That was a porter, whose business it was to carry luggage, and who collected a tip for doing so. There was the sea. This was a seaside town on the east coast. It was all right: it was all clear in his head again.

What, then, had been happening in his head a few moments before—and in the long hours before that? What? . . . Well, never mind now. There was plenty of time to think about that when he had found a compartment. He must find an empty one so that he could be by himself. If he had any luck, he might be alone all the way to London—there oughtn't to be many people travelling on Boxing Day.

He walked up to the far end of the train, and selected an empty compartment. As he turned the handle of this, the hissing of the engine abruptly stopped. The station seemed to reel at the impact of the sudden hush, and then, a moment later, began to carry on its activities again in a more subdued, in an almost furtive way. That, he realized, was exactly like what happened in his head—his head, that was to say, when it went the other way, the nasty way, the bad, dead way. It had just gone the right way, and he was back in life again.

He put his suit-case on the rack, clicked it open, and stood on the seat to see if he had packed his yellow-covered *The Bar 20 Rides Again*. He had. It was on the top. It was wonderful how he did things when he didn't know what he was doing. (Or did he, at the time, in some way know what he was doing? Presumably he did.) Anyway, here was his *Bar 20*. He clicked the bag shut again, sat down, pulled his overcoat over his legs, put the book on his lap, and looked out of the window.

He was back in life again. It was good to be back in life. And yet how quiet and dismal it was in this part of the world. The trolley was still being rolled about the platform at the barrier end of the station; two porters were shouting to each other in the distance; another porter came along trying all the doors, reaching and climactically trying his own handle, and fading away again in a series of receding jabs; he could hear two people talking to each other through the wooden walls of the train, two compartments away; and if he listened he could hear, through the open window, the rhythmic purring of the mud-coloured sea, which he could see from here a hundred yards or so beyond the concrete front which was so near the station as to seem to be almost part of it. Not a soul on the front. Cold and quiet. And the sea purred gently. Dismal, dismal, dismal.

He listened to the gentle purring of the sea, and waited for the train to start, his red face and beer-shot eyes assuming an expression of innocent vacancy and misery.

CHAPTER THREE

The train shuddered once or twice, and slid slowly out towards Heacham.

He put his feet up on the seat opposite, adjusted his body comfortably against the window, and looked idly at his shoes. Something in the sight of the pattern of the brogue on the brown leather all at once gave him a miserable feeling—a little clutch at his heart followed by an ache. For a brief moment he was at a loss to account for this pain: then he realized what it was and all his misery was upon him again. *Netta! Netta! . . .*

He had forgotten! . . . For a whole five minutes—while he had walked up that platform and found a compartment, and taken his book from the suitcase, and looked out of the window while he waited for the train to start he had been somehow tricked into not thinking about Netta! A record, certainly! . . . And he had been reminded of her by the sight of his own shoes. It was because the brogue on his own brown shoes was exactly the same as the brogue on the new brown shoes she had begun wearing a week or so ago. He had noticed the similarity when they were sitting in the Black Hart having gins-and-tonic that morning after that awful blind when Mickey had passed out in the taxi. A nice state of affairs, when you're so in love with a girl that the sight of your own shoes tears your heart open!

Such was the awful associative power of physical love. He took his feet down, because he knew he could no longer catch a glimpse of his own shoes without incurring the risk of being pained.

Five minutes' respite, breathing space—well, that was something—getting on! But wait a moment—what about his "dead" period? Did he think about Netta in his "dead" moods? Or did that strange shutter which fell, that film which came over his brain, somehow cut him off from Netta, from the preoccupation of his days and nights? Perhaps it did—perhaps it was a sort of anaesthetic which Nature had contrived to prevent him going dotty through thinking about Netta. But then if he had not been thinking about Netta, what had he been thinking about? And that reminded him. He had asked himself just that question as he walked up the platform, and he had promised himself to seek an answer to it.

Well, then, what *had* he been thinking about—what went on in his head when the shutter was down? What? What?

It was no good. He had no idea. Not the vaguest idea. This was awful. He must try and think. He really must try and think. But what was the use of thinking? He never could remember, so why should he remember now?

When did it start, anyway? How long had he been "under"? It had been a long time this time, he was certain of that. It went right back into yesterday. What could he remember of yesterday—Christmas Day? He could remember lunch—"Christmas Dinner" as it was called—with his aunt. He could remember that clearly. He could remember the ultra-clean tablecloth, the unfamiliar wine-glasses, the turkey, and the mince-pies. Then he could remember having coffee afterwards. And then he said he would go and "walk it off" and his aunt went up to her bedroom to sleep. He could remember putting on his raincoat in the hall. He could remember going down towards the sea, and then walking along the cliff towards the Golf Course . . . Ah! There you were! That was it. It must have happened while he was walking along the cliff. Yes. He was sure of it. He could see himself. He could almost hear it happening in his head, as he walked along the cliff and looked out towards the sea. Snap. But what then? What? . . . Nothing. A blank. Absolutely nothing. Nothing until he suddenly "woke up," about ten minutes ago on Hunstanto station—"woke up" to find himself looking into the eyes of the man who was clipping his ticket, and hearing the fearful hissing noise of that engine.

Good God—he had been "out" for twenty-four hours!—from about three o'clock on Christmas afternoon to three o'clock on Boxing Day. This was awful. Something ought to be done about it. He ought to go and see a doctor or something.

What was he *thinking* about all that time—what was he *doing*? That was the point—what was he *doing*? It was terrifying—not to know what you thought or did for twenty-four hours. A day out of your life! He could be terrified now, he could let himself be terrified—but the thing had been happening so often recently that it had lost its terrors, and he had too many other worries. He had Netta to worry about. That was one thing about Netta—you couldn't worry about much else.

But, really, it was awful—he ought to do something about it. Imagine it—wandering about like an automaton, a dead person, another person, a person who wasn't you, for twenty-four hours at a stretch! And when you woke up not the minutest inkling of what the other person had been thinking or doing. You might have done anything. You might, for all you knew, have got madly drunk. You might have had a fight, and got in trouble. You might have made friends or enemies you knew nothing about. You might have got off with a girl, and arranged to meet her. You might, in some mad lark, have stolen some thing from a shop. You might have committed assault. You might have done something dreadful in public. You might, for all you knew, be a criminal maniac. You might have murdered your aunt!

On the other hand it was pretty obvious that you were not a criminal maniac—and that you had not had a fight, or done anything dreadful in public, or murdered your aunt. For if you had people would have stopped you, and you would not be sitting comfortably in a third-class carriage on your way back to London. And that went for all the other times in the near and distant past—all the "dead" moods you had had ever since they had begun. You had never been arrested so far, you had never shown any signs of having been in a fight, and none of your relations and friends had been murdered!

Your friends and relations, in fact (though they certainly recognized and sometimes chaffed you for your "dead" or "dumb" moods), had never accused you of doing anything in the slightest way abnormal: nor had anyone whom you didn't know ever claimed to know you.

It was, indeed, abundantly clear from all the evidence that when the shutter was down he behaved like a perfectly reasonable, if somewhat taciturn, human being. How else could he have got to the station? How else could he have packed his bag and put *The Bar 20 Rides Again* on top so that he could take it out to read in the train? How could he have bought his ticket—known where he was going? No—there was nothing to worry about. He had thought out all this before, and he had always known there was nothing to worry about.

It just was that he wished to God he could remember what he had been doing and what he had been thinking.

Chapter Four

The train, rattling in gentle unison with his thoughts as it slid over the surface of the cold, flat, Boxing-Day bungalow-land of this portion of the coast, began to slow down, and then stopped at its first stop, Heacham.

There was a gloomy pause. Then the handle of his door was rudely and ruthlessly seized, and a cold woman, seeming to bring with her all the pain and bleakness of the Norfolk winter outside, violated his centrally-heated thought-closet.

She was apparently of the servant class, and as soon as she had entered she lowered the window and began talking volubly to a friend on the platform, who had come to see her off. This woman on the platform wore no hat, he noticed, in spite of the cold; but instead of that she wore a hair-net over her hair. He looked at this hair-net with dull misery in his heart. Even after the train had started, and the woman had vanished, he retained a picture of the hair-net, and wondered why it made him miserable, why he hated the woman for wearing it, why he obscurely felt she had been giving him cause for resentment.

Net . . . It dawned on him. Of course, that was it. Net. Which equalled Netta . . . He had been quite right: the woman *had* been hurting him—she had been trying, all the time as she talked to her friend, to remind him of Netta.

Oh dear—these horrible off-hand strangers, who knew nothing of Netta, who would care nothing about Netta even if they did, but who yet had the power to remind him of Netta, and obscurely torture him by wearing hair-nets! . . .

Netta. Nets. Netta. A perfectly commonplace name. In fact, if it did not happen to belong to her, and if he did not happen to adore her, a dull, if not rather stupid and revolting name. Entirely unromantic—spinsterish, mean—like Ethel, or Minnie. But because it was hers look what had gone and happened to it! He could not utter it, whisper it, think of it without intoxication, without dizziness, without anguish. It was incredibly, inconceivably lovely—as incredibly and inconceivably lovely as herself. It was unthinkable that she could have been called anything else. It was loaded, overloaded with voluptuous yet subtle intimations of her personality. Netta. The tangled net of her hair—the dark net—the brunette. The net in which he was caught—netted. Nettles. The wicked poison-nettles from which had been brewed the potion which was in his blood. Stinging nettles. She stung and wounded him with words from her red mouth. Nets. Fishing-nets. Mermaid's nets. Bewitchment. Syrens—the unearthly beauty of the sea. Nets. Nest. To nestle. To nestle against her. Rest. Breast. In her net. Netta. You could go on like that for ever—all the way back to London.

But if you weren't in love with her—what then? Net profit? *2s. 6d.* Net? Nestlé's milk chocolate? Presumably. But in that case, of course, you wouldn't think about it at all. It was only because you were crazy about her you went on like this. So crazy that your heart sank when you saw your own shoes, or looked at a woman wearing a hair-net on Heacham station.

Crazy. Perhaps he was really crazy—dotty. With these awful "dead" moods of his—twenty-four-hour slices of life concerning which he remembered nothing—you could hardly call him normal. But he had been into all that and decided there was nothing to worry about. No. He was sane enough. If you didn't count the "dead" moods he was sane enough. In fact, he was probably too sane, too normal. If only he was a little more erratic, if only he had a little fire, a little originality or audacity, it might have been a different story. A different story with Netta and all along the line.

He was, of course, completely without ambition. He wasn't like Netta. He didn't want to hang about film people and theatre people and try to make a lot of money easily. He didn't want anything, except Netta. She, of course, would hoot with laughter if she knew what he really wanted. He wanted a cottage in the country—yes, a good old cottage in the country—and he wanted Netta as his wife. No children. Just Netta—and to live with her happily and quietly ever afterwards. He would love her, physically love her, even when she was old. He was certain of that, though sophistication condemned the idea as absurd. She was, to him, so utterly different from any other girl that the thought of tiring of her physically was unimaginable.

And how she would jeer at him if she knew this was what he wanted—how they would all jeer at him. "I believe poor old George," he could hear Peter saying, "wants you to go down into the country and be a milk-maid or something." And yet he wouldn't mind betting that half the men who were, or had been, in love with Netta wanted very little else—the trouble was they wouldn't admit it.

But they could hide it successfully—which was what, apparently, he couldn't do. Maybe that was because they didn't feel it as deeply, want it as badly, as he did. He couldn't hide it. He had no illusions about himself: he knew exactly what she and all that Earl's Court gang thought of him. They saw him as a poor, dumb, adoring, obvious, cow-like appendage to Netta—ever-present or ever-turning-up. And then there were his "dead" moods, which were a popular joke—a "scream." Dead-from-the-neck-upwards—that was him. Somebody you could really dismiss with easy conviction as an awful fool—a b.f. It was like that at school from Mr. Thorne onwards; it was like that now.

And yet he wasn't such a fool, either. They thought him silly, but he had his own thoughts, and maybe he thought them silly too. They wouldn't think of that, of course: it wouldn't cross their minds. But he had his thoughts all the same. He saw much more than they thought he saw. They would get the shock of their lives if they knew how he could see through them at times—how transparent they were, for all their saloon-bar nonchalance and sophistication.

He could see through them, and, of course, he hated them. He even hated Netta too—he had known that for a long time. He hated Netta, perhaps, most of all. The fact that he was crazy about her physically, that he worshipped the ground she trod on and the air she breathed, that he could think of nothing else in the world all day long, had nothing to do with the underlying stream of scorn he bore towards her as a character. You might say he wasn't really "in love" with her: he was "in hate" with her. It was the same thing—just looking at his obsession from the other side. He was netted in hate just as he was netted in love. Netta: Netta: *Netta!* . . . God—how he loved her!

He hated himself, too. He didn't pretend to be any better. He hated himself for the life he led—the life in common with them. Drunken, lazy, impecunious, neurotic, arrogant, pub-crawling cheap lot of swine—that was what they all were. Including him and Netta. She was an awful little drunk, though she had a marvellous head. She never got up till half-past twelve: just chain-smoked in bed till it was time to drop over and into the nearest pub (only she had to have a man to take her over, because she didn't want to be taken for a prostitute). And she was the daughter of a clergyman in Somerset. Now deceased!

When you met in the morning, all you talked about was last night—how "blind" you were, how "blind" Mickey was, my God, you bet he had a hangover. ("Taking a little stroll round Hangover Square"—that was Mickey's crack.) So-and-so might have been "comparatively sober," etc., etc. And when you had

had a lot more to drink you felt fine again, and went crashing round to lunch upstairs at the Black Hart (the table by the fire) where you ragged the pale waiter and called attention to yourselves. (Of course the tradespeople and commercial gents stared at Netta because she was so lovely and striking.)

He hated it and was sick of it. How long had it been going on? Over a year now—he had known Netta over a year. And when would it ever stop? Never, of course. So long as Netta willed it, so long as she chose to live the life she was living now, never. In the early days he still thought of getting a job in spite of her, still hoped that something would turn up, that he would somehow get his life straight again. But he had given up all hope of that now. He wouldn't look at a job—he couldn't look at one. In that matter he was atrophied. What!—get a job and not be on the spot in the mornings to take her over for her drinks? Get a job and leave her to Mickey and Peter all the day!

And yet he wasn't such a fool even here. He wasn't utterly improvident like they were. He had still got a bit of his mother's money left. He had got three hundred pounds in War Loan and seventy-eight pounds twelve and threepence above that in current account. That wasn't much, when it was all you had against starvation, but if he could live down to four pounds a week (and he somehow did manage, or nearly manage, to do this in spite of everything) it would keep you going a long while. Keep you going until all this Netta business somehow ended, if it ever somehow did—keep you going till you somehow got a job again, if you ever somehow did. He was never going to touch that three hundred pounds if he could help it, and he was going to go on living down to four pounds a week. Two pounds a week for living, two pounds for drinks and smokes and Netta. (And ten pounds extra now, to spend all on smokes and drinks and Netta!)

They, of course, would yell at this providence of his—regard it as meanly cautious, middle-class, poor-spirited, all part of his general "dumbness." It was one of their greatest boasts, one of their major affectations, that they were always broke, always "touching" people—that you would go out and spend your last twelve shillings on a bottle of gin rather than get in groceries. They thought this was clever, and that he was less clever than them. But actually he was one cleverer, because he could see what affectation it was on their part—he could see through them. He was one ahead of them, not one behind.

Not that any of them knew anything in a concrete way about his money. They only knew that he tried to live down to a regular something every week, and despised him as a hoarder. But that was not going to stop him.

It wasn't much, but if it got too low he could live on less, spin it out till something happened, till something turned up.

Till something turned up! What a hope. What could ever turn up now? The year was dying, dead—what had next year, 1939, in store for him? Netta, drinks and smokes—drinks, smokes, Netta. Or a war. What if there was a war? Yes—if nothing else turned up, a war might.

A filthy idea, but what if a war was what he was waiting for? That might put a stop to it all. They might get him—he might be conscripted away from drinks, and smokes, and Netta. At times he could find it in his heart to hope for a war—bloody business as it all was.

But now, according to them, according to Netta and Peter, there wasn't going to be a war at all. They knew all about it, or were supposed to. But he wasn't such a fool here, either—he could see how their minds worked, with what facility they turned their ignominious desires into beliefs. *He* hadn't fallen for all this "I think it is peace in our time" stuff. But they had —hadn't they just! They went raving mad, they weren't sober for a whole week after Munich—it was just in their line. They *liked* Hitler, really. They didn't hate him, anyway. They liked

Musso, too. And how they cheered old Umbrella! Oh yes, it was their cup of tea all right, was Munich.

But it wasn't his. He didn't know much about politics, he didn't know as much as them (not to talk about, anyway), but he knew that Munich was a phoney business. Fine for an Earl's Court binge, but a phoney business, however much you talked. Shame, that was all he had felt, shame which he couldn't analyse. He had felt it all the time they were getting drunk—in fact he had hardly been able to drink at all himself. He was so ashamed he could hardly look at the pictures . . . All grinning, shaking hands, frock-coats, top-hats, uniforms, car-rides, cheers—it was like a sort of super-fascist wedding or christening. (Peter, of course, *was* a fascist, or had been at one time—used to go about Chelsea in a uniform.) And then home again, newsreels, balconies, "I think it is peace in our time," Mrs. Chamberlain the first lady of the land . . . He was ashamed then, and he was still ashamed.

"Peace in our time" . . . Well, we would see. We would see a lot of things . . . His thoughts flowed on, stopping temporarily and looking outwards, through the window, at each station the train stopped at, then sliding inwards and onwards as the train slid on. Darkness slowly fell, and the train slid on towards London on the night of Boxing Day, 1938. Steam collected on the window, which he rubbed away with his hand, seeing nothing but a blotchy yellow reflection of himself, and the yellow compartment in which he did his thinking.

CHAPTER FIVE

The wheels and track clicked out the familiar and unmistakable rhythm—the sly, gentle, suggestive rhythm, unlike any of its others, of a train entering a major London terminus, and he was filled with unease and foreboding as he always was by this sound. Thought and warmth must give place to action in cold streets—reality, buses, tubes, booking-offices, life again, electric-lit London, endless terrors.

Oh dear!—here we were—here was the platform under the huge roof—hollow, hellish echoing noises as in a swimmingbath, and the porters lined up for the attack—no getting out of it now! Foreboding gave place almost to panic. Liverpool Street. Where was he going? What was his plan of campaign? He realized he had made none. He was going along to Netta's, of course, but would she be there? She had said she would, but only in an off-hand way. She never said she'd be anywhere save in an off-hand way. Boxing Night! Of course, she wouldn't be there! She would go out somewhere on Boxing Night, Peter would take her out! She'd be out dancing—people danced on Boxing Night—out with Peter doing God knows what. What was he to do if he found she was gone? This was terrible. He must get over there at once, and find out the worst.

He let the other people get out of the compartment and then rose and stretched his arms up to put *The Bar 20 Rides Again* back into his suitcase on the rack. "Porter, sir?"—"No, thanks. I can manage, thanks." The man went off in a hurt silence. Unpleasant. He stepped onto the platform.

What now? It was half past six. Underground? Central London, and then change at Notting Hill? Unthinkable! In his present state of suspense he couldn't bear it. It must be a taxi. That was what the ten pounds was for, wasn't it? But where to? Straight to Netta's, or back to his hotel first, to leave his bag? Yes, he'd better go to his hotel first. He could have a wash there, and then stroll round to Netta's, fairly composed and clean.

He walked out of the station, and got a floating taxi outside the Great Eastern Hotel. "I want to go to Earl's Court. Do you know Fauconberg Square?" "*Yessir!*"—"Well, it's the Fauconberg Hotel—you'll find it."—"*Yessir—rightsir!*" The man bent down his meter with cheerful briskness, and by his delighted, amiable demeanour, cancelled the unpleasantness of the hurt porter on the platform. The toilers were on his side again.

The City was mauve, misty, empty, cold. Boxing Day. In less than a minute, it seemed, they were jogging and rattling past the Bank. They wouldn't be long at this rate. The lights were going nicely with them, too—shining out with brilliant friendliness like bottles in a chemist's shop.

He was an awful fool to be taking a taxi like this. It was all very well to say he had that ten pounds, but he wouldn't have it if he went on like this. This would be six bob at least—probably seven with the tip. Nearly half of one of your ten pounds gone already!

Why had he taken a taxi! Why did he get into "states" like this? He had suddenly got into a state of panic because he had thought Netta might not be in her flat, and he couldn't wait to find out, couldn't stand a train with a change. But what did it matter if Netta wasn't in her flat? There was tomorrow, there was the day after, there was all next year. Why should he want to see Netta tonight? He wasn't sure that he did want to see her; he would almost certainly go to bed happier if he didn't. But he had got into a state and was rushing to her in a taxi. He was an awful fool.

How empty and bleak the streets were, and how he loathed his shut, shuttered, super-Sunday—the Christmas Holiday. He supposed it was all right for people who had to work all the year, but it made him feel terrible. Thank God it would all be over tomorrow. And Boxing Day wasn't quite as ghastly and undayish as Christmas Day. The pubs were open normally—none of that awful seven-to-ten business. In fact, the pubs were open already. That was a good thought. As soon as he got inside a pub tonight, it would be all right. After that he had only to get home and to bed, and then wake up to a normal world again tomorrow.

The fare came to six shillings and sixpence, and he gave a shilling to the man, who seemed to like it all right: he was obviously a cheerful man by nature. He went up the steps, and into the Fauconberg. He had to pass through the lounge on his way upstairs. It was all decorated for Christmas (he had forgotten that, although he had seen it decorated before he went away), and the only people about were some children who were trying to play blow-football (evidently a Christmas present) on one of the green baize tables normally used for bridge. He knew nobody in the little hotel—the large glorified boarding-house—and he did not mean to. He just slept in a small room at the top, and came down to breakfast when everyone else had gone. For the rest he slunk in and out, only exchanging the time of day with the gloomy porter.

He did a bit of unpacking, and washed in the bathroom along the passage—there was only a jug and basin in his room. He came back and brushed his hair, peering into the wardrobe mirror in the pink light of the fly-blown bulb. He had some gin left in a quarter bottle, and poured a double into his tooth glass, adding water from the glass bottle. He polished his shoes with a light-brown, polish-smeared pad he had got from Woolworth's. Then he put on his tweed overcoat, put up its collar, looked in the mirror again, and decided not to wear a hat. He went downstairs, through the lounge again, and out into the street.

He turned into Earl's Court Road, and walked down towards the station. He passed the station and contemplated having a drink at one of the pubs on the right. No—he might miss her. It was a quarter past seven—she didn't usually go out till about half past. He crossed over Cromwell Road, and looked up to see if there was a light in her flat. He couldn't see one—but you often couldn't if the curtains were properly drawn.

He hoped to God the front door wouldn't be locked, as then he would have to ring, and be let in by that beastly woman. He felt curiously numb. He often did feel numb like this, just before meeting her.

No, the door was not locked. The passage was in darkness, but there was enough light on the first floor landing to enable him to see his way. Her flat was on the top floor. As he climbed up he saw there was a light on her landing. Then, as he climbed the last stairs, he saw that her front door was ajar, and, looking through, he saw the sitting-room door was also ajar, and he caught a glimpse of Peter, talking at the mantelpiece with a glass of beer in his hand.

He knocked with the brass knocker. "Bang-tiddy-bang-bang bang, bang." He saw Peter look in his direction, and he walked in.

"Good evening, chum," said Peter, who had been doing this Syd Walker stuff for a week or so now. "Here's our old Pal, George Harvey Bone . . . Lumme—he don't half get into some funny how-d'ye-do's—don't 'e?"

Though this was said in a superficially friendly and rallying way, he noticed that Peter betrayed, in his look, his dislike and scorn of him. He always gave him this look when he hadn't seen him for a few days. It was a bullying, appraising, remembering look. He nearly always called him George Harvey Bone, too, and the tone in which he said this was appraising, remembering, bullying.

"Hullo," he said, smiling and feigning heartiness. "How *are* we? Hullo, Netta."

He dropped his voice as he greeted Netta, and caught her eye shyly, and looked away again. When meeting her after a parting of any length, he never dared to look at her fully, to take her in, all at once. He was too afraid of her loveliness—of being made to feel miserable by some new weapon from the arsenal of her beauty—something she wore, some fresh look, or attitude, or way of doing her hair, some tone in her voice or light in her eye—some fresh "horror" in fact.

"Hullo, *Bone*," she said from the depths of her armchair. The game of calling people by their surnames, like the Syd Walker business, had been going on for about a week too. He noticed that in her tone and her glance she also conveyed something of what Peter had conveyed in his. There was a difference, however. Where Peter had shown his scorn and dislike, she showed scorn practically without dislike. There was merely cold indifference, mixed, possibly, with a fear of being bored by him, and a slight resentment towards him for being the cause of this fear.

She uttered the word "Bone" with an ironical firmness and emphasis which deliberately brought out the latent absurdity of the word—made you think of dog-bones or ham-bones or rag-and-bone men. This did not displease him at all, however. She had many moods worse than her ironical one. Irony, in fact, was usually a sign of fairly good weather. It might even burst forth into the brief, holy sunshine of kindness.

"So you've got back?" said Peter. "Or so it appears."

"Yes, it seems I've got back."

He smiled again, and looked at Peter so that he didn't have to look at her—in very much the same way as a shy person, having been introduced to a stranger by a friend, looks hard at his friend while the three of them talk, makes his friend's eyes his anchor.

Peter now stood leaning against the mantelpiece, the glass of beer in his hand, warming his legs at the gas-fire. Underneath his grey check jacket he wore a navy blue sweater with a polo collar. On top of this collar was his nasty fair face, with its nasty fair "guardsman's" moustache, which, in combination with his huge sneering chin, made him look not unlike the Philip IV of Velasquez. George could never look at Peter, after having been away from him for any time, without realizing what a formidable, sullen, brooding and curiously evil man this was, behind his off-hand yet fairly good-mannered exterior. Who was he, and where did he come from? He had always been there: he had known him as long as he had known Netta. And yet he knew nothing about him. Above all, what was there between these two, behind the appearance of there being nothing whatever?

He believed, on the whole, that the appearance reflected the reality that there was nothing. But he never found them together without wondering.

He now glanced at Netta, to see if something in her appearance might enlighten him. But she gave nothing away as usual. She lay in the armchair holding a glass of beer on one of its sides, and looking into the gas-fire. She was hardly made up at all, and had an appearance of not having quite finished dressing. She was wearing her dark-brown knitted frock—one which contrived to give him, perhaps, more pain than any of her others—and instead of shoes she wore loosely some red slippers he had not seen before. These matched a red scarf she had put round her neck. He realized that the matching of these two—the red slippers with the red scarf—together with her dark brown dress, and dark eyes and hair—furnished the fresh "horror" he had been awaiting. Although she was not made up, although she was untidy and not trying, she agonized him with the unholy beauty of her red scarf matching her red slippers on her dark self.

She looked, in point of fact, something more than untidy: she looked ill. And he had no doubt she was, very. She and Peter would certainly have been drinking heavily all over Christmas, and the hangover would now be at its dreariest. On countless occasions he had seen her like this, staring into her gas-fire at seven o'clock, waiting to go out and get lit up again. That gas-fire—what sinister, bleak misery emanated from its sighing throat and red, glowing asbestos cells! To those whom God has forsaken is given a gas-fire in Earl's Court.

On the mat in front of the fire was a quart bottle of Watney's Ale. The room was in a state of disorder, and had not been dusted. There were ash-trays full of stubs all over the place, some unwashed, finger-smeared tumblers, and a tea-tray with cups full of old wet leaves. Mrs. Chope had evidently not been in, and Netta never did anything for herself. The room, which she had taken furnished, contained a table, a sideboard, a radiogram, a large settee and two armchairs. A door led from it into her bedroom. You had to go out into the passage to the bathroom and a small kitchen.

"Have some Pale Ale," said Netta, pointing to the bottle with a kick of her red-slippered foot. "You'll find a glass somewhere."

"Thanks," he said, and fetched a glass from the sideboard and came back to fill it on the mantelpiece.

"Well," said Peter, "how's Hunstanton? Bracing as ever?"

"Most," he said. "Well—here's how." And he drank.

"And did your efforts result in pecuniary advantage," asked Peter, "as predicted?"

"Yes. Most successful."

"How much?"

"Ten pounds."

"Ah. Good work."

They knew he had gone to Hunstanton to get money from his aunt—to "touch" her. They had all, and that included himself, made a joke of it. But now, remembering the friendly, kindly woman who had given him the money, who had offered him her seaside hospitality and tried to please him and be "modern" by giving him "cocktails," he was ashamed. That quite pleasant and not undignified little week-end was now lost and to be forgotten forever—converted into a small, cynical joke, to be offered up to the beast Peter and the cruel, dissipated Netta on the altar of a gas-fire in Earl's Court.

"You must have been having one of your brighter periods," said Netta.

"Yes. I was quite bright."

"Not in one of your famous stooge moods?" said Peter.

"What do you mean," he said, "'stooge' moods?"

He knew, of course, what Peter meant. He meant one of his

dumb moods, his "dead" periods. But he had to ask him what he meant out of politeness to respond to the fairly friendly raillery which Netta and Peter had begun.

"Oh," said Peter, "just 'stooge' moods."

"What *is* a 'stooge', anyway?" he asked.

"A dumb person," said Netta in her precise, firm voice. "A feed to a comedian. A butt."

"So I'm a stooge, am I?"

"No. You're not a stooge," said Netta. "It's just that you have 'stooge' moods."

"Well, I can't help it."

"No, honestly, George," said Peter, pouring out some more beer for himself, "what *are* you thinking about when you go all dead like that?"

"Dead like what?"

"Yes," said Netta, "*I'd* like to know what's going on in his head."

"Going on in my head, when?"

"When you go all dumb, and don't talk, and look all vague and automatic."

"Surely a fellow's allowed to be a bit quiet and thoughtful at times."

"Quiet and thoughtful!" said Netta.

"He's probably working out some abstruse mathematical problem," said Peter.

"Yes," said Netta, "or perhaps he's a Trappist Monk or something . . . Vows himself to periods of silence."

"No, it couldn't be that," said Peter, "because he does *answer*. It's just that he's in a dream."

"A somnambulist," said Netta.

"Well, first of all I'm a stooge, and now I'm a somnambulist," he said. "Which is it to be?"

"Neither," said Netta, "just a bloody fool, generally."

And at this they all laughed.

"No, honestly," said Peter, "I wish I knew what went on in your head."

"Oh—I don't know," he said, and by now he wanted to change the subject. For the truth of the matter was, of course, that he had not the slightest conception of what went on in his head at those times, and if he admitted as much to Netta she might think he was ill, or even a little mad. And, if she thought that, she would be able to despise him as an ineffectual human being even more cruelly and destructively than she did already. He had to go on pretending that these moods arose from sheer preoccupation or indifference. Apart from all this, he was genuinely somewhat worried about himself in this matter, and, because he was worried about it, the subject was distasteful to him.

And he said, "Oh—I don't know . . ." and tried to change the subject. "Well, Netta," he said, "how have you been getting on?"

"Excellently, thank you, Bone," said Netta, in that crisp, conclusive tone which she commonly employed when snubbing him, and there was a slightly awkward pause, as it was now clear to all three that he had been caught trying to change the subject.

"Poor old George," said Peter, "I believe he's getting livid with us."

"I suppose," said Netta, still looking into the fire, "that it's because he's so big that he's so silly."

A perfectly off-hand and unstudied observation, yet such was his state, it made his heart leap up in hope and joy. It was the kindest, most cordial thing she had said for weeks. It was the mention of his bigness which particularly delighted him, the naming and friendly admission of his one physical asset. In his very few successes with women in the past, the thing had always begun with his humorous disparagement of his bigness: he was "vast," "huge," "terrific," "simply enormous, of course." And now Netta had called him big and silly—a perfect combination in the language and tradition of flirtation. Could all be lost, if she could still call him big and silly? He looked at her again, trying to read his fate, to find some sign of change of heart, in some look on her face. But as usual there was nothing there: she put out her cigarette in an ash-tray on the armchair, and got up and began to adjust her hair in the mirror over the fireplace.

As he himself was standing at the mantelpiece she was now less than two feet away from him, and here was another ordeal. There was, he knew now, a definite sphere of sexual attraction, a halo, a field of physical and magnetic influence, which Netta carried about with her wherever she walked. This invisible yet palpable influence petered out at a certain distance, about two feet away from her body, which was its centre and source. So if he kept out of range, if he was more than two feet away from her, he was secure from its effects. But if he went towards her and into it, or she came towards him and either consciously or unconsciously smote him with it, he was made to suffer indescribable things. Within this appalling area his love and physical longing for her took on a frightful increase, underwent a complete qualitative change: giddiness supervened; he was in a world in which he could hardly breathe or think, in which he was choked by the mist of his sensuous anguish. And since the only means of abating this anguish, of turning it into delirious joy, was to seize her in his arms and crush her to himself, and since this means was not open to him, all he could do was to stand still in a state of paralysis and suspense, trying to compose his features, trying to appear normal so as not to give himself away, meanwhile praying that she would release him by walking away, he himself not having the physical strength to do so.

Whether she herself was aware of this two-foot emanation from herself, this imprisoning field of radiance, he never knew. Probably at times she did, and at times she did not. At any rate, she now showed outwardly neither consciousness of what she was doing to him, nor any intention to release him at once. She adjusted her hair with deliberation and a serious profile, and then turned and leaned her back against the mantelpiece. She might have been going to stay there for hours. The next moment, however, she strolled into her bedroom, carrying her halo with her, several yards and a solid doorway now being between him and it.

Thus, having assured him, reminded him, warned him of her power, she allowed him to continue his being as before. The whole process had occupied a very short space of time, and was full of mystery. It was as though a policeman, in the night, had shone his lantern on to a dark doorway, held it there for a little while suspiciously, and then walked on.

CHAPTER SEVEN

He talked quite casually and easily with Peter at the mantelpiece, skilfully emptying from his eyes the anxiety and perturbation caused in his brain by every movement and sound he heard from her bedroom—the shutting of a drawer, the opening of a cupboard, the falling of a shoe—and soon there was another "Bang-tiddy-bang-bang—bang-bang" on the door, and Mickey came in.

Mickey was about twenty-six, short, with a small moustache on a pasty face. The romance and glory of his life were behind him. The romance was still the warm East, where he had been a clerk in a rubber firm, and the glory had been the divine facility of living, women and drinking. Now he was unemployed, and wore an overcoat along the hard, frozen plains of Earl's Court, where he lived on and with his mother. His mother was generous, and he was famous for his drunkenness locally, being particularly welcome in drinking circles, such as the one surrounding Netta, because, by his excesses, he put his companions in countenance, making their own excesses seem small in comparison. Your hangover was never so stupendous as Mickey's, nor your deeds the night before so preposterous. The follies of each individual were forgotten, submerged in his supreme folly; by his own disgrace he brought grace to others. For this reason, if he tried to live soberly, and in the desperation of his self-inflicted illness he was sometimes forced to do this, his friends at once revealed their cold dislike of his change of front, and by combined chaffing and indirect bullying soon forced him to return to the character in which he was of such service to them.

George did not dislike Mickey as he disliked Peter. First of all, he had no uneasiness about him in regard to Netta. Mickey was oddly but quite plainly not interested in her as a girl; when near her it was as though he lacked a sense, he did not respond or vibrate in any perceptible way. George also sometimes thought he could discern in Mickey something of his own private loathing of the life they were all leading, and the same occasional, hopeless aspiration to live otherwise. Finally, he felt there was nothing menacing about Mickey, as there was about Peter (and about Netta, too, if it came to that, in view of her power over him). Mickey and he had, in fact, something in common, if only as two weak characters against these two stronger ones. There was, however, no real liking or sense of friendship between the two: they never met or talked save in a communal way in the presence of others.

Mickey shouted through the bedroom door to Netta, and obtained her permission to help himself to the remains of the quart bottle of Watney. Then the three men talked in a gloomy, desultory way about the defunct Christmas, and the prospects of war in the spring, until Netta came back. She now had on brown shoes and a glorious dark navy blue overcoat, but no hat (she practically never wore a hat), and seemed ready to go out. A few minutes later the electric light and the gas-fire had been turned out, and their voices and footsteps were resounding in the stone passage outside.

Now, as always at this precise historical and geographical moment of the evening, he thought only of manoeuvring for the desired position—a position in which he was either behind or in front, alone with Netta, and so could walk along the pavement talking to her and no one else. He was usually successful enough in his tactics, so successful that he could afford sometimes to do the opposite and force Netta to walk behind or in

front with someone else, so as to snub them if they imagined
that any manoeuvring went on. But tonight he wanted to speak
to her alone (he might not get the chance again when once they
started drinking); and when they were out in the street he managed to get behind with her while Mickey and Peter went on
ahead. Then, as they came to cross the road, he took advantage
of an approaching car to put his hand on her arm and hold her
back, while the other two crossed the road and went ahead
completely out of earshot.

A freshly risen wind, coming straight at them as they walked
along the pavement on the other side, under the dull brightness
of the high electric lamps, was piercingly cold, and he put up
his overcoat collar. She did not seem to feel it. (She didn't seem
to feel anything.) They walked along in silence. They would
walk in silence, he knew, until they reached the pub, unless he
opened the conversation, for when they were alone she never
spoke to him unless he spoke to her. It was, really, beneath her
dignity to do so. Having disgraced himself, having put himself
beyond the pale, by being distractedly in love with her without
inspiring an atom of affection in return, he could no longer
expect the normal amenities of intercourse. Only in an excess
of amiability or generosity might she now treat him as an equal
human being. And he knew that her character was devoid of
amiability and generosity.

When he spoke he came straight to the point.

"Will you come and have a meal with me sometime this
week, Netta?" he said.

"How do you mean, exactly, 'meal'?" she said.

He looked at her and saw from her expression that she really knew what he meant, that she was purposely playing "village
idiot." By the word "meal" he had intended to convey several
things all of which she had apprehended instantly and clearly.

He had meant first of all an evening meal; then he had meant
a private meal, particularly excluding the two men walking on

in front; then he had meant a high-grade meal eaten outside Earl's Court. This meant that they would go to a good West End restaurant (as they had done once or twice before when he had been able to afford it), and this in its turn meant that it would be a meal paid for by the money he had brought back from Hunstanton. All these things they both knew, but she was playing village idiot just to make sure, and also to ascertain to what restaurant he meant to invite her. He was aware that, if it was to be in the West End, she was not going to put up with something moderately cheap in Soho. He had tried that one before, and she had made it clear that it would not do. It either had to be the famous, crowded, and expensive Ragloni's (where Peter sometimes took her) or else it had to be Perrier's in Jermyn Street. She had, actually, a passion for Perrier's, he did not quite know why. He had made up his mind, in fact, to name this restaurant.

"Oh, something in the West End," he answered. "What about tomorrow? Could you manage it?"

He was not going to give in all at once. It faintly amused him to set in motion and observe her determination and greed working behind her cool demeanour.

But she was not to be played about with, and she came straight to the point.

"Where in the West End?" she said.

"Oh—I thought we might go to Perrier's again. What about it? Can you manage tomorrow?"

He knew that she was going to accept, for she would not have asked so blatantly where she was to be taken, unless she had intended to do so.

"Yes," she said, "that sounds all right to me—so far as I know."

"Oh—good," he said. "I'll phone you tomorrow, shall I?"

"Okay. You phone me tomorrow."

Though it was not admitted by so much as a flicker of a facial muscle, there was a good deal more than met the eye in this decision that he should phone her. It was, in fact, an acknowledgement of a joint conspiracy—a secret kept from the other two men, from Peter, of course, in particular. Otherwise why did they have to phone tomorrow? Why not appoint a time and meeting-place in due course later in the evening or in ordinary conversation tomorrow? The answer was that later in the evening or tomorrow they might have no opportunity of speaking alone—and this matter had to be arranged in private. She knew as well as he that it was part of the bargain that no one else should be allowed to butt in, that if she went to Perrier's she went with him alone. She therefore, on her side, had to bear the burden of a certain amount of subterfuge: she had so to arrange matters that Peter or Mickey either did not know, or were presented with a *fait accompli* in such a way as precluded them from trying to join the party.

"Fine," he said, and was filled momentarily with a malicious exhilaration at the mere thought of working a deception on Peter, of being able to do something and laugh at him behind his back, above all, of having Netta working with him in such a deception. Such was the reward of his visit to his aunt at Hunstanton. Was there anything which money could not buy?

They were walking down Earl's Court Road in the direction of the station. Instead of making for the Black Hart Mickey and Peter were seen to turn capriciously into a pub on the left which they only used at infrequent intervals, and by the time he and Netta had joined them in its saloon bar they were already throwing darts and had ordered their beer. Netta sat down, and he went to the bar and obtained beer for himself and a large pink gin for her. He sat beside her and watched, in silence, the other two throwing darts in the last hours of the Christmas season, nineteen hundred and thirty-eight.

The Second Part

PHONING

But now her looks are coy and cold,
To mine they ne'er reply,
And yet I cease not to behold
The love-light in her eye:
Her very frowns are fairer far
Than smiles of other maidens are.

H. COLERIDGE

Excitation.—N. excitation of feeling; mental—, excitement; suscitation, gal-
vanism, stimulation, piquancy, provocation, inspiration, calling forth, infec-
tion; animation, agitation, perturbation; subjugation, fascination, intoxication; en-, ravishment; entrancement, high pressure.

Roget's Thesaurus of English Words and Phrases

Being your slave, what should I do but tend
Upon the hours and times of your desire?
I have no precious time at all to spend
Nor services to do, till you require.

W. SHAKESPEARE

"I suppose it's because he's so big that he's so silly . . . " Her words came back to him as he walked along in the cold grey morning to cash his cheque at the bank. He again decided that it was the best thing she had said for weeks. For months. Ever since the earliest days, before he was in disgrace. She was full of such intoxicating insinuations then. She thought he had a lot of money, of course.

She was with that theatrical gang, then. She was working on a film down at Denham. It had happened in the big bar of the "Rockingham" opposite Earl's Court station. They were very noisy, and they couldn't pay for their drinks. The man who had been going to pay had left his money in a car, and somebody else had taken the car, or something like that. He had buttered in and paid. He was as tight as they were. He had paid again and again, amidst their laughing and incredulous applause. Then the man somehow got back his car and his money, and they stood him drinks, and they were all bosom pals. She was there with them, of course, but he didn't think she was so terribly attractive at first. He just noticed that she was frightfully smart, striking, actressy. He didn't really begin to notice her till closing time. Then, as they stood outside on the pavement with bottles of beer under their arms, it was decided that they should go up to her flat and play shove-halfpenny.

It was not until they were up in her flat that anything happened. The three actors were crowding over the board, garrulous and absorbed in their game; but he was sitting with her on the settee, quietly and reasonably talking. She was telling him about herself, the small part she was playing in the film. Then it happened. At one moment she was just something he was talking to and looking at; at the next she was something of which he was physically sensible by some means other than that of sight or sound: she was sending out a ray, a wave, from herself, which seemed to affect his whole being, to go all through him like a faint vibration. It was as though she were a small amateur wireless station, and he alone was tuned in to her and listening. And the message she was tapping out was, of course, her loveliness. Not that he was tremendously moved by what was happening: he merely appreciated the fact that it was happening, and was slightly excited—excited, perhaps, as much by the novelty of the experience as by anything else. She continued talking, and he answered her clearheadedly, and all the time she was talking and all the time he was answering, he was "listening in" . . .

He knew now that those moments on the settee began it all, that he was head over heels in love with her as soon as he had a moment to be near her and look at her, but he had no idea at the time. The party broke up at about half past one. He chivalrously helped her break it up, because she had said she was short of sleep. It was only casually, almost fortuitously, that he arranged to see her again. "Well, don't we meet again or something?" he said as they all staggered in the doorway, and she said they certainly would if he frequented the Rockingham. "Well, I'll be in there at twelve tomorrow. Why don't you come along?" "Right," she said, "that's a date."—"Right—twelve o'clock tomorrow," she said as he went down the stone stairs, and he didn't believe either of them was serious.

But when he awoke next morning he remembered his novel listening-in experience of the night before, and trying, not quite successfully, to recapture it in his mind, developed a longing to recapture it in reality. He didn't expect her to turn up at the Rockingham, but he decided he must see her again by some means or another. He went to the Rockingham at twelve and to his amazement she arrived five minutes later. He at once saw that she was incredibly beautiful, and that he was wildly in love.

He had money, then, of course, and he was spending it. It was just after he had had that mad streak of luck with his Pools, and had made two hundred pounds in a single week. He had that blue suit, too, and those shirts from Jermyn Street. He must have looked prosperous, and behaved prosperously. Perhaps she thought he would back her in a show or something. Why else should she have turned up that morning? Why else should she have acted the part she did, have gone about with him?

And how she piled it on, in her quiet way. So polite, so ravishing, so available! So apparently friendless, or mildly bored by her friends. So serious and hardworking! That week he took to getting up at six in the morning and motoring her down to Denham in a hired car.

He once called her, jokingly yet fondly, a "glamour" girl. "Oh, no, a *fireside* girl," she answered in her own crisp, fascinating way. "A fireside girl, definitely." And he, poor fool, took it to mean that if she was offered a fireside by himself she might accept the offer. There were even moments when he was afraid of committing himself!

How, in that first week, was he to be blamed for falling as he did? Was it his fault that he had caught her at a freak period, when she was working, when her usual friends and background were absent, when she believed he had a lot of money and was pleased to tolerate him, to attempt to attract him, even?

Yes—he ought to have known, he ought to have acted in accordance with the premonition which he sometimes definitely had that this sudden delight in his life was too good to be true, that she was as hard as nails, that she had a virulent, competent life of her own, about which he knew nothing, and in which he could play not even a remotely effective part. On one occasion, on the fourth day of knowing her, he came up to her flat, and found her phoning. There was something in her voice, in her manner at the telephone, in the man's voice at the other end, which warned him of everything. But by then he could not act upon his premonition, because by then he was crazy about her, and the premonition itself, the premonition of her real character and inaccessibility, only served, suddenly and violently, to intensify his longing for her.

Then, even if he ever had a chance, how he had bungled it! That night! He had lost his nerve by then, of course, good and proper. He had told her he hadn't any real money. He wasn't sleeping because of her. When he lay on his bed her face, her colouring, the blend of cruelty and mischief on her mouth, the blend of heavenly kindness and mockery in her brown eyes, stood on guard between him and unconsciousness. Without consulting his will, his whole being had of itself decided to engage itself, to employ and strain all its faculties, in loving her, and now there was no other woman, no other colouring or texture, no other blend of heavenly kindness and cruelty on any other woman's mouth or eyes that would do. He was hers for ever and ever.

It was because he hadn't slept that he made such a mess of it that night in her flat. He had drunk a lot, but he was more exhausted than drunk when he tried to make love to her, tried to kiss her. His mind was in a mist. He had to concentrate to think, to stand properly on his legs. She remained quite cool, and turned him out of the flat, of course. He went like a lamb: he had enough sense to do that. Then, as he stood in the doorway, protesting, apologizing, she said, "All right. Good night," and slammed the door in his face.

Slam. Just like that. Snap. Finished. From that moment his

charming friend, his new acquaintance, his polite companion, the solitary and friendless actress of his imagination, the "fireside girl," became Netta, the Netta he knew. There were no half measures: he was given no period in which to acclimatize himself. When he rang her up next morning her voice and manner proclaimed their new relationship (their permanent relationship—the one existing until this day) with sharp and efficient clarity. It was not that she was tangibly rude in anything she said: she accepted his apologies gracefully; she even let him come along and see her that morning. It was the sudden familiarity of her tone which was so insulting and wounding. She had dropped her pretence of reserve, of reticence, of interest in himself like a hot brick. She was completely at ease with him, "matey," natural, outspoken, good-tempered or bad-tempered at will. Whereas yesterday they behaved and talked like two charmed, tentative strangers, today they might have been old friends for years. ("Can I come round and see you?" "Certainly.") The brief episode of the night before, the fact that his unreciprocated desire for her was fledged, enabled one like herself to make this transition without a qualm, directly and mercilessly. In her mind he was put instantly into a class of men—the class of men who desired her, who sought her favours, and to whom she intended to give no favours.

The coolness and quickness with which she made the change, the arrogance of spirit which her sudden familiar manner over the phone implied, made him hate her more than he could ever have hated her if she had avoided him, or not allowed him to see her again. He still remembered it and hated her for it.

But that was merely the beginning. His peremptory dismissal from the fool's paradise in which he had been living was not to be atoned for merely by bitter disillusionment about this girl and her intentions towards him. He had asked for all he got there; but there was plenty more to come. The blows fell thick and fast. Peter came back, he had been in Scotland for three weeks; there was an awful man called Bermann hanging about (thank God he at any rate had faded out now); he met for the first time her atrocious masculine woman-friend, Enid Staines-Close; her actor friends turned up again. Mickey appeared on the scene. As though under the direction of the evil genius which had made him make love to her that night, in the course of two or three days the whole scene, her entire background, was transformed. He was no longer the sole escort of a delightful girl: he was an interloper in a strange gang, her gang, her crowd, an outsider, a curious hanger-on. He had appeared from nowhere; he was looked at frigidly. He didn't even know their language, their idiom. He would never forget the way Peter looked at him and behaved when they first met around at the "Black Hart." Netta, of course, made no attempt to introduce him. She seemed to take a sort of cold delight in his humiliation. He didn't know to this day how he had stuck on; he had only made the grade because he just couldn't stop himself from seeing Netta, and because he had money at that time. If he hadn't had money they would have frozen him out: but money talks. You put up with a hanger-on, an interloper, if he is paying. He kept on the hired car, and that talked too. His money and the hired car talked for him, while he remained dumb, absolutely silly and dumb; it was not as though he had then, or even would have, any social graces with which to make himself liked.

His money, his fluke Pool money, was gone soon enough, but by then he had established himself with her crowd, created a negative personality and found a place of sorts. He was "George," or sometimes "our friend George," or "poor old George" famous for his stupidity generally, and in particular for his occasional "dumb" moods (which was their name for what he called his "dead" moods). Not that Netta called him "poor old George"; she never called him anything. She remained completely silent about him, both when she was alone with him and when there were others present. Slowly, too, the bitterest aspect of his humiliation as an interloper in a strange crowd, that is, his manifest, dog-like infatuation for Netta, became an accepted thing, a stale joke, something no longer uppermost or even present in their minds.

All that was years ago—a year and a half to be exact. He had stuck on grimly, slowly, patiently, tortoise to their hare, and he had stuck a lot of them out by now. They had either fallen out or gone away. At the moment Peter and Mickey were the only effective survivors from those days, though you never knew who would come back, or who would turn up.

B y now he had reached the bank, and he pushed through its oiled door into the hushed, pervading post-officy warmth of polished wood and pound notes.

He meant to cash his cheque over the counter. No niggling, no putting it into his account and drawing out. This ten pounds was ten pounds of concrete, clearly visualized pleasure, with a beginning and an end—ten pounds' worth of Netta's company. He was going to keep it in a separate pocket, and see when it had gone.

"A very cold day, I fancy, Mr. Bone," said the bank clerk in his emphatic, good-natured way, as he took the money from the drawer. "A very *cold—nasty—day*." This man, who was little older than himself, had, seemingly, a surfeit of good humour, and he never failed to call him "Mr. Bone" or to make a cordial observation of some sort.

They now had a little conversation about the recent holiday, and then he went out into the day again, with the bank clerk's laughter, and richly friendly "*Good* morning, Mr. Bone!" ringing in his ears.

He walked up Earl's Court Road northwards feeling lighter, more resilient in spirit. This was because of the kindness and cordiality of the bank clerk, who had called him Mr. Bone (as though Mr. Bone were somebody), and treated him as an equal.

The bank clerk, of course, knew nothing about Netta, his disgrace, the fact that he was not treated as an equal by her, or by any of her friends, or by people generally. And yet he did not believe that it was because the bank clerk did not know these things that he acted thus. He believed that this bank clerk was one of those few, warm-hearted, indiscriminate, easy-going people, who were naturally unaware of any superiority or inferiority in individuals, or who, even if they were aware of such things, were not impressed by, or at all interested in them. He had known a few people like that—but they were so few. Bob Barton had been like that, of course. He was like that at school. Although you were a fool and a butt to everybody else, he would suddenly come up behind you in break and take your arm and walk round with you, talking like mad about something which happened to interest him at the moment. He had no sense of his being himself, and you being yourself, no envious discrimination, no condescension. And he carried that through into life. When they were together later, when they were "partners" in that awful fiasco of trying to sell wireless parts in Camden Town (*Barton & Bone!*), Bob Barton was just the same—kindly, considerate, talkative, too busy mentally in what he was doing to be conscious of his own superior, or your own inferior, intelligence and quickness. If you made a howler he never made you feel it. He just looked a bit shocked for a moment and a little later he took your arm, as he did in break back at school, and you went round and had a beer, and nothing more was said or thought.

Those were the days all right—the happiest in his life. He had a bit of money; Bob Barton was his friend, and life was opening out and wasn't school any more. It had taken him four or five years away from school to awaken fully to this truth, and it was this period with Bob which had given him the strength and vision to make the mental leap. So long as he was with Bob he was as good as anybody, ready to make friends with barmaids and tell anybody beastly to go to hell. No lessons, no disgraces, no restrictions, no being laughed at, no being snubbed and sent to Coventry. Just beer and fun and phoney projects with your own money. *Barton & Bone!*

But all that was gone. He hadn't seen Bob Barton for five years, hadn't heard from him for three. He was in America (Philadelphia) doing well—or was when he last wrote. If Bob came back now it might be a different story. He might wake up again; throw off his illness; get away from Netta, feel unsnubbed and be able to tell people to go to hell again. But Bob, of course, had gone for good, and he would never feel like that again. Instead of Bob, he had to make do with a friendly bank clerk to remind him that he was a man amongst men.

Bob had genuinely liked him, that was the whole point. There must have been something in his own personality which, whatever its shortcomings (perhaps because of its shortcomings), Bob understood and liked. No one else had actively liked him, so far as he could remember. Except, of course, his sister, Ellen. (He just couldn't bear to think about Ellen, nowadays.) Or was there anyone? What about Johnnie Littlejohn? That dated back from school again. Yes, Johnnie had seemed to like him. And he liked Johnnie. But then he was all part of the Bob Barton period. He had nearly come in on that wireless racket: he had had enough sense to keep out of it! He wondered where Johnnie was now. He wished he could see him again. If only he had some friends to go back to, to have as a background, to show off every now and again, he could keep up his end so much better. It was this complete loneliness and absorption in Netta's orbit which was getting him down.

Yes, Johnnie was one of them—so far as he remembered one of the non-snubbers, the non-sneerers, the people who were too cheerfully interested in things to think about themselves, or others in relation to themselves, to make comparisons, to watch, to suspect, to wound, to hate. The bank clerk was another. You could tell them at sight.

By now he had crossed Cromwell Road, and her window was in sight. Every morning, after breakfast, wet or fine, cold or warm, he made this trip up the Earl's Court Road to look at the house in which she lived. After he had passed it he walked on for about fifty yards, and then he turned and looked at it again as he came back. He had never seen her at this time of the morning, and he had very little hope of doing so; but the habit was now formed, and it never occurred to him to try and break it. He was prompted, perhaps, by the same sort of obsessed motivation which might make a miser ever and anon go and look at the outside of the box which contained the gold which was the cause of all his unhappiness. Then there was the miserable pleasure of mere proximity. For that appalling halo around Netta, that field of intense influence emanating from her in a room to a distance of about two feet, was only the inner, the most concentrated halo. It, in its turn, gave forth another halo, one which came out of her room, and out of the house and into the open street to as far as fifty or even a hundred yards—as far as any point, in fact, from which the house in which she lived might be espied by her lover. This second halo was infinitely weaker, of course, than the inner one which gave it birth, if only because it was more spread-out and in the fresh air, but nevertheless it pervaded the whole, trembling atmosphere amidst the roar of passing traffic, and cast its enthralling, uncanny influence upon every fixed object or passing person in the neighbourhood.

Finally, in this daily walk after breakfast past her house, there yet remained the lurking hope that he might see her "by accident," that she might be coming out of the house for a walk, or on her way to some appointment; that she might be in some sort of distress in which she could make use of him, that he might go in a taxi with her somewhere, or be allowed to be with her or near her. In such a way he might be enabled to discover, and enter, Columbus-like, that unknown world, that mysterious earthly paradise, whose existence he knew about only by logical inference and hearsay, and whose character he could only imagine—the world of Netta's early morning life, her world before eleven o'clock—eleven o'clock being the earliest time she permitted him to phone her, let alone see her.

Chapter Three

As usual, he walked back to the station, bought his *News Chronicle* and went in to the Express nearby for his small coffee.

He bought the *News Chronicle* nowadays because it was "liberal," and he supposed that was what he was, and also because it was getting pretty hot against Munich. He just couldn't stand Munich. Somewhere at the back of his mind it was weighing on him: it had become part of his general feeling of disgrace, of the shame in which he in particular, and the world generally, was steeped. He still couldn't get over the feeling that there was something *indecent* about it—Adolf and Musso and Neville all grinning together, and all that aeroplane-taking and cheering on balconies. And how Netta had loved it! It was about the first time he had ever known her to show externally any enthusiasm over anything.

He scanned the headlines gloomily. "TRAINS CRASH IN SNOW-STORM: 85 DEAD, 300 INJURED." He experienced a momentary feeling that he was about to be shocked, and then saw that the news came from Budapest, which meant that he did not have to be shocked. Train disasters, like Netta, had their own tragic haloes which grew faint and dissipated at a great enough distance.

"PLAYWRIGHT OF MECHANICAL AGE IS DEAD . . . FRANCO CLAIMS 18-MILE THRUST IN GREAT CATALAN BATTLE . . . £4,000 FOR 'PERFECT NURSE' . . . TONGUE-TWISTING RADIO BEE ENDED LEVEL . . . PALACE OUTWIT GRIM ALDERSHOT DEFENCE . . ." He read until his coffee came, and then he put the paper aside, lit a cigarette and began thinking again.

His cigarette, as it always did at this time of day, set him on edge. It was now five and twenty to eleven, and he had to make his plans for the day. Phoning Netta was obviously the first requisite for this, but the question was, what time?

Every day he had this problem to face: every day this morning existence of Netta's, this earthly paradise she created merely by existing, by being awake and moving about in a flat a quarter of a mile away—a paradise made a thousand times more agonizingly interesting and desirable by the fact that he was permanently excluded from it and had no idea of what went on in it—had at last to be interrupted, violated by his own courage and deed. The marvel was that after a certain time of the morning (eleven o'clock) it was possible to make such an assault. It was not necessarily wise—on certain days she might be furious if he phoned at eleven—but it was possible; it was not expressly forbidden. The problem which always exercised his mind was what time to choose, how long he should, or could, hold off. He sometimes tried to get some information on this subject from herself the night before, but she was seldom informative. She was not an informative girl: he had to find out everything for himself by experiment and disaster. From many such experiments and disasters, however, he had deduced certain scientific rules which were of service to him. He had now some knowledge, through deep thought, inference, and hearsay, of the main complications with which, daily, he summoned up the effrontery to interfere. In the forefront of these complications was her bath. There was the bath which she genuinely took each day shortly after she rose; there were also the spurious baths he had foisted upon him when Mrs. Chope was there to answer the phone. The best time to phone her, the time at which she was likely to be in her best mood, was about a quarter of an hour after her genuine bath.

Half an hour after, it was too late: she was often already out of the house. The principal thing to do, then, was to guess accurately the time of her rising, which might, to a certain extent, be deduced from the time she went to bed, and to link up such a guess with the general knowledge he had acquired, over a long period, of the likelihood of the irregular Mrs. Chope having arrived at the flat. For the presence of Mrs. Chope threw out all other calculations based on the premise that she was not there.

Today he did not feel that the same caution and foresight were necessary, for he had been definitely invited to phone her. Moreover, it would be advisable to phone early as, if she intended to keep her promise and come out with him in the evening, she would want to have it fixed up, so that she could tell, if she desired to do so, the appropriate falsehoods to Peter or Mickey, or anyone else who phoned and tried to engage her for the evening. To this day he did not know whether Peter or Mickey knew about these occasions when he took her out by herself. Nothing was ever said about such things in front of them; on the other hand nothing had ever passed between Netta and himself consciously to cause this silence. It was only very seldom anyway, only when he had money, that he took her out alone.

He waited till the clock pointed to eleven o'clock, then he paid his check and went into the station.

In the line of telephone booths there were a few other people locked and lit up in glass, like waxed fruit, or Crown jewels, or footballers in a slot machine on a pier, and he went in and became like them—a different sort of person in a different sort of world—a muffled, urgent, anxious, private, ghostly world, composed not of human beings but of voices, disembodied communications—a world not unlike, so far as he could remember, the one he entered when he had one of his "dead" moods.

As soon as he was shut in, he lit a cigarette, and thought of what he was going to say and how he was going to say it. Then he put in his pennies and dialled.

There was a click, and it began ringing at once . . . *Brr-brr!* . . . *Brr-brr!* . . . *Brr-brr!* . . .

He was mystically transported to the unknown paradise—himself, an imaginary wire, and the bell ringing in her flat being all one instrument—ringing in her flat, ringing on the table by her bed . . .

Brr-brr! . . . *Brr-brr!* . . . He was on the table by her bed, breaking into her privacy, adding another complication to the mysterious complications already prevailing! It was very thrilling to have got right into her flat, right into her bedroom, disguised as a bell, merely by paying twopence; but the suspense was horrid.

Brr-brr! . . . *Brr-brr!* . . . Definitely Mrs. Chope wasn't there.

Perhaps she was in her bath. *Brr-brr!* . . . *Brr-brr!* . . . "Do not dial," he read, "until dialling tone is heard after lifting the receiver . . ." *Brr-brr!* . . . *Brr-brr!* . . . "If you hear a high-pitched 'buzz-buzz-buzz' (the 'engaged' tone) it indicates that the number dialled or the connecting apparatus is engaged . . ." *Brr-brr!* . . . *Brr-brr!* . . . This was getting bad. Perhaps she wasn't going to come to it at all. Anyway, if she did come now, she would be in a temper, because it was obvious that he had interrupted her in something. *Brr-brr!* . . . *Brr-brr!* . . . There was the longed-for click—a click which relieved the tension in his heart in rather the same way as the click in his head relieved him from one of his "dead" moods—and he heard her say "Hullo! . . ."

The Third Part

earnest, wistful, eager, breathless; fer-vent, -vid; gushing, passionate, warmhearted, hearty, cordial, sincere, zealous, enthusiastic, glowing, ardent, burning, red-hot, fiery, flaming; boiling, - over . . .

impressed -, moved -, touched -, affected -, penetrated -, seized -, imbued &c. 820- with; devoured by; wrought up &c . . . enraptured &c. 829.

Roget's Thesaurus of English Words and Phrases

> *I can give not what men call love;*
> *But wilt thou accept not*
> *The worship the heart lifts above*
> *And the Heavens reject not:*
> *The desire of the moth for the star,*
> *Of the night for the morrow,*
> *The devotion to something afar*
> *From the sphere of our sorrow?*

P. B. SHELLEY

indifferent, lukewarm; careless, mindless, regardless; inattentive &c. 458; neglectful &c. 460; disregarding. unconcerned, *nonchalant, pococurante, insouciant, sans souci*; unambitious &c. 866. un-affected, -ruffled, -impressed, -inspired, -excited, -moved, -stirred, -touched, -shocked, -struck; unblushing &c, (*shameless*) 885; unanimated; vegetative. callous, thick-skinned, pachydermatous, impervious; hard, -ened; inured, case-hardened; steeled—proof-against; imperturbable &c. (*inexcitable*) 826; unfelt.

Roget's Thesaurus of English Words and Phrases

H e pressed button A and heard his pennies fall. He said "Hullo."

"Hullo," she said. "Yes!"

She was in a temper all right. He could tell that because there was an exclamation mark, instead of a note of interrogation, after her "Yes." Funny how she got into these tempers—after being so peaceful and saying "Perhaps it's because he's so big that he's so silly" the night before—but oh, how characteristic! He knew his Netta all right by now.

"Oh, hullo, Netta," he said in studiedly polite and gentle tones, though of course this would only add to her fury. "This is me."

"What? Who is it? . . ."

"This is me. George."

"Oh."

"Have I interrupted you in your bath or something?"

"No. I was asleep. What do you want?"

"Oh, I'm awfully sorry. I was ringing up about today—that's all."

"What do you mean—'today'?"

"I mean this evening."

"What do you mean—'this evening'? What about this evening?"

She knew exactly what he meant, of course; but because she was in one of her tempers, which might have been brought about by his having wakened her by phoning, but which was more probably quite spontaneous, arbitrary, and gratuitous, she was going to cross-examine him, make him explain himself, make him look a fool. It was an absolute marvel what he put up with from this woman.

"*This* evening," he repeated like a little boy saying his lesson, "I thought we were going out together."

"Oh."

There was a pause as he waited to see if she would add anything to this "Oh," but he was certain she wouldn't, and he was proved right. It was for him to go on explaining himself, to go on saying his lesson like a little boy.

"Well," he said, "can you come, Netta?"

"Yes, I think I can."

"Oh. Good. Then when shall we meet?"

"You'd better call for me."

"Right. When shall I come along?"

"I don't know . . . When? . . ." Now she was going all vague. "About six-thirty?"

"All right."

"Fine. I'll be along about six-thirty then. Is that okay?"

"All right."

"All right, then, Netta. Good-bye."

"Good-bye."

He waited to hear her slam down the receiver, and he came outside into the fresh air again and began to walk.

He cut up through Cromwell Road and St. Mary Abbotts to High Street Ken., and into the Park. He went by the Round Pond, and watched some sailing, and down to the Serpentine, and along it to Rotten Row and out by Hyde Park Corner. Then up Piccadilly to Piccadilly Circus, where he had a couple of beers downstairs in Ward's Irish House. Then it was a quarter to one, and he went into the Corner House and got a small table to himself on the second floor, and ordered fried fillets of fish, fried potatoes, roll and butter and a lager. He still had his

News Chronicle and he read this and looked down the list for a movie to go to in the afternoon. There was *Astoria*, Ger. 5528. Racket Busters (A), 1.35, 4.20, 7.10, 10. Rich Man, Poor Girl (U), 12, 2.45, 5.30, 8.20. News, etc. . . . There was *Gaumont*, Haymarket. Doors 10.45. Frank Capra's You Can't Take It With You (U), 11.20, 1.45, 4.10, 6.40, 9.10. Don. Duck (U) . . . There was *New Gallery,* Suez (U) with Tyrone Power, Loretta Young, Anabella, 12.45, 2.30, 4.45, 7, 9.20. Disney's Col. Farmyard Symphony (U) . . . He got tired of concentrating and decided to go to the Plaza, because he usually went there when he was up like this. Here there was Say It in French with Ray Milland, Olympe Bradna and Star Cast! (U). Akim Tamiroff in Escape from Yesterday (A), Popeye! IS. *6d.* seats till 1 o'c. Whi. 8944.

He cried a little at the end of each film, came out over the super-soft carpet into the thronged electric-lit darkness of the winter's afternoon at a quarter to five, and took the tube to Earl's Court. He bought a *Standard* and had a cup of tea at the Express. Then back to his hotel to wash and change. He had time to get in two drinks—two large Haig's at two different pubs before he called on her at 6.30 exactly.

He knew, by the darkness behind her windows, and (when he got upstairs) behind her front door, that she was not back, but he rang the bell four or five times, with a pause of nearly a minute between each ring. Then he went down into the street, and looked each way, and went and had another drink. He came back ten minutes later, and rang the bell again four or five times. Then he went and had another drink. He didn't expect she would turn up now, so there was no sense in not getting drunk. But when he went back the next time he saw a light in her window and knew she was back.

When she had let him in she went back into her bedroom, and he followed her in there. She sat in front of her mirror making up her mouth. He didn't think it advisable to mention the fact that she was three-quarters of an hour late, and when she herself did so, with "I'm late—aren't I?" he passed it off with "Oh yes—I *did* look in," and nothing more was said about it.

She spoke to him, or rather answered him, fairly politely—but it was obvious that she was still in one of those moods when she couldn't stand him at any price, and that she would let him know as much before the evening was finished.

S he was wearing her navy blue coat and skirt over a scar-let silk blouse. She was, in fact, in her "best" clothes and she was making herself up with more care than usual, cer-tainly more than she usually showed when she went out with him.

He knew why this was—it was because he was taking her to Perrier's. That was the lovely part about it—she was a wonder-ful little snob at heart. Although it was convenient for her to act this free-and-easy Earl's Court life—irregular, unpunctual, self-consciously "broke," unconventional—she really liked the other things, good clothes, "smart" places and people, snob restaurants. She no doubt thought Perrier's was "smart." She wouldn't be coming out with him, of course, unless he was tak-ing her to Perrier's. She had seen to that last night.

He realized, in a resigned way, that this navy blue coat and skirt thing with the red blouse underneath was the most heav-enly thing he had ever seen her in. But then, of course, it wasn't, either—there was that consolation. Everything she wore, at any time, was the most heavenly thing she could possibly be wearing. To make comparisons was like saying that daffodils in a wood were lovelier than roses in a garden, or that violets in the rain were lovelier than primroses in the evening . . . All the same, what she was wearing now still remained the most heav-enly apparel she could have put on. She was daffodils and roses, and violets and primroses, in a wood, in a garden, in the rain, in the evening, all the time and in every mood or garb. He didn't dare to look at her and think about it: he had to look at her without thinking about it. He could do that nowadays. It gave him a sort of vague backward look in the eyes.

He believed she had had her hair done too. Freshly clean, dry and crisp, it came flowing away from her lovely, serene, yet bad-tempered forehead down low onto her neck behind, in simple, gracious, voluminous lines.

Was this in honour of Perrier's too?

When she had finished making up, she went into the sitting-room to change her shoes, and he followed her. He was always following her, like her shadow, like a dog. She offered him a drink: she had some gin and French, and she told him where to find the bottles and the glasses. He made up the drinks on the mantelpiece, and she went into the bedroom again. When she came out the drinks were ready, and she came and stood at the mantelpiece drinking them with him.

He felt he ought to be very happy. He was getting his ten pounds' worth all right, if only in being alone with her like this for a few minutes, if only in shutting out Peter and Mickey, if only in participating in her private life, for however brief a period, while others were not participating in it.

But he was not happy, because she was not paying the slightest attention to him; and he was not even now participating in her life. He noticed how every now and again she glanced at herself surreptitiously in the glass. She did not often look into the glass at herself like that, and it told him everything. It told him that this evening she had given him was for a definite purpose, and that purpose was, for some extraordinary reason, Perrier's. He was of no more importance, had no more significance, than the taxi which would take them there.

He sometimes marvelled at the way she never said "Thank you" for anything—the way she let him spend his money on her and was bad-tempered or mildly and insecurely good-tempered at will. He not only knew she wouldn't say "Thank you" when it was all over tonight, he knew she wouldn't even *behave* "Thank you" during a single moment of the evening while it lasted. He supposed other women behaved like this with men to whom they were not attracted. But he rather doubted it. He rather thought that the majority of women (except real bitches), if they were making use of you, as Netta undoubtedly was, would get in or suggest some sort of "Thank you" somewhere. Not her. She was in a class by herself.

He noticed this again when she had got into the taxi which he at once hailed when they got outside. How had she known that he, a poor man, wasn't going to take her by bus or Underground train? Would not another woman have somehow subtly suggested an awareness of his gesture, instead of walking into it in the same way that a tired and somewhat irritable typist might walk into a tram, and then sitting looking out of the window without uttering a word?

Then again, when they were half-way there, he was struck by the same thing. He told her that he had rung up and reserved a table.

"Upstairs?" she said.

"No, downstairs. Did you want to go up?"

"Oh yes," she said, "I want to go upstairs."

"Well—I've done it now. I suppose I can change it though."

"Yes," she said, "I definitely want to go upstairs."

She added nothing to this, and the subject was changed. "I definitely want to go upstairs." "I want." Equalling they would. He couldn't help feeling that another man would have asked her who the hell she thought was taking her out, who was paying for the party, who was sacrificing the little he had and getting nothing in return. It would have been different if they were both rich, if ten pounds had been like ten pence. It would have been different if she hadn't known he hadn't a penny. But she did know. She knew that neither he nor she had a penny, yet she "definitely wanted" to go upstairs.

Or was he being morbid, ultra-sensitive? Was she merely employing the convention he was accustomed to with her gang, the convention which he still hated and thought a fake, the one in which you said and did what you liked, were deliberately rude. ("Do you want me to go?" "Yes please"—"Can I have one of your drinks?" "No, you can't," etc.). He supposed this would be her alibi if he accused her of rudeness and ungraciousness. Not that she would go to the trouble of directly using such an alibi. She would just make some retort which would make him feel more out of things, more divorced and excluded from her convention, and so from her life, than ever.

And yet that didn't work, either. The convention of being rude and unpunctual and unconventional and broke didn't fit in with spending a lot of money and going to Perrier's—did it? If she was going to forsake her conventions in one way he didn't see why she shouldn't in another.

However, it was no use worrying. He knew his Netta by now, or ought to. He was getting his ten pounds' worth—the ten pounds' worth he had bargained for—neither more nor less.

As they looked out of the window he put out his hand on hers, and she did not withdraw it. He might even be getting a little more.

Before they ate they had two more large gin things, and he began to feel a bit tight. Two large ones before he called on her—then two while he was waiting for her—one in her flat, and now two more—seven in all, and mixing whiskies with gin. Well, that wasn't eight yet—and the old rule applied with him: he was all right until he had had one or several over the eight large ones, that was to say.

She sat against the wall and he faced her. This small upstairs room was quiet and contained few people, all of whom were behind him.

From behind him, out of the subdued, pink lighting, a man's voice suddenly burst into his ears.

It said "Hullo—how are you?" in polite but rather nonchalant tones. At the same moment Netta's face lit up into a smile, and she shook hands with the man, saying "Hullo—how are *you*?"

The man, without waiting to be introduced, now smiled at him and shook his hand, saying, "How do you do?" in the same polite but off-hand way. He was a tall, dark, slim man, with indolent brown eyes and an indolent air—a young forty, an air of having money, and negligently well-dressed. There was something faintly mocking, sarcastic, challenging in the brown-eyed indolence of this man—a quality which also made itself felt in his quiet, well-modulated voice. He obviously, for some reason or other, impressed Netta beyond measure. He hadn't seen her face light up like that for ages—if ever. And her comparatively eager "How are *you*!" in answer to his cool "How *are* you?" was a turning of the tables indeed! In the ordinary way it was she who threw the offhand "How *are* you!" and the men who grinned and gushed "How are *you*!"

"Won't you come and have a drink," she said, "or are you too involved?"

"No, I won't, thanks," he said in a kindly but unhesitating tone. "I've got some film people here, and we've got to talk. You're looking very well."

"Am I?"

"Yes. Very," he said. "Well. Good-bye." And smiling at both of them he walked away.

He could see that she was secretly in a considerable state of perturbation after having met this man, and so he refrained from asking her who he was. Instead he asked her to have another drink, and she accepted. He stopped the waiter and ordered two more. He was aware that the waiter was decidedly opposed to this drinking and refusal to order a meal, but he was not in a mood to worry about waiters.

By the time the drinks came she had settled down and he said, "Who was that man?"

"What man?" she said. She knew, of course, who he meant, but she was pretending she didn't in order to make it seem that the man had been dismissed from her mind.

"The man who came and spoke to us," he said.

"Oh," she said. "That was Eddie Carstairs."

"Who's he? . . . Something to do with films?"

"No. Not exactly," she said. "He's Fitzgerald, Carstairs & Scott."

Fitzgerald, Carstairs & Scott . . . The plot thickened . . . He had heard of these people who were, as far as he could make out, big theatrical managers, agents, presenters of plays and what-not. He had seen their names on the top of theatre bills, and ever since he had known Netta he had heard talk about

them. He had heard her theatrical gang talking about them—
"Eddie Fitzgerald" and "Eddie Carstairs"—the "Two Eddies."
They always called them "Eddie," though he would bet they
did not know them well enough to do so to their faces—that
was the way with theatrical people.

But they were important people all right—he had gathered
that much. He had sensed profound awe behind the spurious
familiarity with which their names were mentioned. He suddenly remembered a remark of Netta's from some long ago
drunk, he couldn't remember where or when. "Oh yes," she
had said, "they're always upstairs there in Perrier's. It's just
over the way from the office."

"Always upstairs there in Perrier's . . ." He saw it all. This
was why she had made him take her to Perrier's; this was why
she had had her hair done and was got up to kill!

Incredible! Incredible, that the cool, rude, aloof Netta could
nourish in secret such aspirations, could be so ambitious, so
ambitious as to scheme, to prepare and enhance all her charms,
for a doubtful chance of an encounter with an important man!
It might be that she had a soul after all! It might be that she had
no soul as far as he was concerned, but that she had one elsewhere. He was almost inclined to like her better for it.

But what was she up to? Were her motives purely commercial? Was she haunting the haunts of Fitzgerald, Carstairs &
Scott in the hope of getting a job—the job she hadn't been able
to get (and, of course, in her laziness hadn't really tried to get),
for something like a year? Or was she interested in Fitzgerald,
or in Carstairs, or in Scott? Remembering her unusual perturbation while Eddie Carstairs was speaking to them, he rather
thought the correct answer would include both motives. And
was it Eddie Carstairs (of Fitzgerald, Carstairs & Scott) that
she was after? He rather thought so.

Here was a nice state of affairs—he had a big theatrical manager against him now! He managed to turn his head to look at

his distinguished rival. He was sitting where he could see Netta directly, and he was looking at a menu while he talked to the two men he was with. Yes—an attractive man all right—one who would attract women, anyway—they would go for that friendly indolence, that quiet voice, that brown-eyed faint sarcasm, all the time. But would he go for Netta? That was more doubtful. He didn't look as though he was particularly interested in women; or rather he looked as though he was on the whole too successful with women to be particularly interested in them.

"Do you know him well?" he asked.

"Oh no . . . I've just met him at a party or two," she said, and he saw her glance over at him.

"I suppose he's quite an important bloke in your job, isn't he?"

"Yes, I suppose he is."

The funny thing was that he was not made miserable by this new discovery—by the fact that he and his money were being used by Netta to further some obscure design of hers on another man. On the contrary, with the drink he had had, he was rather exhilarated. It was nice to find Netta out in something—to enjoy the brief feeling of superiority which that brought. It was nice to realize that she was human—human somewhere, if not to him. (Who knew? If she had it in her, one day she might be human to him!) Above all, it was nice to think that she probably didn't have a remote chance with this Eddie Carstairs, that there was someone in the world who knew her but didn't think about or want her, that she was for once in a lowly state and had to resort to subterfuge to see a man. He was delighted—almost grateful and friendly, rather than jealous and hostile, towards the man who had brought this about.

She was being nicer to him now, too. She began to talk, to answer him, to enter into something resembling a conversation. This was almost certainly done for effect, because she knew Carstairs might be looking at her, but it made things a good deal easier. The drinks had probably gone to her head a bit, too.

Netta! Foul as she was to him, there were moments when, because he understood her so well, he was almost sorry for her. Piecing together what he knew of her, he could see her as a whole, from beginning to end. He could see her as the bad-tempered, haughty, tyrannical little girl she must have been in the nursery, at home, or at school; he could see her as she must have grown up, encouraged in her insolence, hardness and tyranny by the power of her beauty and the slavishness in others it inspired; he could see her later, with a cold decision to exploit this power to the full in a material way. So she got out of the country and came to London, and, sure enough, got on to the stage and into films in a small way.

But after that she was a flop. Why? Largely because, in spite of her intelligence and quick wits, she couldn't act for nuts (he had ascertained that); but principally because she was spoiled an lazy, and drank too much—because she had expected success without having to work for it, and now drank and was lazy in a sort of furious annoyance at the fact that success was not to be had that way—a vicious circle of arrogance and laziness and drink. In other words, she had never got out of being the bad-tempered, haughty, tyrannical child she was at the beginning. She lacked the imagination and generosity to do so. And that brought him to the present Netta he had in front of him—the one who was making use of him in order to be near a man who might be of use to her. For the moment he was sorry for her, and rather happy.

"Then what do you want from life, Netta?" he asked. "What are you *getting* at in it all?"

When their food had come he had ordered wine, and now, if not drunk, he was careless and bold with drink. Otherwise he would never have asked her a serious, direct question like that. To ask Netta a serious, direct question, in the ordinary way, was simply to ask for one of those hideous cuts across the soul she knew so well how to administer. But now, because of what he had drunk, he felt he could take the cut if it came. If it hurt he was anaesthetized.

They had finished their meal and were having coffee. Eddie Carstairs was still at his table in the corner, though most of the other tables were deserted. There were, however, three people making a good deal of noise at a table nearby, so he could speak in a normal voice without being overheard.

"What do you mean?" she said. "What do I want from life?"

"Just what do you want from it? . . . Do you want to be a success on the films, do you want to be married, do you want children—what?"

"I don't know."

"But you must, Netta. You must know something about what you want."

"No, I don't," she said vaguely, looking at a passing waiter, and speaking as a mother, watching the screen at a cinema, might speak to her talkative child. "Do you know what you want?"

"Yes. Of course I do. I know what I want."

"What?" she said, and looked at him.

He paused a moment, reluctant to start anything. He knew it could lead nowhere, could do him no good. But why *shouldn't* he make love to her once in a way, why *shouldn't* he get something back for the money he was spending, a little of the luxury of telling her he loved her, of speaking his heart. He hadn't opened his heart to her for months.

"I want *you*, Netta," he said, looking into her eyes. "That's all I want."

"All right," she said. "So what?"

"What do you mean," he said, "So what?"

"Just 'So what,'" said Netta, and she was again looking at people in the room behind him.

"Tell me, Netta," he began again. "Don't you *ever* feel you want to get away from this racket?"

"What racket?"

"Oh—just the racket generally. Boozing, doing nothing. It's all such a waste. Don't you ever want to cut it all out?"

"Cut what out? Drinking?"

"Yes. Drinking. *I'd* cut it out if I could only get my life straight—if only things made sense."

"This is a new departure, George," she said. "You as a temperance expert. How long have you been like this?"

"Always. I hate drinking really."

"Yes. That's the impression I got."

"No. Don't be sarcastic. It's the truth. It's only because of this life one leads. Don't you ever feel the same? Don't you ever wake up in the early hours of the morning and feel the same?"

"Alcoholic remorse?"

"No. Not alcoholic remorse. Just wanting to get things straight. You *must* know what I mean. You must feel something of what I feel. *You* can't be content going on living the life you lead."

"Can't I?"

"No."

"Do you mean," she said, after a pause in which she flicked the ash of her cigarette into her coffee saucer, "that I've got to go away and live on a chicken farm in Sussex with you, because you've given me that one before, and I don't want to a bit."

He marvelled at her cruelty but he had known he was throwing himself open to the cuts.

"No, Netta—not a chicken farm in Sussex . . ." he said, momentarily beaten.

"Oh, not a chicken farm in Sussex . . . That's a definite relief Go ahead."

"All right, you can laugh at me, Netta, but there's something in what I'm saying. You must want something in life. You must want to be a success, or to be in love, or something. You must be human somewhere. Don't you want to be in love?"

"There's nothing I'd like better."

"Oh, you *would* like to be in love?"

"Certainly."

"Who with? What sort of a man?"

She paused.

"Oh . . . Boyer," she said, with a little smile which conveyed a world of wicked and selfish meaning, and she again flicked out her ash in the saucer and looked round the room.

"I still think you're wrong," he said, "and that one day you'll come to want what I've been talking about."

"In other words the chicken farm at Haywards Heath?"

"Yes," he said, defiantly. "The chicken farm at Haywards Heath, or something like it. Something with a shape to it. Something which makes sense. I've got to think that. I've got to hope it anyway. If I didn't do that I wouldn't go on hanging about you the way I do—would I?"

"I don't know, my dear George . . . Why ask me?"

He had already noticed that her attention was distracted,

and the next moment her face lit up into a smile, and she held up her hand.

"Good night!" she said.

He heard a man's voice saying "Good-bye" and, looking round, he saw Eddie Carstairs going out with his two friends.

There was a pause in which he looked at her. He had a sudden feeling of tiredness—a feeling that the evening was at an end. Her loveliness and inaccessibility came over him in a fresh wave of misery. He had been a fool to take her out. He had had too much to drink: he would feel awful in the morning; he had again beaten his head against the brick wall of her imperturbability. He had exhausted his nervous system, and it would take him days to get over it.

"Oh, Netta," he said, "I do love you so. Can't *something* be done about it?"

She paused, and then, for answer, she put her hand on her bag.

"Will you excuse me," she said, "if I go to the cloakroom."

And without waiting for him to answer, she pushed back the table a little, rose, and walked away.

While she was gone he thought he might as well call the waiter and pay the bill. It came to two pounds thirteen and sevenpence. He put down three pound notes and said "That's all right" when the waiter brought back the change.

She returned in six or seven minutes (she always took hours in a cloakroom), and sat down opposite him again. It was now twenty past nine. He had an idea of taking her to the pictures, and then of going on drinking down at Oddenino's or at the Café Royal.

"Well," he said, "where do we go now?"

"We go home now," she said. "That is, when we've paid the bill." And she looked round for a waiter.

"I've done that," he said. "But we don't want to go home yet, do we? It's only twenty past nine. We can't go home yet."

"Well," she said, "*I* am. I don't know about you."

"Wery well," he said, abruptly springing to his feet. "Let's go."

All at once he was in a fury. It took a lot to get him into a temper, but that cool, impersonal, indescribably insolent "*I* am" had done the trick. She had just brought him here so that she could see a man, a bloody theatrical manager; she had taken his money, she had taxied, wined and dined at his expense; and now the man had gone, she was going too. "*I* am." He felt he could smack her face; he felt he could kill her.

Chapter Five

Seemingly not noticing his rage (though of course she noticed it because she noticed everything), she rose, and walked out of the room in front of him. As she walked down the stairs he had an insane desire to kick her from behind, to seize hold of and shake her, to make a scene in a public place, anything to humiliate her, to dislodge her from the throne of her effrontery, but instead "Taxi, sir?" said the man at the door, and he murmured "Yes" weakly . . .

The taxi came at once. He was in such a temper with her, with the whole evening, with everything, that he didn't give the man a tip for his hat and coat, and he didn't give a tip to the man who opened the taxi door. Let them go to hell. He was hysterical with hatred. He shouted Netta's address to the driver, and the taxi moved away.

For the time being there was a certain joy in his hatred. Like a local anaesthetic around a tooth, it numbed the pain around his heart—the heart, which, normally, ached with the pain of Netta continually. He could feel, for a moment, that he was through with her; that hatred had killed love; that her beauty and power over him had been rendered null, inoperative, by her loathsomeness of character. If only he could make his feeling last he would be through with her for good.

But how could he make it last? Already he felt it slipping away. She sat silently in her corner as the taxi sped on—sped on home.

In ten minutes' time the evening would be over. How could

he remain silent and sullen when there were only ten more minutes—when he would shortly be dismissed at her door? He couldn't. *She* could. He could see that she knew he was in a temper and that she did not mean to utter a word until he spoke: she would leave him without even saying "Good night" if necessary. Such was her advantage over him, and such was her strength of character. The lights of London whirling across the taxi lit up her wonderful face in bright whirling mauve . . . He looked at her and had to speak.

"Oh, Netta," he said, "you are a beast! Why do you treat me like this?"

And as soon as he had spoken, and felt the self-pity of his own tone, all the hardness, the anaesthetic around his heart, faded away and he was begging for her mercy.

"You've got yourself into a state, haven't you, George?" she said, looking out of the window. "I'd shut up and go to bed if I were you."

"No, Netta," he said, "you are a beast. Even if you *hate* me I don't see why you should treat me like this."

"I'm afraid I don't follow you. Like what?"

"Like *this*! If you're going to come out with me I *do* think you might treat me *decently*! If you're *going* to make use of me, you might give me *something* in return—a little kindness of some sort."

"How do you mean—make use of you?" She spoke sharply, with a note of rising temper in her voice. He had gone too far. He saw that although she made use of him, she was ready to be extremely angry at any suggestion that she did so. If he cared to mention Eddie Carstairs now, if he let her know that he now knew perfectly well the objects she had in mind when she came out with him, he could probably make her lose her temper properly. But he wasn't going to do that. His temper had gone and he could only beg for mercy.

"But you do make use of me, Netta," he said. "After all I

am taking you *out*, aren't I? Can't you be nice if I'm taking you out?"

"I don't know what you're talking about," she said.

"I don't see how you can't see," he said. "After all, I'm paying for everything, aren't I? I know that sounds an extraordinary thing to say, but it's true, isn't it?"

"Most extraordinary," she said. "In fact I've never actually heard anyone say a thing exactly like that before."

"No, Netta, listen." He put his hand on her arm and pleaded with her. "*Do* listen, for God's sake. You *must* be human somewhere. I know I'm a fool. I know you don't care a damn about me. But if you agree to come out with me, can't you even be *civil*? You just treat me like dirt—as though I'd done something wrong. I haven't done you any harm, Netta. The only harm I've done is being in love with you . . ." His voice began to break, and tears came into his eyes as he went on . . . "What's wrong with that? You're civil to other people. Why can't you be civil to me? Oh, Netta, do be kind to me. I can't go on unless you're kind to me. It's all getting too much. Say something civil to me, Netta. Can't you say something *civil*? I'm worn out. I've spent what I've got on you—I've tried to please you . . . Can't you be *civil*? Can't you look at me and say something *civil*?"

There was a pause. He looked at her and she looked out of the window. He waited for her to speak but she did not. In the faint hope that his tears and eloquence were moving her, he went on:

"What have you got against me, Netta—what harm have I done? If anyone else took you out you'd be nice enough to them, but just because it's me you treat me like dirt. You don't treat the others like dirt—you wouldn't treat Peter or Mickey like this. What have I *done*?—That's all I want to know. I love you, Netta—but I don't interfere with you. I only hang about. I'm *harmless*, aren't I? Aren't I harmless?"

"No," she said, still looking out of the window. "You're not at the moment—if you want the truth."

"What do you mean, Netta? What am I doing?"

"You're being a bloody, insufferable bore. And the more you go on the more boring you're being. So won't you shut up? I'm likely to be much more civil, as you put it, if you do."

There was another pause.

"All right, Netta, I'll shut up," he said, and he was silent.

Well, that was that. The evening was over. He knew the rules. When she delivered the final snub, it was always recognizable as such, and it was no use going on.

He hadn't really expected anything else. He had known no good could ever come from taking her out. He supposed he had somehow hoped, in the back of his mind, to make love to her, to woo her, to have her for a few hours to himself and try to bring about a change in her heart towards him. But he ought to have known better than to have hoped for such a thing, even in the back of his mind.

He had known that making love to her was tacitly but utterly forbidden—that he only remained tolerable to her so long as he remained silent about the passion which raged in him. He at any rate couldn't accuse her of not making herself clear on that point. This wasn't the first time he had taken her out and been told he was a bloody insufferable bore—though perhaps she had not before been quite so painfully direct in her speech.

What now? Hadn't he better give her up? Hadn't he better make up his mind to give her up altogether? Hadn't he better go from pub to pub, getting really drunk, and picking up a woman and going with her and deciding all the time to give Netta up? He had done that once or twice before. It hadn't succeeded yet, as far as giving Netta up was concerned, but hadn't he better try again? It might work this time, and he might as well complete the usual circle. And anyway it would be nice to get drunk and go with a woman. He had got five pounds left.

Yes—that was the idea. Then why not start now—leave her in the taxi—let her get home by herself? That was it. Leave her now. It would give her a bird, to leave her stone cold for once. He would do it ever so politely. That would make it more of a bird. He would even offer to pay for the taxi.

"Look here, Netta," he said, "do you mind if I get out here? I think I'd like to stay in the West End for a bit."

"No," she said, "not at all."

But he did not exactly hear her say this. Rather he saw her lips saying it. For before she spoke and while he was looking at her, there was a funny sound, like a click of a camera shutter in the middle of his head, and the world was not the same lively, audible, intelligible world which it had been a fraction of a second before.

CHAPTER SIX

C lick! . . .
Here it was again! He was in London, in a taxi at night, and it had happened again!

"Click . . ." That was the only way to describe it. It was like the click of a camera shutter. Shutter! That was the word. A shutter had come down over his brain: he had shut down: he was shut out from the world he had been in a moment before.

The world he was in now was the same in shape, the same to look at, but "dead," silent, mysterious, as though its scenes and activities were all taking place in the tank of an aquarium or even at the bottom of the ocean—a noiseless, intense, gliding, fishy world.

It was as though he had suddenly gone deaf—mentally deaf.

It was as though one had blown one's nose too hard, and the outer world had become dim and dead. It was as though one had gone into a sound-proof telephone booth and shut the door tightly on oneself.

There were a hundred and one ways of describing it. When it happened to him he always tried to describe it to himself— to analyse it—because it was such a funny feeling. He was not frightened by it, because he was used to it by now. But it was happening a good deal too often nowadays, and he wished it wouldn't.

It was such a weird feeling: it was always novel, and, in a way, interesting to him. It was as though the people around him, although they moved about, were not really alive: as though their existence had no motive or meaning, as though they were shadows—rabbits or butterflies or kangaroos thrown on the wall by an amateur conjurer with a candle. And although they talked, and although he could understand what they said, it was not as though they had spoken in the ordinary way, and it was an effort to understand and to answer.

Take Netta, for instance, who was rather oddly and inexplicably sitting beside him in this taxi. He knew it was Netta well enough—but it was a different Netta. Although he could see her she was remote, almost impalpable, miles away—like a voice over the telephone, or the mental construction of the owner of a voice one might make while phoning—a ghost, if you liked.

She was saying something actually. She was saying "Well, aren't you getting out?"

He could hear and understand the words, but for the moment he couldn't gather what they meant. They seemed divorced from any context: or at any rate he didn't know what the context was. So he didn't answer. For the moment anyway, he was too interested in what had happened in his head.

Then, gradually, and as usual, and without his being aware of it, the feeling of novelty and strangeness, his conscious knowledge of the transition, of the falling of the shutter, faded away. And the world he was in now, the world under the sea, was his proper world, the only one he knew.

And in this world there was something to be done. There was something to be done which he had forgotten about. He had, he fancied, somewhat reprehensibly forgotten about it, and now he must remember it. He could never think of it all at once, but it would come. If he didn't nag at it, but took things easily, it would come.

The taxi sped on towards Kensington; the reflected lights whirled across the inside of the taxi: he looked at the taximan's black bumping back, and he remained silent and waited for it to come. But now she was speaking to him again.

"I am sorry," she was saying, "but didn't I understand you to say you were getting out?"

What did this mean? "Getting out?" Getting out of what? The taxi? Or of some business or concern in which he was a partner with her? What was she talking about? It was a nuisance, her speaking to him like this. How could he remember what he had to remember, if she interrupted him all the time?

"I don't know," he said.

He couldn't say anything else, because he didn't know what she was talking about. He hoped it would shut her up. He looked at the taxi-man's back and tried to get back into a proper state of mind to remember . . .

But she evidently was not going to leave him alone. "Oh Christ," he heard her saying, "you're not going to throw one of your dumb moods now, are you?"

Dumb moods? What dumb moods? She spoke as though he had been dumb, or sulky, in the past. When? That evening? She was talking gibberish as far as he was concerned.

He looked at her, and saw that she was looking at him with a sort of angry curiosity, as if demanding an answer. He was annoyed by these interruptions—the fact that she wouldn't let him alone—but he felt he ought to be polite.

"I'm sorry," he said, and smiled at her. He was aware that his smile was rather foolish, but he hoped that by smiling at her, and being polite, he might make her leave him alone.

It seemed to do the trick. She looked at him, somewhat intently, and then she turned her head and looked out of the window again. Now he could get back to remembering.

He wondered what he was doing in this taxi with Netta. Had they been to a party? Was it the end of some awful binge? They were evidently going home. He looked at his watch and saw that it was only a quarter to ten. What a funny time. But all that didn't matter. All he had to do was to remember and, if he took it easily, and if she didn't interrupt him again, he would be able to do so.

Lulled by the rhythm of the jolting cab, by the whirling reflected lights inside, by the taxi-man's black bumping back, by the smooth, slick change-cycle (red, red-and-amber, green, amber, red) of the traffic lights, it seemed that he almost slept, that he was in a dream, barely conscious of anything.

Then, just after they had passed the Albert Hall, he remembered without any difficulty what he had to do; he had to kill Netta Longdon. He was going to kill her, and then he was going to Maidenhead. At the moment he was not quite clear as to who Netta Longdon was, but that would come back, too . . .

He ought to have remembered before. He couldn't think why he had forgotten. He was always forgetting this. It went out of his head for hours on end, for days. So far as he knew he hadn't thought about it since he was at Hunstanton. He kept on putting it off and kept on forgetting about it. He drank such a lot he was going a bit dotty, probably.

No—he was doing himself an injustice. He kept on putting it off because these things had to be planned. He had decided that at Hunstanton. Fantastically, incredibly, absurdly easy as it all was, it still had to be planned. He wasn't going to have any meddling from the police. The thing had got to be done properly. Not that the police could touch him when once he had got to Maidenhead. But they were clever, and might start meddling before he got there. He was one too clever for them.

Then when was he going to do it? What had he decided the last time he thought about it—on the cliff at Hunstanton? Oh yes—he remembered now . . .

He had decided then to wait until the spring—until it was warmer. It had seemed then that he couldn't kill Netta Longdon while it was so cold. That seemed reasonable enough He heard a voice, a woman's voice in his ear.

102 · PATRICK HAMILTON

"Have you got a cigarette, please?" it said. "I seem to have run out."

He turned his head and saw Netta beside him. She was rummaging in her bag. She had asked him for a cigarette.

Netta . . . There was something familiar about her . . .

She was *like* somebody . . . Who was it? She was the *image* of somebody . . . Good God—he saw it all! She was like *Netta Longdon*. She was Netta Longdon! This actually was the Netta Longdon he was going to kill before he went to Maidenhead. She was sitting in a taxi with him now. How had that come about?

She was sitting beside him as though she was waiting to be killed—had come along with him specially for it. What a delicious coincidence!

She was looking at him truculently now.

"Well, don't sit there gaping at me," he heard her saying. "For God's sake have you *got* a cigarette, or have you *not*?"

"No," he said, limply, apologetically, "I'm afraid I haven't."

H e couldn't be bothered to say anything else, to feel in his pockets to find out whether he had or not. He was too interested in, delighted by the coincidence of her being in the taxi with him at this moment, sitting and collaborating in being killed . . .

Surely he must take advantage of this coincidence—surely he must kill her tonight. Fate had arranged it—had it not?

She was speaking again now.

"Well, do you mind getting the man to stop at a machine," she was saying, "I certainly want some."

He didn't understand this. What man? What machine? Was a man working at a machine somewhere?

"What did you say?" he said, hoping he would understand better if she repeated it.

"I said," she said, still looking at him truculently, "will you stop the man at a cigarette machine. Have you gone stone deaf as well as everything else?"

It was funny, the way she was so aggressive, and shouted at him, when she was really there with him just to be killed. You would have thought she didn't know she was going to be killed. Don't be a fool though—of course she didn't know. He was slipping up. The whole point was that she didn't. She must never know. That was what made the whole thing so clever, the fact that it was so absurdly, incredibly easy, and the fact that she knew nothing about it. He had got to act, pretend—so that she never guessed. He had got to throw himself into a part. He remembered now.

Because, in his preoccupation, he did not answer her, she gave him another angry look, and, rising, spoke to the taxi-man through the window. He heard her tell him to stop at a cigarette machine. He understood what she meant now. When the taxi stopped, he said "All right" and got out himself.

As he fished in his pocket for a shilling in front of the machine he saw even more clearly that this was where he had got to put on an act. He was glad of the fresh air for the moment, so that he could collect himself. If he was going to kill her, and surely it looked as though fate had made it clear that he should kill her tonight, then he had got to put on an act like mad. He had got to try to understand what she said, to pretend he was in her world, to make her believe that everything was proceeding normally, that he was not preoccupied with the thought of killing her and the means he was going to employ. Well, he could act all right!—that was just where his cleverness lay—he hadn't got any doubts on that score. "Here you are," he said, throwing the cigarettes on her lap, and he closed the taxi door, and it started again. "Can I have one after you?"

That was clever itself—the way he said that. Normal, indifferent, casual—just the right note. Now he must give her a light—another beautifully normal thing to do. As he felt in his pocket for the matches he brought out a box of cigarettes along with them.

"Oh, do look," he said, "I had some after all. What a fool . . ."

Clever again! He hadn't pretended he hadn't got them—he had himself pointed to the fact. You couldn't beat him if it came to acting. He lit her cigarette, and then his own. He looked out of the window and saw they were nearing their destination.

"Do you mind if I come up with you for a moment," he said, "and have another gin?"

"No," she said, after a pause. "You can come up and have a last one—if you'll try and behave sensibly."

"Oh, I'll behave sensibly . . ."

The taxi drew up at her door. He got out first and helped her out. Gallantry itself. He overtipped the taxi-man and talked about the weather to him.

She opened the door with her key. There was a dim light on all the landings—reflected from a light on the top floor. She went ahead of him, her high heels clock-clocking and echoing throughout the stone stairways.

She put the light on in the sitting-room and lit the gas-fire. She went straight into the bathroom without saying anything. The sitting-room bore all the traces of their departure earlier in the evening—bits of her clothes, her shoes, the gin and the glasses. He poured himself out a huge gin, added water, and swallowed half of it.

Now he had got to think. Was this where he did it? And if so, how? What with! It was all so easy. He hadn't got to use anything. He had only got to slosh her one, lay her out, and then he could do what he liked. It wouldn't make a sound. Why not do it now? Why worry about plans? He had worried about plans too long. Surely she had asked for it by being in that taxi with him. Surely this was the time.

She came back into the sitting-room. She picked up her shoes and some odd things and went into her bedroom.

"Will you have one of these?" he said.

"Yes," he heard her say. "I'll have a small one. There's some lime-juice somewhere."

He poured out the gin, found the lime-juice in the cupboard, and made her a drink at the mantelpiece.

She came back from her bedroom, and joined him at the mantelpiece. She took a sip at her drink, and began to tidy her hair in the mirror.

He still had the gin bottle in his hand. Watching her carefully, he held it by the neck behind his back. Now! Now! *Now!* he thought.

Lift up the bottle and smash it down on her head. Smash in her forehead with the bottle, and then finish her off at once before she could make a sound.

But there wasn't a cork in the bottle and the gin would spill. Blast it, he must get the cork into the bottle. He couldn't have sticky gin all over the place—going all over her and him. He couldn't be messy like that.

He looked for the cork on the mantelpiece. Where was it! Where the hell was it?. . . She moved away from the mantelpiece, with her drink in her hand. She switched on the radio, and threw herself on to the settee, putting up her feet.

There was a dance band hammering away—with a crooner.

He put the gin bottle back on the mantelpiece. Now he had got to think again. He was glad she had switched on the radio as it meant that he didn't have to talk.

He sipped at his drink and looked at her, pretending to listen to the band. What now? Somehow things were different, now she was lying down. He didn't feel he could hit her, now she was soft and relaxed. She ought to be hard and braced.

Then he must get her off that settee. He must think of a ruse to get her off. And he must do it soon, because she would turn him out in a moment. She had only said he could stay a little while.

But then, of course, if he killed her she couldn't turn him out! She would just be lying dead and he would see himself out. He would have done the job and he could get off to Maidenhead.

Maidenhead! Good God—had he got to go to Maidenhead tonight? Of course he had! What an awful thought. He hadn't got any clothes, he hadn't any money, he hadn't packed, he didn't even know the trains! You couldn't arrive in the middle of the night at Maidenhead without any clothes. The idea was preposterous.

Really, this put a new complexion on things. When he had

thought of doing it now, he hadn't thought about how he had got to get to Maidenhead.

Why hadn't he thought of this? Was he mad or something? Was he drunk? He was losing grip.

He was drunk—that was what it was. He was so drunk he was risking everything—messing it all up! Didn't he know the whole scheme was founded on detailed planning—on infinite cleverness and care? Exquisitely, deliciously simple as it was, it was only that *because* it was founded on infinite cleverness and care. He had forgotten again. He was drunk. He was ashamed of himself. He took another gulp at his gin.

And yet he wasn't ashamed of himself, because he had thought of it in time. He had been clever enough to do that. Somebody else, in his position, might have got confused, might have not thought of it in time. But he was too clever for that.

He was all at once enormously cheerful. So simple. So simple. So simple. And so clever. But not tonight. He had got to plan it tonight. He had better go away and do so now. Tomorrow perhaps. Or the day after. But not tonight.

He looked at Netta again. He was glad he didn't have to kill her tonight. She looked tired. He was tired too. They were both too tired for it: it would have been all wrong. Like trying to make love at an inopportune moment. She was speaking again.

"Well, George," she was saying, "as our conversational efforts don't seem to be making much headway tonight, I think we'd better call it a day."

And she finished off her drink, and switched off the radio, and came and put her glass on the mantelpiece.

He realized she was turning him out. It was really rather funny that, instead of being killed she was turning him out. And yet also rather pathetic. He felt a bit sorry for her. For he was going to kill her very soon now—tomorrow, or the day after, or in the next few weeks, anyway.

"Yes," he said, "I'll go." He finished off his drink, and put on his hat and coat.

"Well, good-bye, Netta," he said, shaking her hand. "I'm sorry you've had such a dull evening."

"Not at all," she said. "Good-bye."

And she went into her bedroom.

"Shove out the light on the landing," she shouted from inside.

He staggered badly at the front door. He was drunk all right: that last gin had done it.

But not too drunk to be too clever for her, to be too clever for all of them.

He shut the front door, and shoved out the light. He was in utter blackness.

He felt his way down the stairs—slowly, staggeringly, blackly, cleverly.

THE FOURTH PART

JOHN LITTLEJOHN

Oft in the stilly night
  Ere slumber's chain has bound me,
Fond Memory brings the light
  Of other days around me:
    The smiles, the tears
    Of boyhood's years,
  The words of love then spoken;
    The eyes that shone,
    Now dimm'd and gone,
  The cheerful hearts now broken!
Thus in the stilly night
  Ere slumber's chain has bound me,
Sad Memory brings the light
  Of other days around me.

                              T. MOORE

J ohn Edward Littlejohn, who had been at school with
George Harvey Bone, and who had also seen a good deal
of him in later life, sat in his lunch hour alone on a stool in
a public house near the Hippodrome.

He was drinking beer, and reading a book. The bar was L-
shaped. Happening to look up from his book, he saw, across
the bar and standing against the other side of the L, his old
friend George Harvey Bone. Thus, although the bar was full of
people, he had an uninterrupted view of him.

It was a fine summer's day outside, but this small Saloon Bar
was lit all the year round by electricity, and was at this hour full
of smoke and fumes and talk. The light shone full on George
Harvey Bone, who was by himself, holding a glass of beer, and
looking in a gloomy and lonely way into space.

John Edward Littlejohn, called by his friends "little John"
or "little Johnnie" (because he was of small stature and his
Christian name and surname excused or invited this slightly
patronizing form of address), had an insignificant appearance
generally. Tortoiseshell spectacles on a nose which was rather
too prominent, a thin face, a chin which receded somewhat, a
pallid complexion—all these gave him, particularly in profile,
something which approximated to a Bateman-drawing look,
and which might delude a casual observer into thinking he was
looking at a fool. But nothing was further from the case. From
the grey eyes behind those spectacles there gleamed the pure,
sober light of experience absorbed, of alert and athletic inter-

est in external things, of a high mathematical intelligence. John Edward Littlejohn, though a kind-hearted and polite man, was no fool: anything but it.

He was now thirty-four, and from inauspicious beginnings (he had been penniless after leaving the public school to which his parents had self-sacrificingly contrived to send him) he had employed his gift—a delightful juggler's nimbleness in the realm of figures—to the utmost advantage, and now earned a good living. After years in the City as a clerk and an accountant, he was now in the West End as accountant to Fitzgerald, Carstairs & Scott, the well-known theatrical agents and producers. He had landed this excellent job because Eddie Carstairs, whom he had met on business apart from the theatre, had taken a personal liking to him and astutely appreciated his worth.

He had taken to wandering into this pub recently at lunch-time because he liked the beer, because it was near a restaurant to which he had taken a fancy, and because here he was not likely to meet any other members of the firm—in other words "the boys." This did not mean that he dissociated himself from the boys, or thought of himself as anything other than one amongst these boys, who at lunch-time, and indeed at several other odd moments of the day, flocked into the little pub almost immediately underneath the office in Jermyn Street, and there did business or had fun. It simply was that he recently had come to believe that in that particular house at that particular time of day he had begun to drink too much bitter, play too much electric pin-table, and waste too much time, and he had decided to give it a miss for a bit. He had also lately, after accidentally reading an English translation of *Père Goriot*, become fascinated by the author Balzac, whom he had never read before; and whenever he was under the spell of a new author it had always been his particular delight to go apart and imbibe him in the lunch hour. Now, as he sat on the stool of the bar, he had the Everyman edition of *The Country Doctor* open on his knees, and he had been reading intently.

On looking up he had recognized his old friend at once and with a great deal of pleasure. He had always had a very warm feeling in his heart for this man, whose personality he could remember from the earliest days at the decidedly tough public school to which they had both been. A tall, shambling, ungainly, shy, haunting, readily affectionate figure he had been then— a noticeably uncruel boy in that cruel and resounding atmosphere. He had been famous for his backwardness, his stupidity, and his "silly" moods, when he seemed to be half asleep. Also, he always wore rather outlandish clothes, which he had always outgrown and which gave the impression (almost certainly the correct one) that he was neglected by his parents. But he was not so silly, as John Littlejohn had slowly come to discover when they had made friends. Much of that apparent dumbness was sheer inarticulacy, or, indeed, a sort of funny inner thoughtfulness manifesting itself in a lethargy of manner. And as for those "dotty" moods of his, they were just something inherent, congenital, a physical defect probably, about which nothing could be done and for which you had to allow.

Then he could remember the uncruel young man into which this uncruel boy had grown. They had been thrown together in London, with Bob Barton as a third, and poor dumb George had blossomed out wonderfully. Those were the days when the three of them were smoking their first pipes, growing their first moustaches, having their first drunks and going with their first women, glorying in their release from meaningless discipline, in the prospect of earthly pleasures and an independent existence. It had seemed then that George was really coming out of his shell. He had gone into enterprises with the indomitable Bob Barton, and had somehow become a different person, with more poise, confidence, alertness. But then those enterprises had failed, Bob Barton had gone off to America, and somehow he had more or less lost touch with him. He had had a night out with him now and again, but gradually and unintentionally they had drifted apart. He supposed he hadn't seen him for a matter of two or three years.

He watched him for a few moments, trying to catch his eye, and in doing this was able to observe the changes which time had wrought upon his old friend. He saw that he looked older and heavier, that his complexion was redder and more swollen; that there were rings under his eyes telling of long drinking and smoking, and the sleeplessness and worry which necessarily accompany both. He looked very miserable, and John Littlejohn wondered what he was thinking about.

Indeed, as George gazed downwards over his beer across the bar, he seemed to be in a sort of trance. Then, slowly, as if a train of thought had come to an end, he lifted his glass for another sip, and put the glass down again. The beery eye began to wander, sorrowfully, disinterestedly, about the crowded, noisy room . . . It alighted upon John Littlejohn. It rested there for a moment, staring. John Littlejohn waved and smiled, and the whole face lit up joyfully. The next moment they had rushed round to meet each other, and were shaking each other's hands and clapping each other on the back.

"Well, here's a surprise?" said John Littlejohn. "I was wondering when you were going to recognize me!"

"Good lord!" said George. "Well, of all people! . . . Good lord this is great . . . Well, of all people! . . ."

It seemed to Johnnie that the other was almost beside himself with pleasure. Johnnie was even a little taken aback. But he let nothing of this be seen and vigorously returned each enthusiastic greeting and compliment.

"Well, *you* haven't changed a *bit*," said George. "Still the same brilliant mathematical genius?"

"You haven't changed, either," said Johnnie. "Still the same bloody fool?"

"Oh—rather! Worse, if possible!"

"*Im*possible," said Johnnie, and they laughed, shyly yet with rich friendliness.

It had always been humorously taken for granted that George Harvey Bone was a bloody fool, and so far from being offended by this query he was only too delighted to have had his personality thus vividly and affectionately recalled.

"Still get your dotty moods?" asked Johnnie, pursuing the joke.

"Oh, rather! . . . They're *much* worse," said George, in the boastfulness and flippancy of his cheerfulness. "I pass out for days on end nowadays!"

They finished off their beer, ordered some more, and soon enough passed into reminiscence. This, naturally, brought them to Bob Barton almost at once, and to what a great fellow he was.

"I know I miss him," said George, in that naive, frank tone of his, "terribly."

"Oh, so do I," said Johnnie, but it occurred to him that he probably did not miss Bob in the same way as George, or to anything like the same extent. Bob Barton, he remembered, had had a curious influence on this big, sad, lumbering man. Whenever they were together George had been a different man, more alive, talkative, confident, happy. He had, as it were, sunned himself in the friendship which Bob had generously yet unthinkingly bestowed. There had, even, been something a little dog-like in George's high spirits and devotion when with his friend—a relationship of which Bob had certainly never taken advantage, for it was true enough that he had been a great fellow. Looking at George now, and the signs of drink, smoking, misery and loneliness which showed so plainly on his face and bearing, it struck John Littlejohn that Bob had unwittingly done George a very bad service, indeed a permanent damage perhaps, by going to America like that.

"Well," said George, "I've found you again now, so you'll have to make up for it. I hope we're going to see a lot of each other now."

"I should say we are," said Johnnie enthusiastically, for he was touched both by what the other had said, and the manner—so simple, and direct, too simple and direct in a hard and complicated world—in which he had said it.

They talked about other things, and a little while later George said, apologetically:

"But I've just been talking about nothing but myself. What about you? What have you been doing? Who are you with now, Johnnie?"

"Oh, I'm in the West End now," said Johnnie. "I'm accountant for Fitzgerald, Carstairs and Scott. The theatrical people. I dare say you've heard of them."

At this an extraordinary change, a look of surprise, wonderment and admiration, came over George's face.

"Good lord!" he said. "Fitzgerald, Carstairs & Scott! . . . Are you with them?"

"Yes . . . What's all the trouble about? Do you know them?"

"No . . . It's just extraordinary, that's all . . ."

"Why . . . what's so extraordinary?"

"Oh . . . nothing . . . Only I know a girl who knows them, that's all . . ."

For a moment Johnnie found it a little difficult to see what might be considered so "extraordinary" in George's knowing a girl who in turn knew the firm. The firm knew millions of girls. Then he shrewdly realized that the extraordinary thing, in George's mind, was not the situation, but the girl. When a man mentions a "girl" to his friend, in just that vague and elusive tone, he invariably means a girl whom he regards as extraordinary. In other words it looked as though his poor friend George was in love. This was a new departure indeed. He wondered whether such an emo-

tion would assist George's happiness, and very much doubted it.

"An actress?" he asked, hoping that George might unbur-
den himself.

"Yes . . ." said George. "Well, she was . . . She had small
parts in films. But she doesn't seem to be able to get anything
now."

"Yes," said Johnnie. "That's the way of it. It's a tough business. Would I know her name?"

"No . . . I don't expect so . . . Netta Longdon's the name . . .
I don't expect you've heard of her."

"No," said Johnnie, "I haven't . . . as a matter of fact . . ."

He added this apologetic "as a matter of fact" in order to
show that it was a mere accident, an inconsequent freak of
nature, that he individually had not come to hear of the girl—
thus hoping delicately to avoid the infliction of any blow to the
pride which George might be presumed to take in her. He was
also now instinctively persuaded, from the look on George's
face when he mentioned her name, that George had "got it
badly." He was faintly amused, and faintly concerned.

George did not seem to want to say any more about it, and
they went on to talk about other things. They ordered some
more beer, decided to have some sandwiches at the bar instead
of going anywhere to lunch, and went on talking. But at last
Johnnie looked at the clock, and saw that he had to go. George
also had an appointment with a dentist, and time was getting
short. They drank up their drinks quickly and came out into the
noise, and traffic, and sunshine. Here, a little dazed by the
brightness and the din of their midday drinking, they made
renewed protestations of their pleasure in having met each
other again, and entered into an arrangement to get into touch
by telephone. They were to have a night out in a few days' time,
and they decided that it would probably be best if Johnnie
came over to meet George at Earl's Court.

When they had parted, Johnnie strolled back through Leicester Square towards the office. His body basked in the warmth and brightness of the day, but this very warmth and brightness tinged his mind with a certain sadness, an apprehensiveness, which had taken to visiting him at this time of day and which he was unable to dispel. Now it had been warm and fine like this for three weeks without a break. In the thick green of the trees the birds screeched and sang above the subdued thunder of the traffic. In the middle of the square the effigy of Shakespeare stared greyly out in the direction of the *Empire Cinema* with its bright advertisements of "Good-bye, Mr. Chips," with Robert Donat and Greer Garson. A pigeon had alighted on the head of the poet, who seemed to be watching the red coat (like an old-fashioned golfer's coat, yet giving a touch of hot exotic colour to the whole scene) of the man who cleaned shoes on top of the Men's Lavatories. Fine, fine, fine . . . Blue and sunshine everywhere . . .

Fine for the King and Queen in Canada . . .

Fine for the salvaging of the *Thetis* . . .

Fine for the West Indian team . . .

Fine for the I.R.A. and their cloakrooms . . .

Fine for Hitler in Czechoslovakia . . .

Fine for Mr. Strang in Moscow . . .

Fine for Mr. Chamberlain, who believed it was peace in our time—his umbrella a parasol! . . .

You couldn't believe it would ever break, that the bombs had to fall.

An unfortunate series of conflicting engagements disabled Johnnie and George from meeting as soon as they would have liked, and it was a fortnight or so after their encounter in the West End that Johnnie took the tube train from his work to meet George at a quarter to seven one evening at Earl's Court station.

Although he was seven minutes too early he found George waiting for him in the Arcade. This struck him as being decidedly pathetic—both because George had nothing better to do than hang about a station, and also because of what it revealed of George's affectionate eagerness to meet his friend again— and a sudden feeling, almost of responsibility, came over the little man in regard to the big one.

They went to the Rockingham over the way and when they had had their first beer George suggested they should go on somewhere else. George had a look in his eye when he suggested this which made Johnnie fancy that he had some ulterior motive in moving on, but nothing was said about it, and they went out into the street.

They went past the Post Office and A.B.C. and then turned down a narrow road on their right which led indirectly towards the Cromwell Road.

Half-way down this they came to a small pub into which George led him. They got beer at the counter, and then sat at a table covered with green linoleum near the door.

The long, warm, bright days still persisted, and the door of the pub was flung and fastened back. It was cool, dark, and restful inside and pleasant with the peaceful beginnings of the little house's evening trade—two men talking quietly, another reading a newspaper, the flutter of a canary in a cage, the barmaid vanishing into the other bars and returning, the occasional oily jab of the beer-engine and the soft spurt of beer. It was good to sit back in this cave of refreshment, and stare at the blinding brilliance of the day outside, the pavement, the dusty feet of temperate but jaded pedestrians.

"This is one of my regular places," said George.

"Oh yes? . . ." said Johnnie. "Very nice."

And he looked around as though politely to appreciate the nature and savour the quality of his friend's background. But, of course, he could not see what George could see—the wet winter nights when the door was closed; the smoke, the noise, the wet people: the agony of Netta under the electric light: Mickey drunk and Peter arguing: mornings-after on dark November days: the dart-playing and boredom: the lunch-time drunks, the lunch-time snacks, the lunch-room upstairs: the whole poisoned nightmarish circle of the idle tippler's existence. He saw merely a haven of refreshment on a summer's day.

In the course of the next forty minutes they had two more beers, and the place began to fill up. Then two people entered, a dark girl without a hat, and a fair man with a moustache, to whom George said "Hullo, Netta . . . Hullo, Peter . . ." and who went to the bar, and stood there talking.

There was something in George's eye when he greeted this couple, which closely resembled the something which had been in his eye when he had suggested they should move on from the Rockingham, and which led Johnnie to suppose that there was a direct casual connection between the two looks. In other words, it looked as though he had been brought in here, either by the conscious or only half-conscious volition of his friend, to see or meet these two. Then, as he continued to talk to George, who was now a little vague in his manner, he remembered the name "Netta" as being the one given to the girl mentioned by George in their last meeting, and he at once understood everything. George had brought him here either because he wanted him to meet or see the girl with whom he was in love, or, perhaps, simply because he was unable to keep away from any place where she was likely to be. Johnnie had a momentary feeling of disappointment, of faint jealousy even, that on this, their evening out, George's real thoughts should be lying in another direction. He also had a slight fear of being bored in the near future as the recipient of confidences. But he showed nothing of this.

In the meantime, while he talked to George, he took what opportunity he could of studying the girl and the man as they stood at the bar. He was not pleased by what he saw, either from his own point of view as a judge of individuals generally, or from the point of view of George's happiness in particular. It flashed across his mind, in fact, that George had got in with a rather "bad lot." He didn't like the look of the man at all. He did not like his general carriage, his fair, cruel face, his fair guardsman's moustache, his eccentricity of dress, his hatless-ness, his check trousers and light grey sweater with polo neck—"sensible" enough, no doubt, but in this case assumed, one was certain, not by a humble man who desired to be sensible, but by a scornful, ultra-masculine man who desired to single himself out from the herd and wear a "uniform" while others made do with a plain shirt and collar.

Here, Johnnie reflected, were the outward signs of the same sort of vanity and exhibitionism as distinguishes the third-rate practitioner of the arts, but the art instead of being that of poetry, of music, or of painting, of Bloomsbury or Chelsea, was of Great Portland Street, of transactions with secondhand cars, of dubious deals with men, of persuasions in public houses, borrowings and post-dated cheques. And he did not like the look of the girl very much better. She was decidedly attractive, he saw, but in an ill-natured, ungracious way. Because of his connection with Fitzgerald, Carstairs & Scott, Johnnie had an extensive knowledge of the external appearance and different modes of behaviour of a great variety of attractive women: they came up to the office in shoals, with their nails dipped in blood and their faces smothered with pale cocoa. And some were charming and simple beneath their masks, and some were complex and arrogant. This girl belonged to the latter type, the type which would ignore or stare surlily at him if he spoke to them, until they learned that the actual money came through him, when their manner sweetened wonderfully. This girl wore her attractiveness not as a girl should, simply, consciously, as a happy crown of pleasure, but rather as a murderous utensil with which she might wound indiscriminately right and left, and which she would only employ to please when it suited her purpose. They were like bad-tempered street-walkers, without walking the street. They walked, instead, the offices of inferior film agencies and studios, and they sat in dirty snack bars with tall, pimply young men, and they went about in open sports cars and they lived in the suburbs, or in Maida Vale, or Earl's Court. They had not the smallest talent for the theatre, nor the slightest interest in it save as a dubious means to a dubious end.

Roughly of this type Johnnie judged this girl to be, though he was aware that he might be misjudging her because of the bar and neighbourhood she was in, and the unpleasant-looking man she was with. As the type of person for George to fall for, however, he was certain that she was disastrous. No type could be less calculated, he surmised, to make his big, simple friend happy. He wondered how far it had gone, and what relationship there was between the two.

After a while the fair, unpleasant-looking man went out, and the girl was left alone on a stool at the bar. At this George became completely distracted in his conversation, and it was obvious that he wanted to go over and speak to the girl. Finally he said "I say—forgive me a moment will you?" and went over to her.

Johnnie tactfully looked out of the door at the street, and a few moments later George came over with the girl and introduced her.

"How do you do," said Johnnie affably. "Come and sit down. What will you have to drink?"

"No—this is my go," said George, as the girl sat down, and when they had decided upon what they would have, he went to the bar to get it.

Left alone with the girl he found nothing to say, and it was clear that she was not going to help him. She was not the type to help in such an emergency. She was the sort of girl who would not be in the smallest way embarrassed by not talking to you or not looking at you as she sat with you. She was also, Johnnie could see, in a hostile mood because she had been forced to be introduced to and to sit with a common-looking little man in spectacles about whom she knew nothing. This, he thought, was reasonable enough. She might, however, have made the best of a bad business, and the fact that she was unable to make the effort was undoubtedly largely due to a general scorn of his friend George. That was one of the first things he noticed about her—her scorn of George. Another thing he noticed was that she was even more attractive near to than at a distance.

CHAPTER THREE

Georgeorge came back with the drinks, pleased, flustered, shy.

"I'm frightfully glad you two have met," he said. "Johnnie's my very oldest friend. We were at school together—weren't we, Johnnie?" He sat down.

"Yes, rather," said Johnnie. "Well—here's how." And they drank.

At this the girl, though still plainly annoyed, evidently realized that she was embroiled for the next ten minutes, and found it convenient to ease the situation.

"Was he always as silly?" she said, and with a hearty, humorous "My God—was he as silly?" from Johnnie, they all laughed, the atmosphere became less difficult and they began to talk.

He noticed that George's face lit up, that he became twice the man, when she spoke about him being silly, and he saw him looking at her on the sly in a puzzled, simple, manifestly adoring way. There was no doubt that he was hopelessly in love, and that the girl was unusually attractive.

It was Johnnie's turn to order drinks next, and they all had short ones. Johnnie went to the bar to get them, and when he returned George let out of the bag a cat which Johnnie had been certain would be released before long.

"I wonder you two haven't met before, as a matter of fact," said George, looking at Netta. "Johnnie works with Fitzgerald, Carstairs & Scott. You know them, don't you, Netta?"

"Oh really? . . ." said Netta in a curious voice. "Do you? . . ."

"Yes, that's right," said Johnnie, and as he took a sip at his drink he was aware that the girl Netta was staring at him, no doubt wondering what on earth such an insignificant little person had to do with these great men. It was not the first time that Johnnie had evoked this sort of reaction in strangers—particularly, of course, those connected with the theatre. To be a member of this powerful firm was to have, as it were, a quick and magic passport into the respect and favour of theatrical snobs and hangers-on on the middle or lower plane, and caused in such circles as much furtive consternation as the news that one had been to Eton and Oxford might cause in a Folkestone boardinghouse for old women. Whether this girl Netta was such a snob and hanger-on remained to be seen.

"Yes. He's their accountant," said George. "He's a genius at figures, is Johnnie—always was."

They talked about other things for a few minutes but soon enough they came back to the firm.

"So you work for the Eddies, do you?" said Netta. The firm was often alluded to familiarly as "The Eddies" or the "Two Eddies" (meaning Eddie Fitzgerald and Eddie Carstairs) by those who had dealings with them, and Johnnie felt that in speaking of them in this way she was trying to establish the fact that she herself had connections with them, and was anxious to get more out of him on the subject generally. Indeed it was quite possible that, as an actress, she smelt afar the possibility of making a connection which might lead her to a job.

"Yes," he said. "They're great people, aren't they? Do you know them well?"

"No," she said. "I just know Eddie Carstairs . . . and I've been up to the office."

She had quite a funny look in her eye when she mentioned Eddie Carstairs, and he wondered how well she knew him. Perhaps she was one of those women who had got a passion for

Eddie: there were dozens of them; Eddie just had that about him. But he didn't imagine she knew him well, as he would have seen her up at the office. He noticed that George was looking mightily pleased at the turn of the conversation, and he thought he could understand why. Probably he believed he was gaining prestige with the girl he loved by introducing her to one whom he could truthfully claim as his oldest friend, and who might be of use to her in regard to her profession. Well, he must help poor old George.

"Yes. He's a great fellow, Eddie Carstairs," he said. "I've known him for years. I got into the firm through him, actually."

They began to talk about the firm, and about the theatre, and the more they talked the more friendly they became and the more pleased George looked. Soon the time came to order more drinks and it became clear to Johnnie that they were all going to get drunk.

He came to this conclusion with a certain amount of gloom, as he always did nowadays, but he realized philosophically that on this occasion it was more or less a practical necessity. His friend George was in a state of happiness he could not spoil; the girl, previously hostile, had become mellow and friendly, and he himself was elated and talkative. So, at a given moment, he resigned himself to the joys of alcohol, wisely telling himself that if there was to be a hateful and repentant morning after the night before, he would at least see that the pleasure of the night before was not marred by the hatefulness of repentance—so that the night before and the morning after, the one in its pleasure, and the other in its pain, might from the true perspective of a long-distance view in time seem to cancel each other out. It was largely a question of time, and Johnnie always thought that if you could only have your morning after first, and your night before afterwards, the whole problem of drinking, and indeed of excess and sin in life generally, would be simplified or solved.

The first thing, of course, for those in the suburbs who realize they are going to get drunk is to hop into a taxi and move
towards the West End. This they now did almost without consulting each other. They rose automatically when the round
was finished, and took their conquering spirits out into the air.

A taxi was found in the Earl's Court Road and at first they
could not decide where they wanted to go. Then Johnnie said he
would take them all to eat in a place he knew in Soho, and its
address was given to the man. But on the way a discussion of
places and pubs arose, and their plans were altered in favour of
Shepherd's Market, because of a place which Netta knew about.

Here they had three more rounds, and talked madly at each
other. Netta and Johnnie talked about the theatre and its per-
sonalities, and Johnnie and George talked about their school-
days and their friends in common. Then they went on to
another pub nearby and began again. But before they had had
two rounds here the lights went down on them and the "All
out" was being called. They rushed a last drink, and made for
Oddenino's, where they could have more drinks with sandwiches on the extension.

Periods of slight gloom and dizziness were now overtaking
Johnnie, as they always did on a long steady drunk without
eats, but he saw that George's spirits were maintained at the
same high level. It was as though he attached some enormous
significance to this meeting of his two friends, and that he was
unable to get over the wonder of it.

When they got to Oddenino's, and were having beer and
sandwiches, this enthusiasm of George's reached a sort of
peak, and caused a conversation which next morning Johnnie
was inclined to regret.

He had happened to remark that on the day after the mor-
row he was going down to Brighton for the night, to see one of
the firm's new shows, which was having a prior-to-London
week at the Hippodrome.

"I wish I could come," said George. "I'd love a bit of sea air. In fact, I wish we could all go."

"Well, why not?" said Johnnie politely.

"Yes—why not?" said Netta, and at this Johnnie saw George look at her in an incredulous way.

"What do you mean?" he said. "Would you come to Brighton, Netta?"

"Yes," she said. "I don't see why not; in fact, if I wasn't so broke, I would."

But still George wasn't satisfied.

"You mean you'd come down to Brighton?" he said.

"Yes," said Netta. "In fact, if you'll lend me the money it's a date."

"Lend you the money," said the intoxicated George, "I'll *give* you the money! Why—this is grand! This is great!"

And in the next few minutes he became quite beside himself.

He got an A.B.C. from the waiter and discussed trains; he discussed hotels, how they were all going to meet, how they would go to the theatre and how long they would stay. Johnnie, of course, had to get back the next morning, but Netta said that she wouldn't mind staying until the weekend. This set George into further paroxysms of joy, and in point of fact, in a mixture of drunkenness and pleasure, he began to make a bit of a fool of himself. Johnnie had seen George like this before when he was drunk, in the old days with Bob Barton.

Trying to get more drinks they were now refused, for it was past twelve. Acknowledging defeat they came out into the cool street, and there, swaying, shouting and affectionate, they said good-bye. George was to give him a ring in the morning, and their next meeting was to be at Victoria Station.

George and the girl Netta got into a taxi, but Johnnie, who had a room in Fitzroy Square, decided to walk it.

On his way back in the summer night his head cleared and

he decided tactfully to get out of this Brighton business. In his life nowadays he had enough necessary drinking to do as it was, and he didn't mean to burden himself by getting into fresh circles in which he had to do more. Besides, if he saw George again, he wanted to see him alone. He liked George, but he liked him for himself and by himself. He still didn't like the girl.

THE FIFTH PART

PETER

Tell me, friends
Am I not sung and proverbial for a fool
In every street? Do they not say "How well
Are come upon him his deserts"? Yet why?
                    J. MILTON, *Samson Agonistes*

CHAPTER ONE

In the mornings, nowadays, George Harvey Bone was awakened by a fluffy white cat belonging to the hotel. At about seven o'clock he would hear a little cry—petulant rather than appealing—outside his door, and he would blunder out of bed in the darkness and open the door. He would blunder back into bed and hear no more.

Then there would be a sudden springy soft weight on his body, and the cat would begin to manoeuvre near his head. Sleepy as he was, he could put out his hand and stroke its fur.

After a while this motion seemed to generate an electrical disturbance within the animal—an aeroplane-like throbbing, slowly growing in volume and drawing nearer—the purring of the cat in his ear. The purring, this surrender of its being to a rhythmic and externally audible throbbing, in its turn seemed to induce in the cat a sort of frenzy, a frenzy manifesting itself mainly in its front paws, which, in an agony of restless pleasure, stretched and relaxed, the right paw stretching while the left relaxed, and the other way about, in eager alternation. George called this "playing the piano." He did not know the name of the cat so he called it "Pussy." "Don't make such a noise, Pussy," the big drinking man would gently murmur in the darkness. "And stop playing the piano." But the cat would not stop until a place had been found under the bedclothes near George's head; then it would go to sleep, and George would attempt to do the same.

But usually it would be too late, and in a few moments he

would be wide awake, grinding out the problems of his life, delving into the night before to see where he had got to exactly, where he had left off. This morning he knew, because of the sickness in his heart, and the giddiness in his head, that he had got drunk, but he couldn't at first remember how or where . . . Then it all came back – Johnnie Littlejohn and Netta! They had all been out together. And something else . . . What else? . . . Brighton! . . .

Yes. Brighton. That was why he had got so drunk—because Netta had said they would all go to Brighton. What a fool. As though it would ever come to anything. They must have all been drunk. Or were they?

To go to Brighton with Netta . . . The old dream of dreams . . . To take her away and have her to himself, away from everybody, from Peter and Mickey, away from London, away from the noise, peacefully, in the country, or by the sea. A small hotel. Not necessarily to sleep with her—just to have her to look at, to talk to, quietly.

That had been his idea of paradise once—but of course it was too late now. Since the cupboard everything was too late. It was all over. He was not in love in that way with Netta any more. At least he was not supposed to be.

The cupboard was weeks and weeks ago now—the cupboard was in early spring—the first real warm spring day—it was like summer. After the glaring sunshine on Earl's Court pavements, the evening had come in warm and velvety, and they had had the window open . . .

They were round at Mickey's playing poker—Mickey's mother's flat with its ground-floor dining-room looking out on the square. There were Peter, Mickey, Netta, himself and the horrible, wise-cracking, self-consciously dour little Scotsman McCrae, a newcomer but insolently sure of himself.

As usual, he, George, was losing, and as usual doubling up to recover his losses, and as usual losing more. By about ten

o'clock he gave in and said he would "watch." Then they wanted to send him out to get sandwiches and bottles of beer. But
at first he wouldn't. He was secretly angry at losing; they had
got all his money; and now they wanted to send him out like an
errand boy. They had done this before: he always lost and he
was always the errand boy, and they thought they could treat
him how they liked. "No," he said, "I'm going to play again in
a moment. Let's all go round if we want anything."

There was a chorus of disapproval at this. "Oh—put a sock
in it."—"Be a pal."—"If you're not playing why can't you be
useful?" etc. But he stuck to his guns, and at last Netta spoke.

"Please don't be a fool, George," she said. "Do what you're
told and behave yourself. I'm thirsty."

They all cheered applause at this, but he still stuck to his
guns, and at last Mickey said he would go. There was then a lot
more argument and finally, because Mickey had at least made
a gesture, he gave in. He knew he was a fool and a weakling to
do so, but they were too much for him. Together they were
always too much for him.

Snubbed, isolated, yet obedient, he went round in the velvety night to the Black Hart, and with the deliberate intention
of keeping them waiting at any rate he had two drinks on his
own. Then he bought a pile of sandwiches and three quart bottles and went back.

When he reached the house there was another car besides
Peter's outside the door, and they were all leaving. Mickey's
cousin, a little moustached man much resembling Mickey,
called Gerald (whom he had met once before), had arrived on
the scene and they were all going off to drink somewhere else
with him. He didn't know where they were going, but he got a
seat in the front with this Gerald, who was driving. They didn't
want the sandwiches or beer now, because Gerald had brought
some whisky, which they were swilling from the top of a ther-
mos flask.

He never knew where exactly they landed up, but it was somewhere in the suburbs—Chiswick or Acton or somewhere like that—in a smallish house in a long row of other houses. They made a lot of noise, so much so that an old woman shouted at them from a window, which caused a lot of hilarity and backchat. Then they were taken into a front room where there were sandwiches and lots to drink. Somebody had got married or won a sweepstake, or both, or something. Anyway, there was lots to drink, and that was why Gerald had brought them round. There were several strangers, and they were all soon screaming and yelling drunk. Somewhere in all this they got to playing hide-and-seek all over the darkened house, and then came the cupboard.

It was in a bedroom upstairs, and he was floundering about for a place to hide. He pulled the door open, and saw them there, Netta and Peter, clearly in the watery light from a lamp in the street outside. He kept his head—thank God—he kept his head.

"Ah-ha—engaged I see," he said casually, jovially as though he had seen nothing of what was going on, as though they were strangers, and he closed the door on them at once, and floundered out of the room. His reaction had been as quick as lightning: they couldn't have known he had seen anything. They must have thought that he thought they were another couple. That was his one consolation, then, as it was now—the one little thing that saved his pride.

When he got out of the room he found his way to the top of the house, and sat on the stairs in the pitch darkness. Netta and Peter! All the time, and he hadn't known it! Netta and Peter! How they must have been hooting with laughter at him, from the beginning. He would never have believed it. So that was it. Well, it was all over now. He was through now. He sat on the stairs, stunned by the shock and anaesthetized by drink, and believed he was almost glad, because now he was through.

After a while the lights went on downstairs—the game was over, and the drunk was proceeding. He wanted to remain on the stairs, thinking it all over, but he decided he must put a face on it. Somehow, sometime, he would get his own back, so long as they never knew he knew. Later, somehow, when they least expected it, he would drop a remark casually showing he had known all the time, showing that he had been wise to them, showing that he didn't care and never had cared. Not now—*later*—when he was somehow on *top*, when he had found another girl. He would have to find another girl—he would have to *pretend* to find one.

He went downstairs and got himself another drink. Peter was getting one at the same time, and he spoke to him, showing nothing on his face, giving away nothing in his voice. Netta was in the room, but he couldn't look at her. She would find out if he looked at or spoke to her.

Soon everything went screaming mad—a woman fell into a lamp-stand and was hurt, Mickey put the lamp-shade on his head, and a few moments afterwards staggered upstairs to be sick. He went up and helped Mickey out, and when they came down it was felt that the party was over.

In the car going back he again sat in front with Gerald, and Peter and Netta sat behind with an intoxicated boy of about twenty-one to whom they were giving a lift, and who sang most of the time—sang while Peter and Netta were silent—cupboard-silent. Every now and again he could see them in the reflector, Peter's mouth crushed on hers and her knee raised in response and pleasure . . . Then they would join in the singing, and then they would be silent again . . . They thought they were fooling him: they didn't realize there was the reflector. Or didn't they care? Both, probably. They were drunk of course . . .

They dropped Netta off at her flat, and he and Peter got out at the station. He went to the coffee stall with Peter and ate sandwiches with him. Peter bought some sandwiches in a bag, and they said good night. Then, trembling with the cold of the night and his fear, he tracked Peter along the Earl's Court Road and saw him go to Netta's flat. Peter let himself in at the front door with the big key which Netta gave you when you went shopping for her.

He saw a light behind Netta's curtains. So that was that. He wanted to hang about, but it was too cold. They were warm and comfy for the night, and he wasn't going to hang about in the cold. They had left him out in the cold. The long, warm, spring evening had ended in deathly cold at two o'clock and he had to get to bed. He had his hangover to face in the morning.

CHAPTER TWO

The odd thing was that that hangover was not as predicted.

When he awoke and remembered, instead of groaning pain he had a funny feeling of calm, of release. He had a feeling only of having behaved well and wisely in drink for once. He had kept his head: he had not given himself or his dignity away: he had established a perfect alibi. They knew nothing: he knew everything. In an odd, inverted way, he felt top dog.

But there was something else, too. There was a sense of release from Netta. By giving herself to Peter she had made herself something other than what she was before—something cheaper, more human, more bestial, less agonizingly inaccessible. Inaccessible to him, of course, but not inaccessible. Instead of being jealous of Peter, he was in a manner grateful to him: he had brought her down to the sordid level of Peter—and on that level she did not hurt so much. She wasn't violets and primroses in an April rain any more: she was a woman in bed with a nasty man in Earl's Court. Good for Peter.

Could this mood hold? Was he what they called "disgusted," and had he a chance of getting out of love with her now?

To his surprise it had seemed for a little that there was a possibility of this. He went round and met them that morning, went and had drinks at the Black Hart, and amazed himself by his coolness. He looked at them both as he talked to them; he thought of what he now knew about them; and all he was aware of was the change in the quality of his feelings towards Netta.

She was still lovely; he still wanted her: but now he didn't want her in the same mad, adoring way. He wanted her only in the way that Peter (and the other men on whom she had no doubt bestowed her favours) wanted her. She was something to be had by men, and as such he could do without her. Or so he believed.

Indeed, after a few drinks that morning, his soul began to smile to itself. It smiled both at this change in his feelings and at the secret knowledge he had of the real facts. He was happier than he had been for months. He was cheerful, almost sparkling. He bought most of the drinks, rallied the sick and repentant Mickey, looked Netta in the eye, and challenged Peter at darts. "You're in very good form this morning," Netta said. And this made him smile inwardly all the more, for it showed how completely he had succeeded in hiding his new knowledge from their sight. It was beyond even Netta's shrewdness to know that he was cheerful because he had found out that she had slept with another man.

He believed, that cheerful morning, that he was through with this filthy gang, that before long he would be rising from this sad circle in hell in which he had been condemned to wander so long. And although, when the evening came, he was no longer cheerful, and had to try and quell the first sickening pangs of physical jealousy and outraged pride, he still contrived to believe that something good, not bad, had befallen, and a few drinks put him right and made him cheerful again.

Eerie days followed. He made a point of going round and drinking with them, of seeing them as much as ever—of behaving normally. Only in such a way could he preserve, for the time being, his secret and his pride. But he found, as he had hoped he would, that the longing as it was before, the old sense of having to hang dog-like on her doorstep, was beginning ever so faintly to fade. He would find himself not ringing her up for forty-eight hours or more, he would find himself staying up in town all day, he would find himself going to the Kensington movie of an evening without consulting anybody, and walking back down the Earl's Court Road and having a cup of tea at the coffee-stall and going to bed.

Then one day, more or less by accident, he got a copy of *David Copperfield* out of the Kensington public library. He had read it years and years ago, and he thought he might try it again. He took it as a good sign that he could even think of reading again, and the experiment was a huge success. He became absorbed in the long book, which almost robbed his life of its bleakness and loneliness in the warm sunny days which followed. The warmth of the weather and *David Copperfield* seemed to conspire together to give him peace of mind. He would sometimes go to bed at nine o'clock, before it was dark, and read *David Copperfield*.

CHAPTER THREE

He began to feel better in himself, to think of taking a "holiday," of going somewhere and getting some bathing and golf. He began to think of health and sobriety as a practical proposition. Among other things he noticed that his "dead" moods had been less frequent recently, and he thought this might be because he was drinking less and not leading such a rackety life. He had had an awful bout of those moods round about and just after Christmas—in fact, they had really begun to scare the life out of him—but now, with the warm weather and *David Copperfield*, they seemed to be passing away.

There were some days when he thought about Netta scarcely at all, and some days when he thought about nothing else. That was all over, he told himself, but he had to go on seeing her and Peter to save his pride and dignity. And he didn't know whether he was lying to himself, and just seeing her because he still couldn't keep away from her.

Then one day, when Peter was away in Yorkshire, she phoned him up (*she* phoned *him* up!) and asked him to come round. She had had a threatening and semi-blackmailing letter from a small dressmaker, and she wanted him to help her. He went round and saw the woman and settled the matter out of his own pocket. That evening she gave him some drinks in her flat, and let it be seen that he might take her out to dinner if he cared. He took her out. She did not insist on Perrier's and they went to a small, cheap place in Soho.

It had been fatal, of course. He had tried to think that it hadn't been, that it hadn't set him going again, but he knew by now that it had. Sitting opposite her in that little, quiet place, was like the old days—those three weeks just after he had first met her, when he had fondly imagined that she had no background, no drunken mob, no Peter behind her. She was wildly, wildly lovely that night. He looked across the table at her, and she was violets and primroses again. He couldn't help it. He just couldn't be bothered about Peter and what he knew. Peter was away—a thing of the past—or at any rate not of the immediate present—and Netta was Netta again.

Then there was one remark she had made which had set him going. He couldn't remember the context, but he could remember the words exactly. "On the contrary, my dear Bone," she had said, "you're very much more presentable these days." That had set him going. He took it back to bed with him that night, and it haunted his nights and days. Was it possible that if he pulled himself together, if he smoked and drank less, he might still have a chance of getting her? If Peter had had her, why shouldn't he? She was to be had, after all. Couldn't he be a man, and pull himself together, and get her? Not that he really wanted her immediately in that way. He wanted to have her for ever, to love and marry her and live in the country. But if he could get her that way, that would be the first step, that would be something. Besides, if he could get her that way, he might fall out of love with her. Things happened like that.

He began to dream and scheme again, and that meant that he went back to drinking.

He finished *David Copperfield*, and did not take it back to the library and followed it up with *Martin Chuzzlewit* as he had planned. The *David Copperfield* period was over.

Then the big day came when he bumped into Johnnie Littlejohn—a very big day. He didn't exactly know why he was so happy after meeting Johnnie again—but he was lighter in heart than he had been for years. It wasn't just because he was fond of Johnnie, or because Johnnie reminded him of the old days: it was something more than that. It was the feeling that perhaps *he* had a friend now—a real friend—that *he* had a background.

It was always Netta who had had the background before, and he who had been isolated—an interloper in her alien and scornful mob. It was always he who had been utterly alone against many, he who had been made the errand-boy, the man to get the sandwiches, the dumb butt of their unfriendly wit. But what if he had had a friend of his own all the time, a background to rival and hold its own against Netta's? What if, after all, he had sources of intimacy and entertainment elsewhere – a circle from which she possibly was excluded and in which he was accorded full human dignity and respect? It was a healing thought, and he very soon made up his mind that Netta and Johnnie must meet.

And what a clever, impressive, prosperous friend, too. He got the shock of his life when he learned that Johnnie was up at Fitzgerald, Carstairs & Scott's. He knew the secret awe in which Netta—the seldom-awed Netta—held his firm. He knew that she was to a certain extent chasing the famous Eddie Carstairs (who, God be praised, didn't seem to be having any). He remembered that scene in Perrier's. That was why she haunted Perrier's—just to try and accidentally meet Eddie Carstairs. And here he had a friend who was in the firm!—a friend who was a personal friend of Eddie Carstairs, who must meet and talk to Eddie Carstairs every day of his life! He would show her! He would show her he had some friends—and some pretty useful and high-up ones, too.

Why, he might be the means, through Johnnie, of getting her in with the firm, of getting her a job. That would be too funny, after all that had passed. How would Peter like that? He must keep Johnnie up his sleeve. There were astonishing possibilities if he only kept his head. It seemed that fate, for once, had perpetrated a kindly instead of a dirty trick, and, out of the blue, had put a weapon into his hands.

Weren't things taking a turn for the better? Hadn't she said, "On the contrary, my dear Bone, you're very much more presentable these days," and hadn't he got this new weapon, this new resource and dignity in Johnnie?

Then, last night, the thing had happened—Johnnie and Netta had met—and he had of course spoiled everything by getting drunk. Just at the time when he wanted to keep sober, he had got drunk. He had been so mad with joy, having Netta and Johnnie together, drinking and apparently liking each other: it had been so exquisitely novel and pleasurable a sensation to have a presentable and by no means unimpressive friend to show to Netta, to be, as it were, alongside of him as two to one against Netta—that he simply couldn't stop himself getting drunk. And then, when Brighton was suggested, and Netta had said she would go, he had gone crazy. He had thought, last night in drink, that all his troubles were as good as over, that Netta, by consenting to come away, had opened a new heavenly era of some sort.

He must have made an awful fool of himself; and he hoped to God he hadn't shocked or disgusted Johnnie: it would be a nice thing if he lost his best friend now he had found him.

And what did it all amount to? Nothing, of course. It was all drunken blah, and it would probably be in bad taste, bad drinker's etiquette even to mention Brighton to either of them again. It just wasn't done to take such things seriously the next day.

Or were they serious? He would have to phone Johnnie to find out. Netta, of course, would never come, but he might have a night by the sea with Johnnie. Not that he felt like it. With a head like his he didn't know how he was going to get out of bed, let alone go to the sea.

He wished he wasn't such a miserable man. He drew closer

to the white cat and stroked its fur. It would soon be time to get up, if he wanted any breakfast, and he had to make himself eat.

He heard the chambermaid creaking and clanking about outside on the landing, and, from dim distances all over the hotel, the hissing of taps turned on, mysterious gurglings in pipes, the running of h. & c. in the bedrooms of his sober, God-fearing fellow-guests. The dynamo in the white cat, again receiving electrical power from the motion of his hand, again began to purr. It was day.

CHAPTER FOUR

When George Harvey Bone telephoned her at eleven
o'clock, Netta Longdon was still asleep.

After a night of drinking, she would invariably wake
up about half past five in the morning, put on the light and
read magazines or newspapers for about two hours, and then
fall into a second sleep until eleven or twelve.

She lifted the receiver and hazily heard George saying something about Brighton. She heard him saying that it seemed to
be off, because Johnnie (that, she remembered, was the name
of the little man they were out with last night) had just phoned
him to say he couldn't make it after all. She had, of course, a
"head," and she couldn't be bothered to listen to him.

"All right," she said, "I'm asleep now. Come round and talk
about it when I'm awake."

George then said he would come round some time after
twelve, and she put down the receiver and went to sleep again.
She woke again about half an hour later, and, brooding dully
about various things, remembered that she had invited George
to come round to her flat in about half an hour's time. She did
not usually let George into her flat in the morning, and she
wondered why she had made an exception this time. Her mind
then went back to the night before, and she realized, dimly, that
she had obeyed a correct instinct in allowing him to come
round and see her.

Netta Longdon thought of everything in a curiously dull,
brutish way, and for the most part acted upon instinct. She was

completely, indeed sinisterly, devoid of all those qualities which her face and body externally proclaimed her to have— pensiveness, grace, warmth, agility, beauty. Externally this Earl's Court sleeper-on, this frequenter of film agents' offices was of the type depicted by the poet Byron.

> *She walks in beauty, like the night*
> *Of cloudless climes and starry skies,*
> *And all that's best of dark and bright*
> *Meets in her aspect and her eyes*
>
> *One shade the more, one ray the less*
> *Had half impaired the nameless grace*
> *Which waves in every raven tress*
> *Or softly lightens o'er her face,*
> *Where thoughts serenely sweet express*
> *How pure, how dear their dwelling-place.*

Her thoughts, however, resembled those of a fish—something seen floating in a tank, brooding, self-absorbed, frigid, moving solemnly forward to its object or veering slowly sideways without fully conscious motivation. She had been born, apparently, without any natural predilection towards thought or action, and the circumstances of her early life had seemed to render both unnecessary. "Spoiled" from the earliest days because of her physical beauty: made a fuss of, given in to, beset with favours, the fulfilment of her desires going ahead at roughly the same pace as their conception, she had become totally impassive; thought and action were atrophied. Having no inherent generosity (as George perceived), having no instinct to "spoil" or make a fuss of anything in return, she had become like a fish.

Alternatively, she had become like a criminal. Lacking generosity, she lacked imagination, and in her impassivity had developed a state of mind which does not look forward and does not look back, does not compare, reason or synthesize, and therefore goes for what it wants, in the immediate present, without taking into account those considerations, moral or material, which are taken into account by non-criminal or normally provident members of the community.

When Netta awoke this morning she was aware that she was feeling decidedly sick and giddy, that she had a "head": but she did not relate her "head" to the night before—to the fact that she had got drunk. Nor was she capable of connecting her present feeling of illness with the future: she had no idea of preventing a recurrence of such a feeling by making an attempt not to get so drunk again. She simply suffered it in a vacuum— as a habitual crook, who spends his entire life in and out of jail, suffers prison bars.

Not that Netta, half atrophied as she was in regard to conscious thought and action, was incapable of living her life or fulfilling the greater part of her desires efficiently. She might get her way more or less unconsciously, but it would be with considerable precision, in much the same way as a somnambulist will step over obstacles and have regard for his own vital interests generally. When she had told George to come round this morning, she had not at the time known why she had done so. There was, however, an excellent reason. The time had come when she had to get some money out of him, and because of all that Brighton chatter last night, when he had talked himself into a money-throwing mood, the time was ripe.

The same dull, fish-like style of thought which she brought to bear on the local exigencies of life characterized her attitude to her existence generally. She was not without ambitions; she was steering a course of a sort; but dimly, without any fervour or coherence. She had at one time hoped to make good at films; she still vaguely hoped to do so, but she was unable to relate this ambition with the labour requisite for its maturing. She expected it to come to her as all things had come to her hitherto, by virtue of the stationary magnetism of her physical beauty. That was how she had got whatever jobs she'd had in the past, and that was how her frigid, inelastic mind conceived of getting them in the future.

Again, she was not without passions. She was, for instance, intensely dissatisfied with her present mode of life—and that might be said to constitute a sort of passion in itself. But also she was not without physical passions: she liked rich and comfortable surroundings, she liked drink, she even liked men. But even here she was without any driving force or power of coordination. She went on suffering sordid surroundings, she got drunk and went with men as it were accidentally, without plan, as opportunity or inclination offered.

George imagined that she had a permanent relationship with Peter, something with a past and a future, but he was mistaken. She gave herself to him only occasionally, when she had drunk to excess and he forced it upon her—spasmodically and lovelessly. On the whole she disliked and despised Peter, if only as part of her disliked and despised surroundings.

If she had any strong feeling for any man at the moment, it was, oddly enough, for Eddie Carstairs, of Fitzgerald, Carstairs & Scott, with whom she was unable to make any sort of satisfactory contact.

She had met him at one or two parties a year or so ago, and she had been attracted towards him for a variety of reasons. She had been attracted by him physically, by his sophistication, his clothes, his personality; she had been attracted by his aloof, offhand air, which was friendly in a slightly mocking way; and above all, of course, she had been attracted by his prosperity and power, the people he mixed with, the places he frequented, the firm of which he was a partner. To go about with Eddie Carstairs was to go about with the high-ups: infinite possibilities were open to you; dispensing with all tiresome preliminaries, you might crash straight from Earl's Court into success,

opulence or stardom. He had made no advances to her whatever, but on the few brief occasions when she had been alone
with him, or when she had been at his flat and only a few other
people were there, he had, she fancied, more than once given
her a curious, humorous, fleeting look. She had been unable to
interpret the exact meaning of that look, but it had at once suggested to her mind the possibility of becoming his mistress,
and no sooner had that idea arisen, with its enormous poten-
tialities, than it had been formulated as a secret practical ambition. From then on, whenever Eddie Carstairs' name was mentioned by her gang, a little light, a faintly absentminded look
denoting an interruption in thought, could be seen on Netta
Longdon's face, and she would be inclined to change the subject, as though her personal affairs were being discussed.

That she had made no headway in this matter, that since she
had been out of a job she had had no practical means of making any further contact with this man, had not failed to add to
her general dissatisfaction with her life, and it was for this reason that George, as he himself had surmised, was occasionally
given the privilege of taking her to Perrier's (the upstairs
room), which she knew he frequented and where she hoped to
meet him by accident.

But Mr. Carstairs did not respond, it seemed, to accidental
meetings, and in the absence of any advance in this direction
Netta, on the whole, was drifting more and more to Peter.
Wanting no other man save the one she could not get, any
other man, the nearest at hand, served her purpose. And
although she disliked and despised Peter, he yet had certain
qualities which appealed subtly and more or less unconsciously to something in her own nature—a coldness, cruelty and
strength, perhaps, which matched her own.

She liked Peter, for instance, because of her knowledge, possessed by few others, of his past—the fact that he had twice
been in jail. He had been in jail on one occasion for assaulting

and wounding a man at a political meeting, and on another for killing a pedestrian with his car while drunk, and this she liked, this stimulated her. She liked the whole atmosphere: she liked the deeds themselves, and she liked the jail. Both provided something bloody, brutal, and unusual which gave him a halo of originality.

Then there were other aspects of the man, too, to which Netta responded, which made him interesting and passable, which enabled her to "stand" him, whereas she could not "stand" the average man who forced his attentions upon her. She knew him inside out, and she knew of his intense, smouldering, revengeful social snobbery. She knew how, behind that pallid, sullen, Philip-the-Fourth-like face, his soul winced when people of the moneyed class, when titled or rich people, were merely mentioned. She knew of the horror, the diseased fury, he harboured in his heart against his own upbringing, the fact that he had not been to a mentionable public school. She knew with what a passion, behind a studied manner of indifference, he clung to each of his few contacts with what were to him the right sort of people. She knew how his political activities, his practical "fascism" in the past, were derived from this sickly envy and passion. Banished, by reason of his birth and lack of money, from the class of which he had so fanatical a secret desire to be a member, he had not turned in anger against that class, or thrown in his lot with any other. That would have been an admission of defeat. On the contrary, he sought to glorify it, to buttress it, to romanticize it, to make it more itself than it was already—hoping thereby, in his ambitious, twisted brain, to gain some reward from it at last, have some place or even leadership in it under the intensified conditions he foresaw for it. Netta knew all this, and, instead of repelling her, it had a decided appeal for her. This was because, in her fish-like way, she had much the same social ambitions and snobbery as he did.

For in spite of her sluttish manner of life, her avowed and somewhat self-conscious "unconventionality," Netta had quite another portrait of herself at the back of her mind. Her true heart was not in the second-hand sports car, the roadhouse, the snack bar and the darts board in the Earl's Court public house; it was, rather, somewhere haunting the society columns, the illustrated pages of *The Sketch*, *The Tatler* or *Vogue*. She would not have admitted this, even to herself, but this was where her inner aesthetic fancy lay. She had not the fanatical anguished social snobbery and aspirations of Peter, but she was all the same, and on the quiet, at one with him in spirit.

And to this was added something else—a feeling for something which was abroad in the modern world, something hardly realized and difficult to describe, but which she knew Peter could discern as well as herself.

This something, which she could not describe, which was probably indescribable, was something to do with those society columns and something to do with blood, cruelty, and fascism—a blend of the two. It had the same stimulus and subtle appeal for her as the fact of Peter having been in jail. It was not the avowed ideology of fascism; she was supposed to laugh at all people who had any strong opinions of any sort. On the other hand it was, in all probability, one aspect of the ideology of fascism. She was supposed to dislike fascism, to laugh at it, but actually she liked it enormously. In secret she liked pictures of marching, regimented men, in secret she was physically attracted by Hitler; she did not really think that Mussolini looked like a funny burglar. She liked the uniforms, the guns, the breeches, the boots, the swastikas, the shirts. She was, probably, sexually stimulated by these things in the same way as she might have been sexually stimulated by a bull-fight. And somehow she was dimly aware of the class content of all this: she connected it with her own secret social aspirations and she would have liked to have seen something of the same sort of thing in this country. She was bored to distraction by the idea of a war, of course, and hence arose her glorious joy (perceived by George) at the time of Munich, when, at one stroke, war was averted and the thing which she was supposed to dislike and laugh at, but to which she was so drawn in reality, was allowed to proceed with renewed power upon its way.

It might be said that this feeling for violence and brutality, for the pageant and panorama of fascism on the Continent, formed her principal disinterested aesthetic pleasure. She had few others. She read practically nothing; she did not respond to music or pictures; she never went to the theatre and very seldom to the movies; and although she had an instinctive ability to dress well and effectively when she desired, she did not even like pretty things. She only liked what affected her personally and physically and immediately—sleep, warmth, a certain amount of company and talk, drinks, getting drunk, good food, taxis, ease. She was not even responsive to adulation, save when, coming fron a man, it promised to further these necessities. She was atrophied. She looked like a Byron beauty, but she was a fish.

Towards George's adulation and adoration, however, she was something other than merely unresponsive, she was hostile. This was not only because of his ineffectuality, his dumbness, his naïvety and his haunting persistence, all of which would have annoyed her in any case. It was also because he was not totally ineffectual, in that, unlike herself (and unlike Peter and Mickey and the rest), he had a curious but ineraseable streak of providence, and possessed a certain sum of money in his bank. The mere existence of this anomalous hoard irritated her beyond measure, the more so inasmuch as she was continually being compelled to make use of it, either in the form of entertainment in public houses, taxis, or restaurants, or in direct loans. His persistence and stupidity, exasperating and humiliating as they both were to her, were both necessary, and therefore the more exasperating and humiliating.

It was for these reasons, of course, that she was seldom able to be polite to him, and enjoyed whatever opportunities arose for watching his humiliation in front of others or in private. The conception of George as the stooge, the silly hanger-on, the errand boy of her set, had actually been originated by her, and was by her perpetuated.

There were occasions, however, when it was necessary to make the effort to be extremely polite, and this morning, as she lay in bed and realized that she had taken the unusual procedure of asking him to come round and see her, she saw that one of these times had come. In drink last night he had promised to give her the necessary money to take her to Brighton. That she could twist this into getting some money and being taken to Brighton as well she had seen at the time. She had even considered it possible that she might get the money without having to go to Brighton. But actually she was not averse to Brighton if this little man (Littlejohn or whatever his name was) was there as well, with his connection with the firm in which she was so interested. But now George had rung up and said that he could not come. How, then, was she to get the money? She wanted as much as fifteen pounds, and she certainly had to have ten for urgent payments of rent and to her charwoman.

She did not exactly know, and as she had her bath, and made some tea, and dressed, she did not bother. Living in a vacuum, with practically no vision of the future, and practically no awareness of the past, she bothered very little about anything, least of all about George, who, oddly enough, and unknown to both of them, at certain seasons directed his mind exclusively to the problem of killing her by violence.

THE SIXTH PART

BRIGHTON

O madness! to think use of strongest wines
And strongest drinks our chief support of health.
J. MILTON, Samson Agonistes

I among these aloof obscurely stood.
  The feast and noon grew high, and sacrifice
  Had filled their hearts with mirth, high cheer, and wine,
When to their sports they turned.
J. MILTON, Samson Agonistes

drunk, tipsy; intoxicated; inebri-ous, -ate, ated; in one's cups; in a state of intoxication &c. *n*; temulent, -ive; fuddled, mellow, cut, boosy, fou, fresh, merry, elevated; flush, -ed; flustered, disguised, groggy, beery; topheavy; pot-valiant, glorious; potulent; over-come, -taken; whittled, screwed, tight, primed, corned, raddled, sewed up, lushy, nappy, muddled, muzzy, obfus-cated, maudlin; crapulous, dead drunk.
Roget's Thesaurus of English Words and Phrases

CHAPTER ONE

Suddenly, as they streamed through Haywards Heath station in the sunny, sticky, streaming afternoon, he became gloomy.

He was in a Pullman car. He sat on the right facing Brighton, and there was no one else at his table. There were only a few other people in the car. Lunch was over, but the lunch-spotted white cloths were still on the tables. He was drinking beer and he all at once became gloomy and saw that he had probably made a fool of himself again, after all.

Until that precise moment his heart had been lifted up with joy and beer and the warmth and splendour of the summer's afternoon. He had been drinking beer since twelve o'clock, ever since Netta had sent him out to get the A.B.C. He had got happier and happier and happier. He had been supremely, gloriously happy when he had got on to the train, and instead of having lunch he had ordered beer. But now, as the train flashed through Haywards Heath, it occurred to him that he was making his usual fool of himself.

It had all seemed so wonderful and simple. He had gone round there at a quarter to twelve and there had been a funny atmosphere from the beginning.

The front door had been open and having rattled the knocker he had walked into the sitting-room and had heard her voice from her bedroom immediately. "Is that you, George?" she had cried. "Sit down for a bit, and I'll be out!"

He had at once sensed something of friendliness in her tone, and, of course, at once presumed that he had made a mistake. Then, "There's some beer in the cupboard if you can find it," she had cried, and he had said, "Thanks, Netta," and poured himself out a flat half-tumblerful remaining in an old quart Watney. He still, of course, didn't believe there was anything behind this odd cordiality he sensed in her tone, but all the same he couldn't help feeling a bit cheered.

Then she came out of the bedroom, and through the sitting-room, on the way to get something from the bathroom. She was fully dressed except for her skirt. That is to say, she wore a jumper, shoes, stockings and underclothes, but no skirt. Thus you could see, if you cared to look, her legs above the knee and her underclothes up to the waist. She frequently walked about like this in her flat when Peter and Mickey were there, and it never failed slightly to shock, embarrass and irritate him. He knew that he must not show by the flicker of an eyelid that he was embarrassed; he knew that it was assumed in her set that it would be conventional and genteel to a degree, libidinous even, to show any consciousness of her not being fully dressed. But he was secretly of the opinion that this was an affectation, and he was displeased both by the affectation itself and by his being forced to share in it. Also he hated to look at her under-clothes, because, of course, they had the same murderous love-liness of everything else that she wore and he was seeing for the first time.

Then it had occurred to him that she had never before come through into the sitting-room in this way while he alone was there: always there had been others present as well—a crowd as it were, to deprive this affectation of negligence of any per-sonal or intimate significance. He noticed this; and taking it in conjunction with the cordiality, or at any rate lack of rudeness, in her voice, he again felt cheered, dared to believe, almost, that something was afoot.

Then she came back into the sitting-room, and instead of

going back into the bedroom she came to the mantelpiece, took a cigarette, lit it, and flopped down in the settee.

"Well," she said, "what's troubling you?"

He told her about Johnnie, and how he had phoned that morning and said he couldn't make Brighton after all. And then they had talked for a little. And then, somehow, he didn't remember how, she had said, "Of course, I'm in an awful spot, anyhow."

"Spot?" he said. "How do you mean, Netta? What sort of spot?"

"Oh, just money and things generally," she said. "I couldn't have made Brighton anyhow."

"Oh, but I was going to treat you to Brighton," he said.

"Were you?" she said. "Well, even that wouldn't have seen me out. I'm in a real mess. Of course, you're so astonishingly provident you don't get into these troubles."

The atmosphere was most odd—he couldn't make it out at all.

Her quiet, confidential tone; her smoking a cigarette and sitting in front of him in her underclothes; the mere fact that she had invited him round in the morning; it was all puzzling. Was it conceivable that she was "making up" to him, that she had a favour to ask of him? No—with Netta it was inconceivable—the harsh, proud, independent Netta he knew. All the same a sudden inspiration prompted him to take advantage of the situation, to exploit this weird new atmosphere which he could not understand, and he said, hardly knowing why, or what answer he expected:

"I suppose you wouldn't come to Brighton with me?"

To his amazement, he saw her pause before replying (as though she was considering it!), and then as she flicked the ash from her cigarette and looked at the floor, she said, "How do you mean exactly, George? When?"

"I mean *now*, and not bother about Johnnie," he said, and

then added laughingly shyly, "I don't mean living in sin! . . . Just going . . ."

Again, to his utter astonishment, she paused, still looking at the floor and smiling faintly yet not ill-naturedly at his crack about living in sin. Then she rose, and, apparently with the object of putting out her cigarette in the ash-tray, joined him at the fireplace. She was only two feet away and he was within the awful halo. But he was so interested in what she was going to say next that he could hardly respond to the halo. At last she spoke.

"Well, I don't know," she said. "If you'll pay some of my bills, I wouldn't mind going away for a bit."

From that moment, of course, he had gone mad with joy.

"Pay your bills!" he had said. "Why, of course I'll pay your bills. Why, Netta, this is wonderful. Of course I'll pay your bills! Why, this is grand!"

"Well," she said, "they're pretty stiff," but he just wouldn't listen to her. He found out later that he had to give her fifteen pounds, but by that time he was so worked up he would have scarcely cared if it had been fifty.

After a little more talk she said she couldn't actually go today, because she had certain things to do, but that she would go tomorrow; and finally it was decided that he should go down first and find a hotel, and she would join him. This pleased him beyond all measure. What a task! To go down to Brighton and find a hotel in preparation for Netta's arrival!

And what a task even preparing to go to Brighton! He must go today—he decided that at once. They had to look out trains, of course, and for this they wanted an A.B.C. "Well, we can soon settle that," he said. "I'll go and get one now!" He was so happy he wanted to be on the move. He even wanted to get away from her, so that he could think about her, think about it all. He left her, promising to return with an A.B.C., and of course the first thing he did was to go to the nearest pub and order a pint of beer. After this he had a gin and French, and managed to borrow an A.B.C. from the pub, who said he could take it away if he brought it back.

"I'm afraid I got so excited I went and had a drink," he said when he got back, and she smiled with quiet indulgence. Then they got down to talking about the trains, while she walked about from room to room finishing her dressing, and they decided on the 5.5, arriving 6.5, as the train she should catch, and he would meet her at the station. "All right—that's a date," she said. Then he gave her the cheque for fifteen pounds which he had written out when he was in the pub.

"Really, this is most accommodating of you, George," she said in that funny crisp way of hers in which she as it were parodied formal speech. "You'll get it back all right, but you may have to wait a bit."

"Oh—don't bother about that," he said, and he didn't really know whether it was a loan or whether he was giving it to her.

At last the time came to go, because she had a lunch date with a woman. As he said good-bye at the door he felt so full of himself, so affectionate and grateful in a frank and almost brotherly way, that he wanted to kiss her. He hesitated and then decided against it. It might look as though he was taking advantage of the favour he was doing her, as though he expected something more than usual from her in the future, as though, even, he crudely imagined there was some bargain or significance in her consenting to come away with him to a seaside town with a reputation. So instead he just shook her hand, as he always did, so sadly, oddly, shyly, clumsily, when he left her.

He went straight back to the pub, and ordered another beer. He usually tried to keep from drinking too much in the middle of the day, but today he meant to have as much as he liked. Hadn't he got something to drink and think about?

He thought and drank, and drank and thought and smoked.

What in God's name did it all mean? Was this a change? Had her feelings somehow changed, had his persistence somehow prevailed, so that in future she was going to be kinder to him, so that in future he might, even, have a chance with her?

And if there was a change—why? Had she just changed because she had changed, or had she some motive? Was she just getting something out of him? Yes, fifteen pounds. But Netta, the shrewd, cruel Netta who scorned him, could never resort to so vulgar and obvious a ruse as that—she would be too proud. Or would she not be too proud? Was she, perhaps, just a common little schemer playing him up just to get some money out of him? Like a prostitute? Perhaps she was just a common little prostitute. Ah—if only she was! If only she was something you could buy and have and be rid of!

Then her walking about the room without her skirt like that. Perhaps he had got this woman all wrong. Perhaps (you could never tell) she only went with Peter because he gave her money! Perhaps he himself ought to try and make love to her like a man (instead of like a forlorn shepherd in an Elizabethan poem) when they got to Brighton. Perhaps she expected it. It was not impossible.

Then there was the question of Johnnie. She was impressed with that connection of his—he saw that clearly enough. She was, for whatever ultimate reason, tremendously interested in this firm, Fitzgerald, Carstairs & Scott, and Johnnie being a member of it, and he being an old friend of Johnnie, had raised his stock enormously. What if her change of manner was due to this connection of his with Johnnie—which she had only discovered last night? What if he had a trump card in Johnnie? That again was not impossible, and he must play it for all it was worth.

But what did it matter? What did it matter whether her manner had changed for purely selfish, shrewd and material reasons, or because for some reason she suddenly liked him better? The point was, her manner had changed and she had promised to stay in Brighton with him alone.

What a one in the eye for Peter! What a one in the eye for Mickey and for them all! For a few days he had got Netta—Netta Longdon—the proud, coveted beauty—alone. Alone and away from them all. He would have her to talk to, to listen to and watch, to walk with, to be seen with, to consort with quietly or even gaily, by the gleaming sea. He might even make love to her, kiss her in the darkness to the sound of the sea—make love to her like a man—anything might happen.

He honestly believed a change had come, that the tide had somehow turned. He was so very happy. He drank and thought and thought and drank and smoked. Finally he went back to his hotel, packed a bag and took a taxi through the gorgeously sunny streets to Victoria. Then he had another beer at the buffet, and then got on to the train.

And then everything had remained all right and lovely until, suddenly, as the train flashed through Haywards Heath, it occurred to him that he had got drunk at midday and made one of his usual fools of himself.

She would never come, of course; she would find some excuse; he was in a train on his way to Brighton simply as a result of a mad midday binge; he had thrown away fifteen precious pounds from his precious store, and all was lost.

As though sensing his sudden return to misery, the train itself all at once began to hesitate, to slow down, and, finally, to stop, not at a station, but, mysteriously, miserably, bewilderedly, in the open country . . .

The sun streamed in upon his head. Now that the wheels were still, a wasp or bluebottle could be heard buzzing from the other end of the car . . . A bored fellow-passenger rattled a newspaper in turning it . . . And you could hear the clinking of crockery and the conversation of the attendants in the kitchen behind . . .

London, Netta, everything was so remote and hot and becalmed . . . How could you ever imagine her packing and taking a taxi and a train and joining him in Brighton?

He wished he hadn't made such a fool of himself. He wished he wasn't such a fool.

There was a huge outing of violent girls, down for the day from the "Lucky Tip" cigarette factory in London, shouting and sprawling over the town, permeating it with colour and affecting its quality much as a drop of permanganate of potash will affect a tumblerful of water.

They went about in threes or fours, and looked boldly, nastily, and yet perhaps not uninvitingly at him as he passed on his way to the sea. They wore American sailor hats and carried strange coloured favours. He had not counted on this, and it added to the strangeness both of his existence generally, and of his sudden transportation to London-by-the-Sea.

They were thickest about the Palace Pier, and so he walked along the front towards the West—but it was crowded everywhere, with the shelters and deck-chairs full, the blinding satin-blue sea glistening and purring on the one side, the traffic hooting and swirling by on the other, and the tar and dust and people all smelling of heat.

And behind, and mingling with all the noise and colour and heat and haze and smell, there could be heard, if you cared to listen, the faint distant church of people walking, or rather slithering about, on the crowded beach below—the characteristic noise of Brighton at the height of its season.

He had left his suitcase at the station, and told himself that he was strolling about looking for a suitable hotel for himself and Netta. But he was not really doing this, because he knew really where he was going to stay. He was going to stay at the

Little Castle, a small commercial just off Castle Square, because this was where he had stayed with Bob Barton in the Bob Barton days, and because he wanted to be on ground he knew, and because he knew it was reasonably cheap, and because he didn't have the energy and initiative, anyway, to break new ground and find an unfamiliar hotel.

He hadn't bargained for all this noise and crowd and the "Lucky Tip" girls. He couldn't conceive Netta in such a setting, even if she came. What was he to do with her, where was he to take her, in all this heat and hubbub? Well, perhaps he could take her out to the country during the day, and they could have quiet meals at inns, and, anyway, the "Lucky Tip" girls would be going back tonight. And then Brighton would be quiet at night, anyway, and they could have a quiet meal somewhere and walk quietly along the front, and go back to the Little Castle which he knew was quiet.

He turned at the West Pier and walked back to Castle Square. He went into the Little Castle, and the porter remembered him, and so did the woman at the cash-desk, and they said they had a room for him tonight, and another for his "friend" tomorrow.

He took a bus back to the station, got his suitcase from the cloak-room and then took a taxi back to the hotel. He unpacked, discovered, whether to his satisfaction or not he did not quite know, that the room promised for Netta was next to his own, and then went out to get a cup of tea at the Lyons in North Street.

The "Lucky Tip" girls were in here too, and it was ages before he was served. When he came out it was past six o'clock—time to have a drink.

The "Lucky Tip" girls were in the pubs too—making a frightful noise. They were getting tight, and you could hardly hear yourself think, they were screaming so, and you had to fight and wait for hours to get served. He tried pub after pub, five in all, but he couldn't shake them off. Suddenly he got sick of it and decided to go back to the Little Castle and have a meal on his "all in" terms—an early night. He had got drunk at lunch and was dead tired, anyway.

He came out onto the front, which was steeped in the pink of the sunset, whose mighty, cloudy architecture shone aloofly over the mighty ocean at whose edge the puny "Lucky Tip" girls, in their sailor hats, had chosen to hold their brazen festival. When he reached the Little Castle, the lights were on in the small, old-fashioned, rather stuffy dining-room, where he at once sat down for a meal. Except for a man and his wife and their child at a table by the window, all the other diners had gone.

He ordered sole and chips and read his paper. The man and his wife and child modulated their voices awkwardly, because every word could be heard across the length of the room.

Later, the porter, who remembered him from the Bob Barton days, came and talked to him, and finally went out for him with a wire to Netta:

"IN CASE ACCIDENTS ADDRESS LITTLE CASTLE HOTEL CASTLE SQUARE SEE YOU 6.5 TOMORROW LOVE GEORGE."

After his supper he sat on a long while reading his newspaper, and then went out for a little stroll. He was set on a quiet evening.

Night had fallen now, and there was a faint rain coming down in the cooler air. He felt cooler and happier. He passed through the fairy-lights of Castle Square to the sea, and walked along the glistening front. The sea was rising and pounding against the beach in the freshening breeze; a few stars twinkled in spite of the rain above the high white lamps; and there were little lights on the sea facing the majestic Metropole between the two piers outlined with blazing jewels. He wondered what it was all about—the pounding sea, the beach, the rain, the stars, the lights, the piers, Brighton, Hitler, Netta, himself, everything. *Why?* . . .

Impossible to say. But it was somehow all bigger and cooler and darker and nicer than himself, and he was glad of that. He walked back to his hotel, went straight to his room, undressed, put out the light, got into bed, and in a few minutes was himself utterly at one with the big, cool, dark, nice thing—with the sky, the rain, the sea, Brighton, and the "Lucky Tip" girls at that very moment singing and screaming their way back to town in lit, crowded train-loads.

C ooler and happier. That was his thought as he woke, and saw from his watch that it was nearly ten o'clock in the morning and that he had almost slept the clock round. He had been cooler and happier last night, and he was cooler and happier now. In other words, he had gone to bed sober and had a grand night.

He heard the busy traffic in Castle Square outside and felt he could face it. He felt he could face life, enjoy it even. He had a quick bath, dressed quickly, and was down in time to get some breakfast.

He couldn't remember eating such a breakfast for years. When he came out the porter said there was a wire for him. It was from Netta.

"BONE LITTLE CASTLE HOTEL ARRIVING 7.5 NOT 6.5 NETTA."

So she was coming! He could hardly control himself in front of the porter, as he went out and talked with the excellent man on the steps of the hotel, and watched the sunny people in the sunny street. She was coming! He was sober last night; he was cool, well, and happy, and she was coming! She—Netta—the holy and terrible one—had taken the trouble to wire him!

How was he to spend the delicious day? The porter left him and he looked at some notices on the board. Visitors were requested, etc. etc. . . . Then, "*Ringdean Golf Course, 2s. 6d. per round.*" The porter came out again and he asked him about it.

The porter told him you could get there easily by tram from Castle Square, and a heavenly "Why not?" sprang up in his soul. Why not borrow some clubs from the pro and mess about? He would! He got his hat and was on the tram in five minutes.

Golf! How long was it? Not since the Bob Barton days—he had simply forgotten about it. And they used to make such a fuss of him—Bob and all of them—even the nasty ones—it was the one thing he was any good at. That was the one decent thing at school—the nine-hole golf course they were allowed on a mile or so away. "Well, Bone," old Thorne once said in his pompous way, "with a drive and iron play such as yours I think you may be said to have lived not *wholly* for nothing." And he *could* play, too, if it came to that. He was down to two when he left school, and everyone said that if he could only keep it up he could be a crack. But of course he hadn't kept it up and he hadn't thought about it for years.

The pro was a nice man, and let him have quite a decent bag, and explained the lie of the course, which began high up at the back of the town and led over the Downs. It was half past eleven when he started, so there was no one about.

He teed up at the first hole—a long short one—a difficult three downhill to a banked green. With delicious pomposity (how it brought it all back!) he looked at his card for the length, and decided that against the wind it was a spoon. He teed up his ball and had some swings. There was nothing to it, there never was anything to it—you had only got to relax, relax, relax, and keep your chin pointed at the back of the ball all the way. No clues or nonsense, just relax and your chin pointed. Just pretend you've been playing frightfully well for the last few holes, and keep your chin pointed. He went up to the ball.

He was on! He was on! He was on! All the way! He had socked it bang in the middle—the spoon was the club all right, and he was on! He was about twelve feet from the pin . . .

He knew his putt was going down before he hit the ball, and

in it went! A two. Thank you very much—that would do all right for a beginning.

He pulled his next drive, but it lay well, and he hit a screaming number four up to the back of the green. He was playing golf! He knew he was playing golf! You either had that feeling or you didn't! He had got it. He was going to hit the blasted ball all the way round!

He got his bogey four, and at the next hole—a five—got his four with a glorious chip (like a pocket-knife closing) and a putt. Nothing could stop him now. He was out for their blood. He had gone "mad" and he was going to keep mad.

He was out in thirty-four. He chuckled aloud as he sunk his putt and he breathed deeply and braced himself for the battle home . . .

He walked alone along the Downs, this sad, ungainly man with beer-shot eyes who loved a girl in Earl's Court—carrying an old bag of borrowed clubs and thinking of nothing but his game of golf. His face shone, his eyes gleamed, and he felt, deep in his being, that he was not a bad man, as he had thought he was a few hours ago, but a good one. And because he was a good man he was a happy man, and if he could only break seventy he would never be unhappy again.

He got a six at the fourteenth, but he didn't let it rattle him, and he came to the last hole, a long five, with a five to get for his sixty-nine.

He wasn't going to get rattled. Nothing could rattle him now. His drive went into the rough on the left, that didn't rattle him. It didn't lie too badly. He debated whether to take his three (he hadn't got a two) and play safe, or try it with a spoon. He decided on the spoon—he wasn't going to get rattled.

It was a rotten shot . . . but it was on, it was on, it was *on*! One of those awful low, curly S-shaped things, right over to the left and then fading away to the right, but it was on! It was about twenty feet away from the pin on a hilly green.

He didn't want a sixty-eight—he only wanted sixty-nine. He wasn't going to try for a sixty-eight; he was just going to hit it firmly up to the hole—so firmly that it went well beyond the hole—for two putts and his sixty-nine. He took the line carefully and he knew the moment he had hit it that his sixty-eight was in the bag. It went less than a foot past the hole on the right, and he knocked it in with one hand.

Sixty-eight! Hadn't played for years—borrowed clubs on a strange course, and sixty-eight! He was giddy with joy. He wanted to tell somebody. He saw two men approaching the first tee and he wanted to go and tell them. He only just kept himself from doing so. The pro, fortunately, was still in his shop. "Well," he said as he handed him the clubs. "They're all right. I did a sixty-eight, anyway. Not bad on a strange course. I haven't played for years either." And his voice was vibrant with pride. The pro congratulated him warmly and they had a little talk about the course.

He went to the rather ramshackle club-house, which was empty, got a half of beer, ordered some sandwiches and sat down.

Sixty-eight! Golf! How had he come to forget golf—the fact that he could play a game well—the fact that he was good at something, anyway?

Good at something. The thought brought Netta back. He hadn't thought of her for three hours, and she was joining him tonight. What would she think of his sixty-eight? Nothing, of ourse. But it wasn't nothing. He'd like to see Peter shoot a sixty-eight! Perhaps, tomorrow, she would come and play with him. Perhaps she would come and *watch* him play. She might . . . But it wasn't the sixty-eight so much as the golf—the fresh air and sanity. What with his quiet night last night, he hadn't felt so well for years. Why not take up golf and give up drinking? A holiday, a golfing holiday—that perhaps had been what he had wanted all the time. If he had had a holiday before he wouldn't have got into such a mess. Now was the time to pull himself together. Yes. Now. Now or never.

And Netta joining him tonight. Alone with Netta, quietly for the first time in his life, and feeling well, on top of his form. Surely this moment had come, and everything was conspiring for his good. If only he could take the opportunity and keep calm. Like in golf, confidence and relaxation—that was all there was to it.

He wasn't going to get drunk. She could drink if she wanted to, but he wasn't going to—at least only a little. He was going to keep his head.

And then, if he couldn't make any headway with her, he'd cut her out. For the first time since he had known her, he felt he could cut her out. He would play golf, and cut her out and start all over again.

But why cut her out? Hadn't she been entirely charming to him recently, and wasn't she joining him in the most delightful manner at a seaside resort? Why should a sane man talk of cutting her out? Wasn't this the very moment when he might hope to get his way, to make her respect him, to make her love him?

It was all very exciting—this almost clandestine meeting in Brighton. It was like being in love when you were a boy for the first time. That was how he was going to think of it, and that was how he was going to treat her when he met her. He was going to pretend to himself that he had only met her a little while ago—forget all the past. Already he had a plan at the back of his mind. Down here he wasn't going to be just a boozy hanger-on. He was going to spend money and do the thing properly. He was going to meet her in his best suit: his hair would be brushed: and he would just have had a bath. She would be taken aback by his appearance. Then he would take her in a taxi to the hotel; and then, when she had unpacked, they would go out in another taxi to Sweetings. Sweetings was the place, he didn't care what it cost. There they would have dinner, and afterwards, if she liked, they would go to a theatre or the movies. Sober. Civilized. Unruffled. Sane. He would show her that he knew his way about.

He had another beer. He had done a sixty-eight and was on top of the world. His sandwiches came and he saw that it was nearly three o'clock.

He ate his sandwiches. No more beer. He was a sober man now. He lit a cigarette, left the club-house and took a tram back to the hotel.

He lay on his bed and slept, slept to sleep off his golf, and to be fresh for her at seven. The porter, on his instructions, woke him at a quarter to six, and he went and had a bath. He put on his best blue suit and brushed his hair.

No drinks. Plenty of time for that when he met her. He took a bus and was at the station at a quarter to seven. The station was very crowded, and it made him feel a little scared—so many people and so much rolling, echoing noise, and not having had anything to drink. And then you didn't meet Netta alone, in a seaside town, when you were feeling well and knew that your one chance had come, exactly every day of your life! But he still wouldn't have a drink. His feeling of wellness and freshness, his sixty-eight that morning, his resolutions, his blue suit and his bath would see him through until she came.

The train was very punctual—came wobbling grimly into its hissing standstill almost before he was ready for it. The doors opened and crowds poured out and bore down upon the barrier.

It was not long before he saw Netta. Then, through the bobbing heads, he saw Peter, who was holding her arm.

Then he saw that on Peter's other arm there was a stranger – a young man, about twenty-two, wearing his hat at an absurd angle over his eyes, and slouching along absurdly. As soon as they had reached the barrier, and Peter had hailed him, he relized that they were all three aggressively drunk—had been aggressively drunk for several hours.

"Hullo, Bone!" cried Netta. "How are you!" And she waved her hand and smiled without a flicker of guilt in her eyes. "Where's the bar? We want a drink."

She was quite tight, though, as usual, she did not show it, like the men, by complete silliness, but by a voice much louder, harsher and crisper than usual, a brighter eye, a manner at once inconsequent and dictatorial.

"Hullo, George Harvey Bone," said the strange young man. "I've been hearing all about you. Sorry I can't shake hands. I'm the beast of burden." (He was carrying Netta's suitcase.)

"Come on," said Peter, "park that bloody thing and let's go and have a drink."

"No need to park it," said George, "I'll take it." And he took it from the stranger. He presumed the two interlopers were shortly going back to London, and he felt that by taking charge of Netta's suitcase he was making manifest the private nature of his assignation with her, and also hinting that their early departure would be desirable.

"Good old George!" said Netta. "Good old beast of burden. We're all very fond of you, George." She took his arm. "Come on. You may now conduct us to the ale-house."

"The ale-house, *ho*!" said the young man. He was a nasty-looking piece of work short, virile, stocky—with a darkly tanned, scarred, pugilistic, Rugby-football face—a full mouth and the burning brown eyes of the school bully. When they had lined up at the buffet bar, he ordered double whiskies for all of them without consulting anybody.

"Who's this?" said George, quietly aside to Netta, as they waited for the drinks to come.

"Who's what?"

"This," he said signifying whom he meant by his eyes.

"Oh, him. I don't know," said Netta. "Here! You! Whatsyourname! Who *are* you? George Harvey Bone wants to know!"

"Me?" said the young man. "I don't know. Who am I? Here. You. Excuse me." He called to the barmaid. "Can you tell me who I am? There's a gentleman here wants to know."

"I don't know I'm sure," said the barmaid, smiling wanly as she passed.

"But this is disgraceful. I come into a bar and ask in a perfectly reasonable way who I am and nobody can tell me. I mean to say it's absurd. I mean . . ." He started a long wrangle with the barmaid, which finally became boring even to Peter and Netta.

"No, who is he, really, Netta?" asked George, while this was going on, and she replied as she looked into her bag for some lipstick, "I don't know. We just picked him up. We all got blind at lunch-time and just picked him up."

"I don't like the look of him a bit," he was bold enough to say.

"Don't you?" said Netta. "I rather like him."

"Well, George," said Peter, "you don't look very bright at seeing us."

"On the contrary. I'm delighted. It's just that I haven't had any drinks, that's all."

"Really . . . This is most unusual. You must have some quickly and make up."

"Well, I was aiming to have a meal," said George. "What's the general idea? When are you two going back?"

"Oh—we're not going back," said Peter quickly, swaying slightly with drink, and looking at him, his glass in hand, with a look of pure malice such as George had never seen quite so vividly on his face before. "I rather thought you thought we were going back."

"No, I didn't," said George. "I just wondered what you were going to do for luggage."

"Oh, that's all right. It's all in Netta's. We all dashed about collecting things and packed up at Netta's."

"What's all this?" said the young man, to whom the barmaid would no longer listen. "What's this about packing?"

"I was just telling George how we packed," said Peter. "He thought we were going home."

"Going home? What do you mean? We're staying with you, aren't we! I understood we're staying with you. What's the matter with you, George Harvey Bone?"

"Yes, of course, we're staying with him," said Netta. "We're at the Little Castle Hotel. He got us rooms. Shut up, Bone darling, and buy me a drink."

They had two more rounds at the buffet, and then went to a pub a little way down Queen's Road. Here they had three more rounds and played pin-table, and when they came out it was dark and raining again. They went back to the station and got a taxi.

"Where to?" said Peter, swaying about outside. "The Little Castle Hotel," cried Netta, "and drive like the devil, my man!"

She was tighter than he had ever seen her. She put her arm through his and began to sing.

They sped through the bright lights of the gleaming town, and as they passed the Regent—"What's the matter with you, George?" said Peter. "You're still looking very dumb."

"Yes, he is," said the stranger. "I don't think I like your friend. What's the matter with him? Doesn't he like us? You told me he was dumb, but I didn't know he was this dumb."

"Why," said George, "have you been discussing me?"

"Yes, darling," said Netta. "We discussed you in the train."

"Well, I'm sorry if I'm dumb, but I didn't know it was going to be a binge. I thought I was meeting Netta alone."

"My God," said Netta. "You didn't think I could stand you alone, my sweet Bone, did you?" And at this they all laughed, and a few moments later they drew up in front of the little hotel.

CHAPTER FIVE

The staff looked askance, hesitated, and then decided good-naturedly to treat it as a joke. "No, do shut up!" whispered George. "Shut up!" And Netta actually joined him with, "Yes, shut up or we'll be hoofed out."

"I don't *want* to register," said Peter. "I want the bathroom. Where's the bathroom?" But he signed, and went off in search of the bathroom, and the other two signed more or less quietly. They had only one room left in the hotel itself, but the odd man could sleep in the annexe. "All right, that's not *me*," said the young man, and he bagged the key for the room in the hotel, which was found to be next door to Netta's.

They asked how late they could have dinner, were told they had half an hour, and went through into the bar. George sneaked out to the office and said he was sorry. The woman was nice about it, and the porter, his trusty friend, said, "Don't you worry sir. They'll settle down when they've had something to eat."

He got them in by a quarter to ten. He had now had quite a few himself, and could stand up to it better. There were, unfortunately, two other diners still in the room, who stared but took it in good humour, and soon enough they went out. The waiter was good-humoured, too, and the porter hung about, as though willing to come to the rescue if things got too tough.

Netta was the toughest to begin with, taking it out of the waiter. "Waiter, I want some household bread!" Then, when it didn't come at once, "WAITER!—I want some household *bread*—I want some household *bread*—I want some household *bread*—I want some household BREAD,"—chanting rhythmically and banging her hands on the table. He had never seen her, had never expected to see her as bad as this, and yet he was seeing nothing new, making no fresh discovery about her character. He was seeing only what he always saw beneath her normal composure—the harsh, cruel, beastly, tyrannical little girl he knew she must have been as a child and which she had never ceased being. To see this while she was wild and raucous was hardly more painful than to see it when she was calm and collected, and, anyway, he was really beyond pain at the moment.

Soon enough Peter began throwing whole rolls of bread about the room, as he always did when he was really lit up, and this the new member of the circle enjoyed enormously. They threw catches to each other the whole length of the room, and Netta cheered.

Then they began to play football, Peter lying down and holding the roll, while the newcomer took a flying kick to convert a try, and then the latter lying down and Peter taking the kick. And every now and again Netta cheered, and her bright eyes rained influence and judged the prize. Then the waiter came in and said excuse me, but would they be a little more quiet, as some of the guests had already gone to bed. And Peter said Blast him and Damn him, he would *not* excuse him, but all right if he would bring some more beer they would see what they could do. And actually they were quieter for a little, and the waiter brought them some more beer, and they went on with their dinner.

Then all at once Peter was demanding an evening paper, and sending the porter out for one, because he wanted to see what *Em* Molotov was up to. Blast him. There was a lot of dirt going on, and he wanted an evening paper. And soon enough they were talking about *Em* Molotov and *En* Chamberlain, and were getting quarrelsome.

"Excuse me, *En* Chamberlain is nothing of the sort," said

Peter, and "Excuse me, *En* Chamberlain is *everything* of the sort," said his opponent, and Netta cried, "Good old *En* Chamberlain! I say he's a bloody hero."

"Bloody hero? He's a bloody weakling," said the newcomer, and, "Please don't talk rot, both of you," said Peter. "Neither of you know what you're talking about. Listen. *Mister* Chamberlain . . ." And he went off into a lecture, to which the other two did not listen, but to which they gave an appearance of listening by remaining silent in a dazed, glassy way for a few moments before interrupting simultaneously. *Mister* Chamberlain . . . *Mister* Chamberlain . . . *Mister* Chamberlain . . . Adolf . . . Munich . . . *Mister* Chamberlain! Excuse me! . . . On the contrary! . . . On it went and they ordered a fresh round of drinks. *Mister* Chamberlain . . . Munich . . . Good old Adolf . . . "Well, *he* did something for his country, anyway," said the newcomer, and "Hooray!" said Netta. "That's what *I* say. I'm all for my Adolf . . . !" "Listen—you don't understand," said Peter wearily, "you're *children* politically—*children*."

"Well, you're a bloody fascist, anyway," said Netta . . . "You don't *understand*," said Peter, and, "Well, there's a lot *in* this fascist business if it comes to that," said the newcomer, and the reconciliation slowly set in.

He sat there, smoking and drinking with them, and not saying a word. He knew they would be reconciled. He knew they all loved Chamberlain and fascism and Hitler, and that they would be reconciled. Finally they became maudlin.

"You're right, old chap, you're right," said the newcomer. "You're perfectly right. You've *shown* me something. No, I'm not flattering you—I *don't* flatter—you've *shown* me something. You're right."

"Well, I think I'm right," said Peter. "I've been in jail for it, anyway!" And he laughed in his nasty, moustachy way.

"Jail?" said the newcomer, politely, his head lurching over his pint can of beer. "Really?"

"Oh, God, yes," said Netta. "Poor old Peter's been in jail twice. Come on, Peter, tell us how you've been in jail!"

"I have been in jail *twice*, to be precise," said Peter, lighting another cigarette, and suddenly employing a large, pompous professorial tone. "On one occasion for socking a certain left-winger a precise and well-deserved sock in the middle of his solar plexus, and on the other for a minor spot of homicide with *motor-car . . .*"

He sat there, smoking and drinking with them, and saying not a word. He was frozen inside. So it was all coming out now—it was all coming out! Jail-birds and proud of it. No doubt it would soon transpire that Netta was a shop-lifter. Never mind. He could take it. He was frozen inside.

He wondered whether Peter would remember having made these revelations when he woke tomorrow morning. It was amazing how this secret had been kept from him all this time. And Netta in on it, too—they were very close, these two, closer than he had imagined. You'd have thought it would have come out before: they'd both been tight in front of him often enough. But of course tonight Peter was raving tight.

The little virile, pugilistic newcomer was delighted, inspired, humbled by these revelations—the sudden distinction accruing to his drinking companion—and with Netta's assistance egged him on to talk. Mr. Chamberlain was forgotten and Peter held the stage.

"Jail? . . . Yes . . . Jail is a curious thing . . ." He sat back, he leaned forward, he made large gestures. He was absolutely blind. Finally he called the waiter for some more drink, but the porter came up instead and said he was sorry but it was after twelve and they couldn't serve any more.

What the *hell* are you talking about?" said Peter. "We're staying at the hotel, aren't we?"

And then, as the argument rose, a curious thing happened. Instead of supporting Peter, and arguing, quite correctly, that as residents they had the right to order drinks at any time, Netta all at once said, "Oh, well, if we can't we can't—let's go to bed." And as she said this, stabbing out her cigarette on a plate, she gave a funny little sidelong glance in the direction of the newcomer, who glanced at her in the same sidelong way, and then said, "Yes. Let's call it a day. I've had enough, anyway." And George saw both glances and believed he understood them. *No! No! No! Please God, No!*

He lay on his bed and tried to relax. He was fully dressed, but he had turned out the light. He faced the bed and held his head in his arms. He would be able to think soon—if he relaxed for a little.

The last door had closed. Peter was over in the annexe. They had sorted out their belongings from Netta's suitcase in the hall and the porter had taken Peter over. They had all said "Good night." "Good night, Bone," she had said. The last door had closed. The lights were out. He relaxed. Outside it was beginning to rain.

The last door was closed. They had closed the last door cleverly. No sneaking in. They were too clever for that. They had closed it boldly, slammed it almost, as though in the general hubbub of going to the bathroom, of sorting out the luggage, of to-and-froing before going to bed . . . But he had heard the first giggle through the thin wall, and the long silence and creaking after the first giggle.

Now they were getting bolder—now they were beginning to talk. A few moments ago they were whispering, but like all whisperers at night they couldn't keep it down; they kept on breaking into the vocal tone, and then shamefacedly whispering again. It was like the first twittering of birds at dawn; it would grow and grow; and soon they would be in full chorus.

Why did they have to talk? What was he to do if they went on talking? Didn't they know he could hear them? Or didn't they care? Why had they chosen Netta's room—next to his?

Why hadn't she gone into *his* room? They were too drunk to care—too *hard* to care.

And only this morning he had done a sixty-eight! He had walked on the Downs and found that he was a good man, that life was good, that he could start afresh, cool and calm, that Netta might yet be his. But now it was half an hour after midnight and to this strait had his coolness and calmness brought him, and in this manner was his passion fated to find consummation!

If only they wouldn't talk . . . They were getting louder and louder, and he heard Netta giggle, and someone walk across the room. What were they up to? He heard the clink of a glass. Oh, God—they were going to have a drink. They were going to drink from the half-bottle of whisky he had seen in Netta's suitcase. They would drink out of the tooth-glass. Yes—there it went—faint as it was he heard it—the gurgle in the pipe and the hissing of the tap as they filled up with water! They were doing it in style. Nothing brief and bestial. A night of love.

And that morning he had done a sixty-eight, and flattered himself. And while he was flattering himself, and breathing life and fresh air into his lungs, they, up in London, were brewing this for him. He saw it all: he could piece it together from their conversation during the evening. She had gone over with Peter to the Black Hart in the morning and they had got talking to this stranger. She had probably taken a fancy to him at once, this aggressive little boy of twenty-two with the pugilistic nose and the school-bully's brown eyes—he was probably her type. There must have been an understanding between them from the beginning. A depraved woman. Then, as they all got drunk, the scheme must have materialized. She must have originated it, told them of her date in Brighton, told them what a bore it was, asked them how she could get out of it. Then the moment of inspiration, as they all chimed in and said they would all go! and had another drink to celebrate it! How Peter must have gloried in that moment, gloried in the knowledge that George wasn't going to get away with it after all. Well, Peter, actually, had been one too clever. He was in the annexe.

A pleasant holiday. A pleasant holiday by the sea. And he had given her fifteen pounds for this.

If only they wouldn't talk. Mumble, mumble, mumble. They had given up trying to whisper now—they were settling down to it. That tap again!—and the soft gurgle in the pipe! Filling up. Running h. & c. in all bedrooms—every modem convenience. A tinkle, a creak, a subdued laugh . . . Mumble, mumble, mumble . . . Liquid, intimate . . . Didn't they *know* he could hear them?

Why did people do these things to him? Was it his fault? Did he deserve it? Had he done something wrong? Had he done wrong to get a sixty-eight this morning and try and start life afresh? It looked as though he had, because this was the result.

Or was there something wrong with his character? Did he ask for all he got? Ought he to go and make a scene, burst in on them, bash this little horror's face in, kick him out? Wake up the hotel? Would another man do that? He couldn't see it. It was her business, her affair. You couldn't wake up a hotel. He was probably wrong, but he couldn't see it.

Mumble, mumble, mumble . . . He couldn't stand it. He had got to do something. He sat up on the bed, and stared at the window, the mauve watery light from the lamp outside on the rain-spotted pane behind the lace curtains. He couldn't stand this all night. He had got to do something. What? What? Go outside and knock on the door and tell them to shut up? Knock on the wall and shout? Pretend he knew all about it and was indifferent—that he just wanted to go to sleep?

That tap again, and that gurgle . . . They weren't even subduing their voices now; they were drinking, giggling, and talking as though they were in a public room. There would be

complaints from one of the other guests soon—that would settle it, perhaps.

He heard the tap again and another tinkle of a glass, and
all at once he remembered that he had a full bottle of whisky
in his own case. That was it!—the only thing. He must open
up the bottle, and drink himself—drink himself to sleep.
They weren't the only ones who could drink in the small
hours.

He crept over to the switch and turned it softly. Why was *he*
creeping? Why did *he* put on the light softly? Why was *he*
ashamed?

Because, oddly enough, of his pride. He had been through
this before, when he found out about Peter. The only thing he
could do now was to save his pride, or a little of it—not let her
know that she had exploited him, insulted him, trampled on
him—pretend he was the complete fool she thought him. It
was better that way—awful as it was. That way he saved a little pride. If she ever knew that he meekly suffered what she
had chosen to dole out to him and came back for more, he
could never look her in the face again.

He must be fast asleep, and a fool—a complete fool—a hog.
He crept slowly over to his suitcase and got out his whisky. He
opened the stopper stealthily, got his tooth-glass, poured out a
huge amount without a sound, and went to the tap. Now the
rain was pouring down outside—an accomplice in his crime.
Gently turned, the tap poured with the rain—he could hardly
hear it himself. Thus the two taps in the two rooms, gurgled
and answered each other in the wicked hours of the night.

He switched off the light again, and took an enormous swill.
He looked at the rain-splashed window behind the lace curtains in the watery light of the lamp. He felt better almost at
once. There was nothing like drink. He groped in the darkness
for the bottle and splashed some more in. This was the way—
this was the way!

Mumble, mumble, mumble . . . Cosy, liquid, intimate. Would they never stop? He took another swill. Hullo—what was this? Had they stopped at last? Had they stopped? He put his head to the wall and listened intently.

Oh, God, they had stopped . . . They were silent. What was he to do now?

If only they would talk he could stand it, but this he couldn't stand. What was he to do now?

He listened again, but absolute silence shuddered through the wall.

The rain poured down outside. He drained off the remains of his glass, and stumbled about the room for the bottle.

He was awakened by feeling cold about three hours later. He had lain on the bed without putting anything over him. He awoke abrubtly and remembered everything with extraordinary clearness.

He sat up on the bed and looked at the lace curtains in the mauve light of the lamp outside. It had stopped raining.

They weren't silent now: they were mumbling again, very softly. Perhaps it was this very soft mumbling, and not the cold, which had awakened him.

He listened to their mumbling for about five minutes, and then it subsided again into silence. Silence. He wondered what he ought to do. He had got to do something. He had got to get away from that silence. He had got to get away.

Get away? What was stopping him? Why hadn't he thought of it before? Why hadn't he walked out of the hotel? He sprang from the bed and looked at his wrist-watch in the watery light of the lamp.

A quarter past five. It was still very early, but it was summer and it would soon be dawn. He would have a walk—a walk along the front in the early morning—a constitutional!

He hadn't got to dress—that was something. He thought of washing; but that would mean turning on the tap and they might hear it. He turned the handle of the door with infinite care, and crept on to the landing.

He crept downstairs. There was a dim light in the hall, lighting his way down. He hoped no one was about, but just as he was turning the latch of the front door, a voice said "Yessir? Do you want anything, sir?" It was the night porter, whom he had never seen before.

"That's all right," he said, grinning. "I'm just going for a walk. I'm a guest all right. I'm not a burglar!"

And they both laughed in a subdued, sleeping-guest-respecting way, and the next moment he was out in the wet, glimmering lamp-lit street.

He walked through Castle Square to the sea. When he reached the sea he saw that dawn was breaking over it, dimly, bluely, feebly, amidst the torn clouds of rain. He smelt the air and felt better. He was glad he had done this. He felt like a walk. He was doing the best thing.

And then he felt a curious snap in his head.

THE SEVENTH PART

END OF SUMMER

They, only set on sport and play,
Unweetingly importuned
Their own destruction to come speedy upon them.
So fond are mortal men,
Fallen into wrath divine,
As their own ruin on themselves to invite.

J. MILTON, *Samson Agonistes*

CHAPTER ONE

Snap! . . . *Click!*—just like that . . .

He was walking along the front at Brighton, in the sombre early dawn, in the deep blue cloudy not-quite-night, and it had happened again . . .

Click! . . . It was as though his head were a five-shilling Kodak camera, and someone had switched over the little trigger which makes the exposure. He knew the sensation so well, yet he never failed to marvel at its oddity.

Like a camera. But instead of an exposure having been made, the opposite had happened—an *enclosure*—a shutting down, a locking in. A moment before his head, his brain, were out in the world, seeing, hearing, sensing objects directly; now they were enclosed behind glass (like Crown jewels, like Victorian wax fruit), behind a film—the film of the camera, perhaps, to continue the photographic analogy—a film behind which all things and people moved eerily, without colour, vivacity or meaning, grimly, puppet-like, without motive or conscious volition of their own . . .

A moment before his mind had heard and answered; now he was mentally deaf and dumb: he was in on himself—his mute, numbed self.

Numbed and sensationless. But there was something to be done. That was the whole point—there was something to be done. Always, a little while after the shutter had fallen, he knew this.

It was all most odd and obscure—odder and obscurer than

usual because of the darkness, the circumstances, the time, the dim, rain-washed dawn on the Brighton front . . . What on earth was he doing there at such a time?

Oh yes—he had just left Netta and Peter—no, not Netta and Peter—Netta and the new young man—the young man with the pugilistic nose and brown school-bully's eyes—he had just left Netta and this young man in the bedroom next door to him. He hadn't been able to stand it. He had decided to take a walk, he had hated it so. But he couldn't be bothered by Netta and the young man at the moment, because there was something to be done, and he had got to find out what it was.

It was a great relief, really, to be dead and numbed like this, not to have to bother about Netta, and just to have to concentrate on finding out what it was that had to be done—a great relief after all he had been suffering.

But what was it? He could never think of it at first. Never mind, it would come. If he didn't nag at it, if he relaxed mentally, it would come.

While Brighton slept—North Street, West Street, East Street, Western Road, Preston Street, Hove, the hotels, the shops, the restaurants, the movies, the baths, the booths, the churches, the Market, the Post Office, the pubs, the antiques, the secondhand books—slept and gleamed and climbed up from the sea under the dark-blue dawn, the enormous gloomy man walked along the front, hardly visible in the darkness, seemingly the only wayfarer, the only one awake. And he looked out at the sea and wondered what it was he had to do.

When he remembered, he was about opposite the Grand. He remembered without any trouble, any strain. He had got to kill Netta Longdon. He had to kill her, and then he would go to Maidenhead. He would be happy in Maidenhead.

But what was this? Who was this Netta Longdon? Didn't that mean Netta?—the girl he knew—the girl he had left behind in the hotel? Of course it did! How odd. It was Netta he had to kill. And she was here in Brighton with him.

He had got to kill her because things had been going on too long, and he had to get to Maidenhead and be at peace with himself. Why hadn't he killed her before? Why did he keep putting off killing her?

Yes—he remembered now. This was his great fault—he kept on putting it off. Something kept on stopping him—in some extraordinary way he kept on forgetting about it and putting it off. Why, he could remember as far back as Christmas, when he was at Hunstanton with his aunt . . . Then he was thinking about killing her, but he had put it off to the spring—the warm weather. And now the spring had gone and it was summer! If he didn't look out it would be getting cold again and he wouldn't be able to kill her till next year.

Yes. He must get down to it; he must do it at once, now—start thinking it out. It didn't really need much thinking out, because it was so absurdly easy—but there had to be a certain amount of planning.

He passed the West Pier, and saw that the dawn was brightening. It was very queer, to be walking along the Brighton front a this hour. He was usually in Earl's Court. And here was this girl—Netta Longdon, whom he had to kill—down in Brighton with him. It looked like the hand of fate. It looked as though she was chasing him, following him down just so as to be at hand to be killed.

How had they got down here? He must try and remember . . . Oh yes—it was coming back. He had thought he was going to have a holiday with her. He came down first, and she was coming down, and they were going to be alone together. But when he went to the station there were three of them there, and they were all drunk.

That was awfully mean. They were a mean lot, really. It was beastly of Netta—she must have known how it would hurt him; but she didn't care. She was like that. Getting killed would serve her jolly well right, really. All her life she had had things too much her own way. He didn't have any grudge against her, but he didn't have much pity for her either.

Peter was mean too. He, actually, deserved to be killed more than Netta. He was a bad lot, this Peter, a criminal really. He had killed a man himself—that had come out last night. And he had assaulted another man criminally, and been in jail twice. If that wasn't criminal, what was?

He was a sinister brute, Peter. He had always known that in his heart, but last night it had come out good and strong, for all decent, sane people to see. But Netta hadn't seen it, nor had the little school-bully who was in Netta's room now. They thought it was clever to have killed a man in a car while drunk, and to have knocked another man out. They were a thoroughly nasty lot and deserved what they got.

And yet, Peter, apparently, got off scot-free, and it was only Netta who was to be killed. That didn't seem quite right. He ought, really, to kill Peter too.

But that was impossible, wasn't it? It was only Netta that he had to kill, so that he could stop it all and get to Maidenhead? He didn't see how Peter came in on it.

Or *did* he? Did he? The sudden thought trickled into his brain. Had he been making another mistake, had he got the whole thing muddled? Surely it wasn't just Netta he had to kill in order to get clear, to get to Maidenhead—surely it was Netta and Peter, surely it had been Netta and Peter all along!

Of course! He must kill Peter too! This was most interesting. He had got it all muddled. It was like him to get things muddled like that, just as it was like him to keep on putting it off. But he was going to pull himself together now.

Why, Peter and Netta were one. He knew for a fact that they

were one. He had found them in the cupboard. You could no more kill Netta without killing Peter than you could kill Peter without Netta.

He was glad of this because it made things more just—he hadn't liked the idea of Peter getting clean away with it. He had killed a man; now he would be killed too.

What about the little newcomer who was in bed with Netta now? Oughtn't he to be killed, as he was one with Netta too? No, no. That was quite a different thing. He had only just appeared on the scene. He wasn't in on the thing at all. He hadn't been going on too long, like Netta and Peter. He only had to kill them for going on too long, and keeping him from Maidenhead. It didn't make sense otherwise.

How odd, them being in Brighton like this, lying asleep back at the hotel, Netta with her boyfriend, Peter in the annexe, and never guessing they were going to be killed almost at once. They'd never have come to Brighton if they had known this was going to happen!

Was he, then, going to kill them *in* Brighton, *now*: today or tomorrow? Yes. Of course he was—no more putting off. He had got wise to himself now. Here was half the summer gone: it would be cold soon, and he would have to wait another year. Another year in Earl's Court!

But it had to be planned. He would have to make them stay down by the sea, pay their bill if necessary. Then the trouble was where to do it: he had always thought of it up at Earl's Court, in Netta's flat. And there were two of them now—that didn't make it any more easy. Then Peter being a man—that was a slight snag—he would have to use a clever trick, hit him while he wasn't looking and then finish him off. It wasn't quite as absurdly easy as it was with a girl.

Then the trouble about Brighton was the distance from Maidenhead. It wasn't near Maidenhead, like London was, and if there was any meddling from the police he couldn't get there so quickly, so that they couldn't touch him. He would have to go up to London first, and then on.

Yes—meddling from the police—"questions asked"—there mustn't be any of that. That was the whole point. Or if there was any meddling he had got to be on his way to Maidenhead. Perhaps it was dangerous, this Brighton business . . .

No!—there he was, shilly-shallying again—trying to put it off. He meant business this time—he was going to do it now. If he didn't do it now he would somehow forget again, and the cold would come, and he would be in for another winter in Earl's Court . . .

If he could only plan it, think it out, it was as easy as pie . . . Then why not plan it and think it out now, while he was walking, while he was alone in the dawn?

He must go on walking and go on thinking. He would walk and think until he had found the plan. He wouldn't go back, he wouldn't turn round, until he had found it. Then he would go back and do it. It might be today: it might be tomorrow: but it would be in Brighton, and he would do it. He meant business this time all right.

He passed the King Edward Peace statue (a fat lot of peace with Hitler about!) and walked along by the Hove lawns. The dawn glowed redder and brighter: it would soon be day. He noticed he was not entirely alone; ahead of him a fat man, clad in a dressing-gown, a bather, climbed over the railing, and scrambled down to the sea—a raving lunatic, of course, but it took all sorts to make a world.

Hove and Brighton slept. The dawn glowed pink—the front shone in the recent rain. The raving lunatic bobbed up and down in the decidedly rough waves. He noticed that he himself wore no overcoat and no hat—that he had come out just as he was from the hotel, in the blue suit he had put on for Netta, and stayed in all night. He walked towards Worthing.

*C*rack! . . . It almost knocked him down. It made him reel. It was as though he had been hit by something. And yet he knew what it was. It was only his head, cracking back. And with the crack everything came flooding, rushing, roaring back—noise, colour, light, the fury of the real everyday world. It was almost more than he could bear. It would settle down, he would adjust himself soon, but for the moment it was too much for him. He leaned against a wall, giddy and faint.

That crack! Usually it was a little click, a pop, a snap. But this time his brain had almost burst in two: it had practically knocked him off his feet. These attacks were getting worse. He was an ill man.

Coming up from the depths, the impact of the real world was too much. He simply couldn't collect himself. He still leaned against the wall. Where was he?

A woman came up to him. "Excuse me," she said, in a frightened way. "Can I help you?"

She was a middle-aged working-class woman wearing black. She carried a straw shopping-bag.

"No. It's all right, thanks," he said. "I'm just a bit giddy. It's all right. Thanks very much."

"Sure you're all right?" she said.

"Yes. Thanks awfully. Just a bit giddy. I get these attacks. I'll be all right. Thanks very much."

She smiled doubtfully and passed on. Where was he? Where in God's name *was* he? He raised his head.

He was in a narrow street. He saw the mast of a ship: a wood-yard—a coal-yard—a canal—the sea—ships—tugs—cranes—wharves—warehouses. He couldn't *collect* himself. Where was he? He must be in a port somewhere. Where was it—Southampton, Portsmouth, Yarmouth, Plymouth, Cardiff? How had he got to a narrow street in a port? He had nothing to do with ports.

Oh, God—this was terrible. He was up against it this time. . . He didn't know where he was—he didn't know *who* he was—he just didn't know. He wore no hat; he was dishevelled, cold, exhausted. He had on his best blue suit. He might be in Dublin: he might be in America: he might be in France—he just didn't know. No, not France, because the woman spoke English.

He must keep calm. He must ask somebody, go to the police.

They must find out for him. This was the end.

How had he *got* here? If only he could remember how he had *got* here!

He began to walk. He must go to the police, and ask them to explain it all to him.

But couldn't he find out for himself?

He saw an errand-boy propping up his bike outside a small tobacconist's. He crossed the road to him.

"Excuse me," he said. "Where is this?"

The errand-boy stared at him in a scared way.

"This? . . ." he said blankly. "This is Portslade . . ."

"Oh—thanks . . ."

He seemed to be frightening everybody. The woman first and now the boy. But they weren't as frightened as he was!

Port Slade . . . Slade . . . Where was Slade? He had never heard of Slade. The Slade school of art, but not port. Port Slade.

No . . .

And yet there was something familiar about it . . . Port Said!

That was it—it was like Port Said? But he couldn't be in Port Said—you wouldn't have women with shopping-bags, and errand boys and tobacconist-shops like that, in Port Said . . .

No—it was Port *Slade* all right. Or perhaps Port Slaid. And there was such a port—he had somewhere vaguely heard of it. He just couldn't place it.

A green motor-van came by. He saw written on it, in neat gold letters, "THE PORTSLADE MODEL LAUNDRY."

"Ah! Portslade! Portslade! *Portslade!*" The little green van had saved his life—his sanity! Portslade!—the little town next to Brighton. Brighton!—it was all coming back. He was staying down at Brighton. It was all perfectly normal. He was there with Netta, with Netta and Peter and the little school-bully they had brought down with them.

But how had he got out to Portslade? What was the order of events? He had met them at the station and they had all been drunk; then they had gone back to the hotel and made a row; and then—oh dear, yes, it was coming back—they had gone to bed. The last door had closed. The gurgle of the tap, the creaking, the giggles, the mumbling all night, the ultimate silence. All night long they had driven him out of his mind. That was Netta's clever revenge on him for giving her fifteen pounds, for forcing her to come to Brighton. And at last he hadn't been able to stand it any more, and he had run out into the dark dawn.

Then blank. Complete blank until that awful crack in his head, and he woke up in Portslade. Why Portslade? How had he got there? Had he taken a bus? Or a train? Or had he walked? He looked at his wrist-watch and saw that it was five and twenty past nine—breakfast time. Presumably he had walked. He felt as though he had been walking forever: he was exhausted, cold with exhaustion, sleeplessness and general shock. Since he met them at the station last night he had taken it on the chin as he had never taken it before.

That crack in his head. That had really frightened him. Usually his coming up from the depths, his clicking out of a "dead" mood, was a more or less pleasant exhilarating sensation, was accompanied by a gratifying clarification of mind. But that crack, and the subsequent utter confusion—that was something new. Was this a turn for the worse in his strange mental disorder? Was the strain he had been through beginning to tell on it? He ought to do something about it; he ought to see a doctor.

And he had flattered himself that these "dead" moods of his were getting better. He had had a bad bout of them round about Christmas and for a little while afterwards; and then he had had one or two in the early spring; but after that he had been almost entirely free. They went in bouts, he knew that by now.

He ought to go and see a doctor. And a doctor would tell him to go away somewhere, and take a rest. But he was "away"—wasn't he? Wasn't he at Brighton, supposed to be having a "holiday"?

And now, actually, he was at Portslade. He was within full sight of the sea again, and walking back to Brighton. He saw some bus-stops, and hoped he might soon catch a bus to help him along; but he didn't really care much.

A pleasant holiday. The wind was rising, hitting him in the face, and the sky was full of rain. It was blowing up for a storm. The still days, the long summer, had crashed, fallen into tempest and misery, as he had done. He was indescribably unhappy.

At last he caught a bus, and was physically grateful for the warmth inside, the padded seats, the smoothness and speed with which he was wafted along.

What now? Go back to the hotel to them? To his bedroom? The thought made him feel faint with pain.

It was now half past nine: he would be there by a quarter to ten, and they almost certainly would not be up. They would, of course, have a frightful hangover, and be sleeping on. No—not *back* to the torture! He couldn't face his bedroom: he couldn't go upstairs while they were there. He doubted whether he could face them at all.

Then how was he to get back to his things—to wash and tidy himself up? He was in an awful state: he had to do something. He was hungry, too.

He supposed he would have to face them some time. But no—not until they were out of bed, not until they had come downstairs where he could meet them on his own ground.

Then he must wash and shave and eat outside—go to a barber's and a Lyons'. Yes—that was it—be fresh and tidy before he saw them.

What attitude was he going to take—how was he going to meet Netta's eyes? How was he going to save his pride before them both? How was he going to meet the little school-bully's eyes? She had no doubt told the latter all about him—of his long-standing and ridiculous inclination towards her. They were probably giggling about it last night over their whisky.

All he could do was to pretend he wasn't hurt, that he hadn't noticed, that he was well and happy, on top of the world. To pretend, really, either that he was a complete fool or that he didn't really care a damn about Netta. It wouldn't really wash, either way, but it was the only thing to do: and it might mystify them, even annoy them, if he seemed to be in good form. For all they knew he might have a secret of his own.

That was the thing. He must be looking well and in good form. So he would go to a barber's, and have a shave, and wash and brush-up, and then to Lyons' for a meal, and when he met them he would just act—pretend that there had been no night-before—no gigglings, no gurgling taps, no silence—and that he was feeling fine. They would have a hangover, but he would be feeling fine. It wasn't much good, but it was the only thing.

He saw West Pier approaching. He had better get off here. The bus stopped at Preston Street, and he got off.

He walked up Preston Street, and found a barber on the left. He went in and was shaved soothingly in warm electric light. The barber did not talk, but beat up a rich sweet-scented lather with the brush on his face, and then scraped with the razor in a sacramental hush. Only once he asked, in a formal voice, "Is the razor to your liking, sir?" and George Harvey Bone replied, "Fine, thanks." Thus these two, the barber with his own past and private life, and George Harvey Bone with his, met, touched, were silent with each other under electric light, and then parted never to meet again.

When he came out, carrying, as he walked along, the fresh electric-lit memory of his shaven face, his brushed hair, his brushed clothes and tidied collar and tie—seen in the barber's electric-lit mirror—he felt wonderfully better. He walked up to the Western Road and along towards the Clock Tower, whose clock pointed to a quarter past ten. A tremendous wind was banging up West Street from a lead-grey sea, and he went down North Street to the Lyons' at the bottom.

He ordered egg and bacon and household bread and coffee. He began to feel warm all over, and he read a paper he had found at his table. When he had eaten, he smoked a cigarette. Soon enough it was eleven o'clock. They would be up by now, and he supposed he ought to go. Instead, he lit another cigarette, and sat on reading his paper. Let them wait. Let *them* wonder what *he* was doing, for once.

The time crept on to a quarter past eleven, and then to twenty past. Perhaps now he had better go. He got his check from the girl, paid his bill, and came out into the street.

The hotel was only two minutes' walk away, and he suddenly felt frightened. It was, after all, something of an ordeal after last night. But he pulled at his coat and straightened his body, and remembered that he had had a shave and was in his best suit.

He walked straight up the steps of the hotel. He looked into the dining-room, but they weren't there—only the waiter laying the things for lunch. Then he looked into the little lounge over the way—but they weren't there either. Then he went to the reception office, but there was nobody there either. Nobody seemed to be anywhere.

Finally the woman—the receptionist—appeared from a door behind her office. "Oh, good morning," he said, smiling. "Have you seen anything of my friends?"

"Oh . . . Them?" she said, staring at him in rather the same frightened way the woman in Portslade had stared at him when was standing against the wall. "They've gone . . . Didn't you know?"

"Oh," he said. "Have they . . . ?"

And he stared back at her.

CHAPTER THREE

"They went this morning—about ten . . ." she said. "Oh . . . really? . . ." He could think of nothing else to say.

"They said you'd pay the bill," she said. "Is that all right?"

"Oh . . . really? . . . Yes, that's all right . . . Did they leave any message for me?"

"No. They didn't say anything."

"Oh," he said. "How funny . . . Well, if they've gone, they've gone, I suppose." He smiled. They were still staring at each other.

"To tell you the truth," she said, "I think there's something I ought to tell you."

"Oh—really? . . . What? . . ."

"Well, to tell you the truth, the manageress had to ask them if they'd mind going. You see, there was such a noise last night, and one thing and another, we really felt we couldn't keep them. I thought I ought to tell you. I'm sure you'll understand."

"Oh dear. I'm sorry. I'm afraid it's my fault . . . I'm sorry."

"Oh no—it's not your fault at all. We're very glad to have you here. But we really felt they were a little too much for us. I'm sure you'll understand."

"Oh yes. I do. Thank you very much. I'm afraid they were very noisy."

"Yes. They were, really, weren't they? And it wasn't only the noise, really . . ." She smiled, and changed the subject. "Anyway, I hope *you'll* be staying on?"

"Oh. Yes. I think I'll stay on. For another night, anyway . . . I'll let you know . . . Well, thank you very much. I'm awfully sorry." He began to move away.

"No, not at all. I just felt we ought to tell you . . ."

"Yes. Thanks very much," he said, and walked in a dazed way along the hall to the front steps. Here the cheerful, friendly porter was now standing.

"Good morning, sir," he said. "How are you, sir?"

"Oh, I'm all right," he said. "I hear my friends have been thrown out."

"Oh, I don't know, sir," said the porter, grinning shyly. "They were a bit noisy, weren't they? And I believe there were certain complaints."

"They didn't leave any message with you, did they?"

"Message, sir?"

"Yes. Message for me, I mean."

"I don't know, sir. Have you asked at the office?"

"Oh yes. I've asked there. I was wondering if they left any message through you."

"No, sir. Not through me, sir. I'm afraid not, sir." And there was an embarrassed pause, in which they both looked out at the street.

"Hullo," he said, noticing it for the first time. "It's started to rain."

"Yes. It's started now, all right, sir," said the porter, and a moment later he said, "Excuse me a moment, will you, sir," and went away on his business.

He stood there, staring at the rain. He wondered what he did now. Up till now he had hardly reacted to this new turn of events, had made his answers to the woman and the porter automatically, in a dream. Now he had to see what thing it was that had happened, and what its implications were.

It was no use standing here, staring at the rain. He must get out and walk. He ran upstairs for his hat and raincoat.

His room was neat, the bed made, "done." He heard the chambermaid moving about in the room next door. (She had a mess to clear up!) He ran downstairs and out into the street.

He went down East Street towards the sea. It was pelting with rain, and the wind boxed his ears. Oh—how the summer had crashed, and he with it! Tempest and disaster lay ahead—only tempest and disaster!

He knew he would get soaked if he went on walking, but he couldn't bother about that. He had to walk. What fate was it which made him always walking, always by himself?

No message—no attempt at a message—and he was left to pay the bill! He had thought to save his pride, but now this last, this smashing blow had been dealt it. They had just crashed down, scorned him, wrecked him, torn him to bits, disgraced him publicly in the quiet hotel he had chosen, and crashed back again. Surely this was the end: he couldn't put up with it any more, could he?

They were a dirty lot, and Netta was the dirtiest. He felt he would like to beat her up, do her some physical damage, smash her face and tell her to go to hell. He could understand men wanting to hit women.

Unfortunately, that wasn't his way. He wasn't the woman-hitting type. Too late to try and do a Cagney now! But why should he have to pay the bill? Why not refuse to pay it, and let the hotel recover from them? No, that wasn't his way, either. He had brought them down, and he was responsible. The hotel had been very nice and it wasn't their fault.

What could he do, then? Only one thing—cut them out, never see them again. Go away somewhere—start again. But he *was* away, and where could he go?

He was on the front and the rain was impossible—impassable.

He turned into a pub near the Grand. He was in a saloon lounge, with bar and tables. He ordered a bitter, and noticed that the fire had been thoughtfully lit in spite of the season.

The summer had crashed. He went over and warmed his wet legs, made them steam in front of the fire.

He sipped his beer, and wondered where he was to go, what he was to do. He had got to get away, get a job—start again. But not in London, and not in Brighton.

Of course, he would have to go back to London—he had all his things there. He would go back tomorrow. But after that, where? And where could he get a job? Who could help him, who did he know? No one. Except Johnnie. Perhaps Johnnie would help him. Yes. He would go back tomorrow and ring up Johnnie. He wouldn't see them ever again.

He would ring up Johnnie and perhaps Johnnie would help him get a job—a job somewhere else—away from London. Then he would get well. He ordered another beer and came back to steam his legs again.

To get away—that was all he could think of now. But where was there, apart from London and Brighton? The "country" . . .

What was the country? Somerset? . . . Devonshire? . . . Cornwall? . . . Hampshire? . . . Yorkshire? Or down the river somewhere, where he had been when he was a boy, and his sister Ellen was alive . . . Shepperton, Cookham, Maidenhead? . . .

"Maidenhead" . . . A faint, rather funny feeling came over him as he mentioned Maidenhead to himself—a feeling as though he had been reminded of something—as though there was some thing he ought to remember about Maidenhead . . . It was like one of those sensations you had when you went into a strange room, or a strange place, and felt you had been there before . . . (And people said it was reincarnation or a trick of the brain, "Maidenhead" . . . What was it? . . . He puzzled for a little, and then gave it up, and went on thinking and steaming his trousers. He had four beers altogether, and then went out on to the front. The rain had stopped now, but the wind was thundering madly all over the streaming esplanade, and he sought the shelter of the town. In a side street he passed a sports shop, and, seeing some sets of golf clubs on display, stopped to look at them.

He could never resist looking at golf clubs in a window, and he remembered his sixty-eight of yesterday. Yes, it was only yesterday, incredible as it seemed after all he had been through Then he had felt well, then he had planned to become a golfer again. Now he was a ruined man, drinking beer in a summer which had crashed over a seaside town.

He had planned to become a golfer, to start again. Well, wasn't he planning to start again now? Then why not get some clubs and start his new life with golf—the one thing at which he was any good? No—that was absurd—he couldn't afford clubs, But why not buy a club—just one club—to remind him of gall? A number five, say, and take it back with him and perhaps play on the little approach course—what did they call it?—at Holland Park at the top of the Earl's Court Road, opposite the Kensington Cinema?

Golf. The one thing you could do. He went into the shop, and came out a few minutes afterwards with a number seven. He had decided that a number seven, on the whole, was the best thing for Holland Park.

He felt astonishingly cheerful. The club was wrapped in brown paper—a sort of brown-paper bag made specially for golf clubs—but he knew how sweet and gleaming and sticky-gripped it was underneath, and he saw the shots he was going to make with it. He approached holes and made the shots as he walked along. You couldn't be anything but cheerful with such a thing under your arm.

He was so cheerful he decided to have lunch, instead of having any more drinks, and then to go to a cinema.

He had lunch at the restaurant on the first floor of the Regent, and then went into the cinema below, carrying his brown papered club.

He was out at six and had a few more drinks and went to

bed at ten. So his holiday at Brighton ended. He slept well. In the morning he packed, and tipped the cheerful porter, and took a taxi for the 9.5 to London. It was not until he was nearly halfway to London that his head clicked again.

Chapter Four

He was reading his newspaper . . .
"*It was only when Miss Fields herself pleaded 'Please make way,'* he read, "*that she was able to enter Broadcasting House.*

LOOKED EXHAUSTED

"*She looked pale and exhausted when she reached the vestibule.*

"*Miss Fields said to listeners: 'My goodness, it is wonderful to be back at this old microphone again and to be able to speak to and thank you all wonderful people for the great love and affection you have shown to me during what has been the most dreadful ordeal of my 41 years.*

"*'Thank heaven and Mr. Searle, the surgeon, and all those wonderful sisters and nurses at the Chelsea Women's Hospital.*

"*'I want to say 'Thank you' to the Bishop of Blackburn. The day he came to see me was I think the most critical day of my illness. I felt that all the life had gone out of me and I could feel myself slipping back.*

IT WAS WONDERFUL

"*'After your prayers, dear Bishop—if you are listening—a miracle seemed to happen. I felt myself slowly gaining strength again, it was wonderful.*

"*'Now I want to say 'Thank you' to all you wonderful people from all over the world, who have written me such beauti-*

ful letters, and for all the wonderful flowers, telegrams and presents.

"'I tell you that you have made me cry. I have been so over-come by your devotion.

"'Maybe you would like to hear the old voice—they haven't been mucking about with that. I am going to sing some verses of a song that you all know. The words express all that I . . .'"

Click! . . .

Click . . . Here it was again. He was sitting in a damp, stuffy, third-class compartment, reading his newspaper, and it had happened again.

He tried to read on.

"She sang, 'I Love the Moon . . .' At the end of her song she said, 'Thank you, Mr. B.B.C. Good night and God bless you . . .' Miss Fields will leave for Capri today. It is expected . . ."

But he couldn't make any sense of the words. He could only think of what had happened in his head.

He looked slyly around, over his newspaper, at his fellow-passengers, to see if they had noticed what had happened, observed some change in his appearance, but they didn't seem to have done so.

He sat there, very, very still, pretending to read his news-paper. He looked like one seized in public with a sudden pain which he endeavours to hide—an earache, a toothache, colic. Like such a one his eyes strayed furtively, and then became fixed . . . strayed again, and again became fixed, thoughtful, dead.

He was, he realized, in a train on his way from Brighton to London. A moment ago such a realization would have had some comprehensibility and point, now it was merely a dead-grey thought in a dead-grey world . . .

The third-class compartment, the people in it, the sky

splashing drops of rain on to the pane, the newspaper in front of him, all were grey and dead. But he had something to do. The wheels clicked and rumbled beneath him, and he waited to find out what it was. Lulled by the sound of the wheels, he went into a sort of doze for a few minutes, and when he came out of it he knew all about it. He had, of course, to kill Netta Longdon. Netta Longdon and Peter. He was probably on his way to do so now, he couldn't quite remember.

Yes—that was right. He remembered working it out as he walked that morning along the Brighton front to Portslade. He had at first thought of doing it at Brighton, but then as he had walked he had decided that that wouldn't be safe, first of all because there wasn't a really useful private place to kill them in in Brighton, and secondly because he would be too far from Maidenhead. He would have to journey up to London before he could get there, and the police might get him, they were so quick. Why, they might have arrested him on the train! He had been one too clever for them. You had to be careful. He kept on forgetting you had to be careful.

And now where was he? He was on the train, very wisely having not killed them. And where were they? Oh yes—they were back already: they had left early in the morning yesterday—tuned out of the hotel. Everything fitted in wonderfully. He had decided not to kill them in Brighton, and they had most obligingly gone back to London for him at once. And now he was following them back to Earl's Court, where he had arranged to do it at once on his return. He had worked out his plan on the walk to Portslade. He couldn't quite remember the details, but he knew he had arranged to do it at once on his return.

"At once." Did that mean now—today? That was a bit stiff, wasn't it? He ought to have some time to think about it.

No—there he went again! Putting it off—vacillating, delaying! What was wrong with today—it was as good as any other day, wasn't it? . . . And go to Maidenhead tonight? . . .

What a funny idea. But wasn't his bag packed? Wasn't everything ready? It looked like fate.

Maidenhead! Tonight! Peace! A thrill ran through him such as he had never quite felt before. Maidenhead tonight—away from everything—the whole bloody thing which had been going on too bloody long! Maidenhead, peace, the river, an inn, a quiet glass of beer, and safety, utter safety . . . Maidenhead, where he had been with poor Ellen, the river in the sun, in the shade of the trees, his hand in the water over the side of the boat, the sun on the ripples of the water reflected quaveringly on the side of the boat, his white flannels, tea in a basket, the gramophone, the dank smell at evening, the red sunset, sleep! Tonight!

Curse it, it was raining . . . But it would be fine tomorrow. It was still summer. He would get up early and would be down in a punt at Cookham by midday. And the sun would shine, and he would get under the trees, and there would be no Netta, and no policemen, and no killing and sordidness. It was on! It was a date!

There was just the sordid thing to be done. Well, he had never shirked a duty. "Yes, I'll admit that you have a certain—er—torpid conscientiousness of sorts, Bone," old Thorne had once said. Which meant that he was a plodder, that he got things done, in his own dull way. Well, he would show old Thorne he was right. He would get the thing done before dark.

What was his plan? He had worked it all out on the walk to Portslade, but now it had slipped away again. He had got to get them both together in Netta's flat, that was the thing. And that was the difficulty, to make sure of having them both together. It had been child's play when there was only Netta, but now he had both on his hands.

Blast Peter, for butting in like this. Couldn't he leave Peter out of it! No, no—that was out of the question now. There could be no Maidenhead, no peace down there, with Peter left out loose and alive—the thought was absurd—he might just as well kill Peter and leave out Netta! They were both in it together—two in one, and one in two.

Then how had he planned to get them together? Ah, yes—it was coming back—the bottle of gin and the blunt instrument. He was to get them together with the bottle of gin, and hit them with the blunt instrument.

The blunt instrument was for Sir Bernard Spilsbury—"evidently some blunt instrument." It wouldn't be right unless he made it a blunt instrument for Sir Bernard Spilsbury. He remembered deciding that.

But what instrument had he decided upon? What was blunt? He looked round the compartment. An umbrella? That wasn't blunt. A suitcase—that was blunt but too unwieldy. Then, on top of his suitcase, he saw his golf club wrapped up in brown paper.

A golf club! . . . What about a golf club? Perfect? What could be more harmless-looking, what could he himself wield more skilfully or with direr effect than a golf club? Innocence itself! This was genius . . . Practising in Netta's room—practising swings, and then the appalling accident. He had no idea that Peter was standing there! Peter laid out, and then settle with Netta anyhow—settle with both of them.

This was sheer genius. The uncanny cleverness of it. He was really quite excited now—both by what lay ahead and by his own cleverness. He looked around at his fellow-passengers, to see if they noticed how clever he was, the sort of man they had amongst them.

"Excuse me, sir," said the rather pompous man opposite, "if you've finished with that paper of yours, would you exchange it with mine? I've exhausted this."

"No. Certainly," he said, "good idea." And he handed over his *News Chronicle* and took the *Daily Mail*.

"Nothing much in any of them, I'm afraid," he said.

"No," said the man, "very little new."

He opened the *Daily Mail* and pretended to read it. There was cleverness for you. "Nothing much in any of them, I'm afraid." So completely natural. Here he was, plotting a killing in the next few hours, and he could make entirely natural conversation in a train. "Nothing much in any of them, I'm afraid."

Just like that. And now he was opening the paper, and pretending to look at a column which interested him, fooling the pompous gentleman opposite. He could fool anybody. It was almost too easy.

But he must not be vain. In that way he would cease to be clever. He was so clever that he could see even that. He had to be clever, cunning, right up to the very end, right until he got to Maidenhead. Then there would be no cunning and no sordidness any more; only peace, the bright, watery, quavering reflection of the ripples on the side of the boat . . .

He walked along the platform at Victoria towards the barrier. His head bobbed amongst the other heads, and he entered the dense bottle-neck of human beings by the ticket collector. For a moment he felt a little disquieted: he had a nasty sensation of being in a complete dream. He had to force himself, as it were, to keep awake in this dream. He couldn't understand what all these people, none of them about to kill anybody, were up to what they were getting at. They had no reality; nothing had any reality. There was only his plan: he had his plan and he was going through with it now. His plan was all he had to stick to, in a confused, meaningless, planless world.

He was feeling disquieted, so he went and had a beer at the buffet. He felt it would put him right. It did.

He came out and went straight to the telephone booths, dragging his suitcase and brown-papered golf club with him.

Because they were all filled and electric-lit, he had to wait some time before he could get into a booth; but at last he seized his chance and dragged his suitcase in and propped his golf-club parcel against the cork wall on which people had drawn drawings and scoured chocolate-coloured circles with impatient pennies. He had his plan, and put his two pennies in without hesitation.

He got her almost at once.

"Hullo," she said.

"Hullo, is that you, Netta?"

"Yes, who's that?"

"This is George, Netta."

"Oh—yes? . . ."

"What happened to you? You just vanished. I've just arrived at Victoria."

"Oh . . . have you?"

"Yes . . . What happened to you, you just faded out? You didn't even leave any message."

All part of the plan . . . He had worked it out. He had got to be natural, to pretend to be hurt. They'd think there was something phoney if he wasn't.

"Didn't we?" she said. "Well, we couldn't as a matter of fact. We were turfed out. I'm sorry."

"How do you mean, 'turfed out'?"

"Turfed out. They told us to go."

"Well, I still think you might have left a message."

"Do you? I don't see why . . . I'm very sorry, but we just didn't think about it."

"And I had to pay the bill, didn't I?"

"You're very quarrelsome, George. We'll pay you back, if you're worried about the money. What's the matter with you?"

"Oh, nothing . . . Netta. Listen."

"Yes."

"Can I come round and see you? I've just found a bottle of gin in a suitcase. I'd forgotten all about it. I thought Peter might come round and we'd open it up together."

She paused.

"All right," she said, "come round if you like."

"Is Peter there?"

"No, I haven't seen him."

"Oh well, I'll phone him up. I'll be round about twelve. Is that all right?"

"All right. Yes."

"All right then. Good-bye, Netta."

"Good-bye."

He came out into the station. He still felt dream-like, dull, bewildered, but he knew he had done all right.

Now for the taxi to Paddington! . . .

Things were getting close, drawing near, becoming very real! Paddington to Maidenhead—it had come to stations now! He had so many times thought of this trip in his mind, but he had never quite thought of it as it would be when it was a near reality. Victoria to Paddington, Paddington to Maidenhead. It was all very exciting.

There were plenty of taxis drawing up in the station yard. He waited while one of them ejected its passenger, and then said to the driver, "Paddington Station, please," and got in with his suitcase and golf club.

It was pouring with rain. They went up by the wall of Buckingham Palace, and then into the Park up to Marble Arch, and then along the Bayswater Road, and then into Hyde Park Square, and past the chemist who called himself Chymist, and up again to Paddington.

A porter opened the door and took his suitcase and golf club. He paid the taxi-driver, and said to the porter, "I only just want to park that in the cloak-room," and the porter said, "Very good, sir" and led the way to the cloak-room.

While they were waiting in the noisy station for the cloak-room attendant to take in the suitcase, the porter said: "What time'll you be wanting this, sir?" And he hesitated and replied, "Well—I don't really know—sometime today."

"Where's it for, sir?" asked the porter.

"Er—Maidenhead," he said. "How do the trains go in the evening—do you know?"

"Well—there's the 5.15, the 6.13 . . ." said the porter, and reeled off a lot of trains.

The attendant came at last, and snatched the suitcase and golf club.

"No, I'll keep that," he said, referring to the golf club, and it was given back to him. He paid his threepence, received his slip, gave the porter a shilling, and went into the buffet and had another beer. Then he walked out of the station and caught a taxi in the street.

"Earl's Court Station, please," he said to the driver.

CHAPTER SIX

As the taxi sped through streets he vaguely wondered why it was he had to take another taxi, and why it was that he had to do things just in this order. When he reached Earl's Court, he realized, he had to phone Peter from the station. Why? Why hadn't he phoned Peter at Victoria, directly after he had phoned Netta, and got it done with? Why did he have to park his suitcase at Paddington first, and then take a taxi to Earl's Court to phone Peter?

It was as though somebody had told him to do these things in just this order. Who had told him? Anyone? No . . . Of course. No one. He remembered. What a fool he was—forgetting. This was his plan. He was obeying the plan he had worked out in the train.

Obey the plan, and all would be well. Rather an expensive plan, he noticed, with all this taxi-taking. But, of course, money didn't matter now—that was the joy of it. He would be in Maidenhead tonight, and money wouldn't matter. That was the divine simplicity of the whole thing.

But he had to have enough money before he got there. A fine state of affairs, if he found he couldn't get there because he hadn't enough money! He felt in his pockets and found he had two pound notes and some silver. That wasn't enough: there might be some hitch, and he would want a lot more than that. He would have to go to the bank. It hadn't been on the plan, but he would have to do it all the same.

It wasn't so easy, all this. You had to keep your brain going all the time. You couldn't just sink into a dream and obey the plan absolutely without thinking. Well, he could do the thinking all right. He would be glad, though, when it was all over, and there was no more thinking.

He arrived at Earl's Court station, and paid the driver. It was five to eleven. It was pouring with rain. Now for phoning Peter. He felt again curiously bewildered and curiously frightened, as he entered the phone-box. If he didn't get Peter he would have to make a new plan, and that would be awful. He pulled himself together and put in his two pennies.

He got Peter at once. Amazing, how he got these people! It was almost as though, when he made the plan, he had the gift of prophetic insight. Perhaps he had. It was a strange world and there were more things in it than were dreamed of in your philosophy, Horatio.

"Hullo," said Peter.

"Hullo, is that you, Peter?" he said. "This is George."

"Oh," said Peter. "Hullo."

"How are you?"

"I'm all right. How are you?"

"I'm all right. Look, Peter. I've just been on the phone to Netta. I discovered a bottle of gin I'd forgotten about and I thought we'd open it up. I'm going round there at twelve. Are you coming along?"

Peter hesitated. "Oh. . ." he said. "All right. I'll be along."

"I hear you were turfed out at Brighton?"

"Yes. We were . . ."

"I think you might have left me a message. Just barging off like that."

"Sorry. We didn't think about it."

"Well. All right. See you at twelve."

"Right. Good-bye."

"Good-bye."

So that was that . . . Very brief, very clever. Just enough complaint about Brighton to make it seem natural, and it was in the bag.

They just fell into his hands. They couldn't resist the free gin, of course—they never could resist free drinks. You'd think they'd have some shame, really, after what they'd done to him, you'd think they'd be embarrassed and try to avoid him. But not they. He came back from Brighton, a kicked dog but with his tail still wagging and a bottle of gin to offer, and they were ready to admit him to their company again.

Rather grudgingly mind you. "All right, come round if you like." "All right, I'll be along." Really, they had a nerve! They were awful fools. It served them right.

He had now reached the bank and he went inside and got ten pounds from the cashier who was always kind and treated him as an equal. It occurred to him that this was a farewell, that when he had got to Maidenhead there would be no more banking, and so he would never see this man again. He felt a little tinge of regret.

When he came out he looked at his watch and saw that it was ten past eleven.

There was now only the gin to get, and then he was all set.

CHAPTER SEVEN

He had to get the gin not at a pub, but at a shop—a wine merchant's. He didn't know why this was, but it was in the plan, and against anything in the plan he dared not go. It had served him well enough so far.

He found a shop, bought the gin (the money he was spending!), and then walked along the Earl's Court Road to a pub the gang had had a row with and never used. He had to be alone, as if anyone came up and spoke to him now (if he met Peter, for instance, by accident) the whole thing might fall through.

As he walked along the crowded street in the rain he was again beset by that nasty feeling of being in a dream, of only being able to keep himself active and conscious by an effort of will, by concentrating mentally on his plan, and obeying its demands. Again he couldn't understand what all these people, none of them about to kill anybody, were up to, what they were getting at. They had no reality or motive. Nothing had any reality or meaning. There was only his plan: he had his plan, and he was going through with it now.

He ordered a pint of beer at the pub, whose saloon-bar clock pointed to twenty past eleven. As it was no doubt five minutes fast, that meant it was a quarter past. That meant he had three-quarters of an hour. Not very long, that. In an hour's time it might well be all over.

He was absolutely cool, though surprised, slightly mystified, by the fact that he was at last going to do what he had planned to do for so very long—years it seemed. It was like planning in the summer to get up and have an early morning bathe, and putting it off and off day after day, and then getting up one morning and finding yourself on the diving plank. Here he was. He had only got to go in now and all his troubles would be over.

Yes, he was quite cool—bored almost. Nor had he any doubts. As to his capacity to do the job quickly and without fuss. It would all be over in a few minutes. Slosh Peter with the club, and then do Netta in anyhow, she was only a woman. If he was quick enough, he could see she didn't make any noise. Then he would come back here and have another drink. Then what?

Lunch? It wouldn't be later than half past twelve.

Half past twelve . . . He perceived a snag. It would still be daylight. It would be daylight for hours, and of course, you couldn't go to Maidenhead till it was dark. That was the whole point about Maidenhead—he had to arrive there in the dark.

Maidenhead didn't make sense unless he arrived in the dark, and then awoke next morning to the sun, the peace, and the river. The police could meddle, could get him, even in Maidenhead, if he arrived there before dark. He knew the rules all right, and you needn't think he was going to slip up and forget them. Here, then, was the snag. He would have to wait hours in London before it was dark and he could get to Maidenhead. And while he was waiting in London the police might interfere.

Why hadn't he thought of it? Was there something wrong with his plan after all? Surely he had allowed for it: he couldn't have been such a fool as not to have done so. If he hadn't allowed for it he must think something up—and mighty quickly too—it was half past eleven and time was getting short. This was definitely bad.

Then he remembered. Of course. The note on the door. "Back at 9.30." He hadn't been a fool, he hadn't tripped up, after all. He had been brilliant. He had just forgotten. He had arranged after he had done it, to pin a note on the door saying "Back at 9.30 Netta." They would think Netta had written it, and that meant that nobody would ring a bell, nobody could interfere, until 9.30, and by that time it would be dark enough, and he would be on a train to Maidenhead, which would be quite dark by the time he reached it. Actually, he believed he would be quite safe directly he was on the train—quite apart from reaching Maidenhead. He wasn't quite sure on this point. It was interesting. It didn't matter, though, anyway. They couldn't find anything until 9.30.

That was all right, then. But he must write the note. He'd better do that now. He pulled out an old letter from his pocket and asked the man behind the bar if he had a pencil.

He was given a pencil and wrote, in large printed letters:

BACK AT 9.30. NETTA AND PETER and gave the pencil back to the man.

He wasn't quite sure about the "and Peter" but thought on the whole it was best in case some busy-body was looking for Peter too.

It was now a quarter to twelve.

What about the pin—to pin it on the door with? Ask the man if he had one? No. That might create suspicion—give a clue. You couldn't be too careful. You either did this thing properly, immaculately, or not at all.

"Mind my beer for a moment, will you," he said to the man behind the bar. "I just want to pop over the road."

"Certainly, sir," said the man cheerfully, and he went out and walked over the Earl's Court Road to the little draper's immediately opposite.

"Have you got some pins?" he said to the girl, and the girl said, "Pins?" and produced a drawer, and put it on the counter; and he chose a pink folded packet of innumerable silver pins, and paid threepence for them, and walked back to the pub, where his beer was still intact upon the counter.

He swilled off the remains of this and looked at the clock. It was six minutes to twelve.

Well, all was set now. The last snag was cleared up, and it was plain sailing. Should he have another drink, or go straight at it? One more, perhaps—a half. "Can I have another half in this?" he said to the man.

He drank it off quickly—in two gulps. He reckoned it would take three minutes to get to Netta, and it was now three minutes to twelve. "Good morning," he said to the man behind the bar, and he picked up the golf club in brown paper and went out into the street.

It had stopped raining now, and he felt remarkably cheerful. The beer had gone to his head a bit—not enough to affect him, just enough to make him cheerful and cool-headed.

He was glad he was cool-headed and not nervous. The time, in some extraordinary way, had come at last: that was all. There was no fear—only a slight sense of mystification, of weirdness, that at last he was going to do what he had meant to do for so long.

He was glad he was cool and competent for their sakes, too. Being cool and competent, he would get it done with quickly, without bungling, without hurting them. He would never forgive himself if he hurt them. In fact, the whole thing would be off if there was any question of doing so. That was one thing he had never done in his life, hurt anybody.

The front door was open, and he went up to the stone stairs—his dear old friends. The last time, he reflected, the last time for all three of them. He would come down them once more, just once more, on his way to Maidenhead, but they would not come down them any more. He felt oppressed by the sadness and incomprehensibility of existence generally. He was sorry for them, and made up his mind again that they should not be hurt.

He reached the top landing, and rang his old friend the bell. There was a pause, and then Peter answered the door.

"Hullo, George," said Peter, and leaving George to close the door, he went into the sitting-room. George followed him in.

Netta was sitting in the armchair. She wasn't dressed yet. She was wearing dark-blue pyjama trousers, a dressing-gown to match her red slippers and a red scarf. She had never looked lovelier. She was drinking beer.

"Hullo, Bone," she said. "How are you?"

"Hullo," he said. "How are you?"

It was rather odd and disconcerting, her being in her dressing-gown like this. He hadn't pictured killing her in her dressing-gown: he had seen her properly dressed, ready to go out. It didn't make any difference, really, but he had to adjust his mind, see the thing differently.

"What on earth's this you've brought with you?" said Peter. "I thought you were going to bring some gin."

"This?" he said. "This is a golf club."

"Oh, that's a relief," said Netta, looking him up and down in that cynical and piercing way she had. "I thought it was an umbrella."

"Yes, so did I," said Peter and they both laughed, a little nervously it seemed, and looked at him . . .

"No. Only a golf club," he said, laughing with them, and tearing the brown paper away from the club. "I'm taking golf up again. I got this at Brighton. I did a sixty-eight that day you came down."

"A sixty-eight?" said Peter. "What's a sixty-eight?"

"A sixty-eight? It's a score. How do you mean?"

"It sounds like something dirty to me," said Netta, and "Yes, *most* obscene," said Peter, and they both laughed again. They were evidently in a flippant mood.

"There," he said, throwing the last of the brown paper on to the floor, and holding up the club. "Isn't that lovely? Just feel that." And he offered the club to Peter.

But Peter kept his hands in his pockets.

"I don't want a bloody golf club," he said. "I want some gin."

And they all laughed again.

"Oh yes," he said. "I've got the gin all right." And he hauled the bottle out of his overcoat pocket, and put it on the mantelpiece. Then he propped the club against the table and began to take off his overcoat. "Shall I get some glasses?" he said. "They're in the kitchen, aren't they?"

"That's right," said Netta, and he went into the kitchen. "Have you got any Italian, or anything?" he shouted from the kitchen, as he collected the glasses. "We can't have it neat, can we?"

"No," she shouted back. "But there's some lime on top of the cupboard. Bring that in, and some water."

"Right!"

He put the Rose's lime juice on the tray with the glasses, and filled the Marks and Spencer's glass jug with water from the tap, and put it on the tray, and carried it all in.

Peter had already opened the bottle, and he and Peter assisted each other in concocting the drinks. He gave Netta her glass, and then took his own, and then said, "Well—here's how . . ."

After they had drunk there was a gloomy pause, in which nobody said anything, and he saw that the time, more or less, had come. He put down his glass on the table, and picked up the golf club, and swung it vigorously in the air, and scrutinized its shaft and swung again.

He was glad to have got hold of the club so naturally, and to be holding it in so highly natural a way, as now it was pretty plain sailing. He could pretend to be playing with it, fondling it, practising shots, until the right moment arrived. The right moment had not come yet. He felt they ought to have a drink, and he would like Netta, if it was possible, to be out of the room. He didn't want her to see him hitting Peter; it might frighten her, and there would be a panic.

The moment came, soon enough. They talked for a little, and he had another sip at his gin-and-lime (while still holding on to the club) and then Netta said, "Well, if you're just going to stand here playing golf, I'm going to dress. I've got a date at one."

And she lit a cigarette, took up her drink, and went into her room, closing the door except for a few inches.

Peter flopped down into the other armchair and picked up his *Daily Express* and began to read.

He went on playing imaginary chip shots on the carpet, and looked at Peter out of the corner of his eye. Well, here we were. Now. To it, my boy. Now. Swing back. Slow back. Eye on his head just behind his left ear . . . Eye on his ear and follow through . . . But he went on playing chip shots, and he heard his heart pumping, and he felt a singing noise in his ears.

He went over to the window, and looked out on the giddy, wet, weird street below.

"It's frightfully wet, isn't it?" he said.

"Yes," said Peter, who was reading, and not inclined to conversation. "It is."

Why this pumping and singing noise? Was he afraid? What was the matter with him? He had got a job to do. He wasn't going to funk it now. Come now, pull yourself together. You were standing on the plank. Dive in; and it would all be over. Dive in and swim hard! Count ten and dive-in! Was he a coward? Was he going to fail at the last moment?

No—he was no coward. Now for it. He was a bit nervous, but that didn't matter. He walked back to the carpet and began looking at his club, playing chip shots again. He heard Netta closing her cupboard in the next room. Peter went on reading.

Now then—count ten and dive in. All right . . . Ten shots. One, a little chip . . . Two, a little pitch and run . . . Three . . . Four . . . Oh, *stop* all this nonsense and *do* it! Now . . . Look at his ear . . . *Now* . . . Slow back . . .

All right, then, since you asked for it! NOW!

He swung the club furiously back, aiming at Peter's ear, but something funny happened. Before he reached Peter's ear, he himself, it seemed, was hit on the head. *Crack!* It simply knocked him out—stopped everything. Most odd. Instead of hitting Peter he must have hit himself. Or had someone else hit him? He felt utterly dazed—everything was going round, going far away and coming back again. He felt he was going to faint. He stumbled forward into the room, and supported himself on the table, upsetting his own drink with a clatter.

*C*rack! . . .
He was in a room somewhere, supporting himself at a deal table on which a drink was spilled and it had happened again.

Crack! . . . He knew what it was all right. It was only his wretched head, cracking back. But it was such an awful crack that it had almost knocked him out. It used not to crack like this. It used to be a funny click, a pop, a snap—rather fascinating. Now it was this frightful crack. He was getting worse.

And now, of course, everything was flooding back—noise, colour, light, the real world—roaring and rushing back. But he was so confused by the crack in his head, and by the rushing and roaring back of reality, that he couldn't collect himself. He would be all right soon, but for the moment it was a bit too much for him. He couldn't make out where he was.

"Are you all right?" he heard a voice saying, and he was aware that this voice had made the same inquiry only a moment before.

"Yes, I am all right," he said. "I'll be all right."

Where was he? He had got to keep up pretences until he found out where he was.

Still leaning for support against the table, he lifted his head. A room, evidently. But what room, and how had he got there? Had he walked into a strange room? Had he got drunk? Had he been hit over the head and robbed? Had someone taken him into their house to recover?

Now he heard the same voice speaking near, right in his ear.

"What's the matter with you, man? Are you doped or something?"

He turned, and saw a fair man with a moustache staring into his face. He didn't know that he had ever seen his face before. And yet he had a sensation of hating it for some preconceived reason, an intuition of its having an evil, nightmare familiarity.

"No, I'm all right," he said, "I've just had a come-over. I'll be all right."

He felt that if he could only put a name to this evil face it would cease to be evil, and that everything else would come back. It was bound to come back soon. All that had happened was that his head had cracked back from one of his "dead" moods. In the meantime he must keep up the pretence of knowing where he was.

"Netta," he heard the voice say. "Our friend's had a come-over and spilt his drink. Where'll I find a rag to mop it up?"

"Netta" . . . He knew who "Netta" was all right. That was the girl in Earl's Court he was so crazy about, who gave him such hell. But how was *she* in on this? Where was *she*? Why was *her* name mentioned?

He heard a voice from the next room. "What's the matter? What's he done?"

That was Netta's voice. No mistaking that. Netta! Here! In a flash he saw it all. This was Netta's flat. He recognized it. The evil man was Peter. He recognized him too. It was as clear as day. But how had he *got* there? What was the time? What was the day? What were they doing? In the meantime he must pretend he knew.

"All right," he said, "I'll get a rag. Don't bother. There'll be one in the kitchen."

He went into the kitchen, found the rag, and came back.

"What did I do?" he said, mopping up the mess and trying

to pump Peter who was now in the armchair again. "I came over all dizzy."

"I don't know exactly," said Peter. "I was reading. You were swinging the club, and then you seemed to throw a sort of fit and plunge forward and grasp the table."

"Oh . . ."

Swinging a club? What club? He could only think of an Indian club. Had he been doing Swedish drill or something?

Then he saw the golf club lying on the floor. How in God's name had that got there? He had bought that at Brighton! He'd thought he'd like some golf on the approach course in Kensington. What on earth could have induced him to bring it up here? Netta and Peter didn't understand about golf.

Having mopped up the mess, he took the rag back to the kitchen. He turned on the tap, and washed the rag out. He was glad to be alone. He had to think this out. It was coming back slowly. Brighton. His "dead" mood on the front—the waking up at Portslade. His coming back and finding them gone. His long wet day hanging about, and then taking the train next morning to Town . . . Then blank—another sudden "dead" mood—completely blank until his head cracked back into position a moment or so ago and he had nearly passed out.

How long had he been "under"? It might have been for days for all he knew. But he was fairly certain it was only since that morning. He was wearing the same shirt and suit he could remember wearing on leaving Brighton, and he had an unmistakable feeling of having been in a train recently. He looked at his watch and saw it was half past twelve.

What had he been doing in the meanwhile? Where was his suitcase? He had taken it to his hotel presumably. He supposed he would find it there when he got back. Then why and how on earth had he got round here with a golf club? He was going completely mad and must see a doctor without delay.

In the meantime he must put the best face on it he could. He went back into the sitting-room. Netta had now come out. She was dressed and was putting on her shoes.

"Hullo, Bone," she said, "have you recovered?"

"Yes. All right now."

"I'll have another of your very nice gins," she said, "if you can pour it out without throwing another fit."

Your very nice gin? Had he provided the gin, then? It sounded as though he had. Best to say nothing about it.

"Right," he said, and poured it out, and put in the lime and handed it to her.

"Are you having one, Peter?"

"Oh . . . Thanks."

He poured out one for Peter and gave it to him, and poured out one for himself. He took a good pull at it, and began to feel a bit drunk.

He looked at them and remembered Brighton—all he had suffered at their hands in the last sixty hours.

Why had he come back here of all places? What devil, or angel, or whatever it was that guided him in his "dead" moods (about which he knew absolutely nothing) had brought him back to them? After what they had done he had only hated and wanted to get away from them.

He marvelled that they had the nerve to face him. No mention of her treachery in bringing the others down, no mention of the bill he had paid, no mention of their walking out without leaving so much as a message. They just took everything for granted, because it was "George." He felt he must get outside.

"What's the programme, by the way," he said, "shall we go and have a drink outside?"

"There's no programme," said Netta. "I've got a date at one at Gloucester Road. That's all."

"Right then. Let's go out and have a drink, shall we?"

"All right," said Netta, "I'm agreeable." And "All right,"

said Peter, and a few minutes later they were all clattering down the stone stairs together.

It was still raining. He wondered what Netta's date was. With the little brown-eyed school bully? He didn't really care: he was too confused and tired to care.

They went to the Black Hart as that was near the station and Netta could get a train to Gloucester Road quickly. It was very crowded, and the moment they got in they were assailed by Mr. Montague (the vast, burly, rich-voiced, appalling Jew who had got matey with them lately, and always just had to tell them the other little one about the man who had just married his wife, see? . . .). Mr. Montague bought them all drinks, and told a story to Netta and Peter to which he couldn't even bother to listen. He found a seat and sat drinking his beer alone amidst the hubbub and confusion of the lunch-hour trade.

At about twenty past one Netta left (so nice for whoever was waiting for her!) and Peter was in an argument about Jews with Mr. Montague . . . Mr. Montague, like Peter, was on the whole *against* Jews, but there were infinite subtleties . . . He could hear it, through all the noise, from where he was sitting. He was very tired. He would have another beer, and a cigarette, and then he would go back to his hotel and sleep. He presumed his suitcase was there all right. He pushed through the crowd and got his beer, and sat down, and felt in his pocket for his cigarettes. He pulled out a pink, folded piece of paper, pierced with innumerable bright silver pins . . .

Pins! . . . A golf club, a bottle of gin, and a packet of pins. Things were getting interesting. Was there anything more?

He felt in his pockets. He found ten, new, crisp pound notes in his hip pocket, and in his waistcoat pocket a Paddington cloak-room receipt.

Paddington. So that was where his suitcase was! He somehow always knew at the back of his mind that it wasn't at his hotel.

Pins . . . gin . . . pound notes . . . golf clubs . . . Netta . . .

cloakroom tickets . . . It was too much for him. He was drunk, anyway. He had better go and sleep.

He walked out of the noise without saying good-bye to Peter, and, putting his head against the rain, he walked to his hotel in Fauconberg Square.

The white cat was in the passage outside his door. Seeing him, it opened its mouth and made a half plaintive, half irritable noise. He took this for a welcome.

"Hullo, pussy," he said. "Let's go and have a sleep, shall we?"

It was funny, going to bed at twenty to two in the afternoon without any lunch. Downstairs the guests were no doubt having theirs. As he took off his coat and trousers, the white cat, crossing one paw methodically over the other as it walked, weaved itself in and out of his legs, and purred like mad.

He drew the flimsy curtains to quickly, and jumped under the bedclothes in his shirt. There was a pause, and then he felt the sudden springy weight of the cat on his body.

He lifted up the bedclothes so that the cat could come in. The cat, hesitating, came half in, and began to paddle and purr.

"Come on, pussy," he said. "Stop playing the piano and go to sleep."

But the cat went on paddling and purring and he still had to keep the bedclothes held open for it.

Finally the cat dived down under, and turned round laboriously, and went on purring, but stopped paddling.

"Come on. Let's go to sleep, pussy," he said.

The cat purred, and he began to breathe heavily . . .

Pink packets of silver pins, bottles of gin, pound notes, golf clubs, Netta, his "dead" moods, cloak-room tickets, Paddington . . . It was all too much for him.

The cat, warm against his side, suddenly stopped purring and slept. The warmth of the cat beat up against his side, beat up against the pins and the pound notes, and George Harvey Bone slept too.

THE EIGHTH PART

MR. BONE

Desire of wine and all delicious drinks,
Which many a famous warrior overturns,
Thou could'st repress; nor did the dancing ruby,
Sparkling out-poured, the flavour or the smell,
Or taste, that cheers the hearts of gods and men,
Allure thee from the cool crystalline stream.
                    J. Milton, *Samson Agonistes*

CHAPTER ONE

In the year 1939 there came from Lewes, in Sussex, to Earl's
Court, in London, a young man of eighteen of the name of
John Halliwell. He was employed by a firm of insurance
brokers in the City who thought highly of him for his industry,
integrity, and good nature.

He was a fair-haired, clean-shaven young man with a fresh
skin and a rather prominent nose, and he occupied a small,
cheap and slightly sordid room at the top of a house in Nevern
Road.

Here he slept and was given breakfast; but most of his spare
time he spent out of doors in the immediate neighbourhood.
For he was alone in London for the first time, and at an age
when the external world generally bears a totally different
aspect from the one it bears to its more battered and jaundiced
inhabitants—at an age, indeed, when even the scenery of S.W. 7
might be associated with the beginning of life rather than the
end of all hope, and its streets and people charged with a
remarkable mystery and romance of their own.

Sometimes, of an evening, he would just walk about, and
sometimes he would go to the pictures; but most of all he preferred to go to the saloon bars of public-houses, and, having
one or two drinks, watch and listen to people who were older
than himself. On these occasions he would drink small glasses
of port, which was the only alcoholic drink he at all liked. He
was not even certain that he liked this, but he was anxious to
acquire the worldly feeling of liking and taking drink, just as he

was anxious to acquire the worldly habit of going into public-houses.

Sometimes he would get into conversation with someone, and might have as many as five or six of these small ports in the course of an evening (going home pleased with the spiritual achievement, rather than the physical sensation, of being slightly intoxicated), but usually he stood by himself in a cor-ner and watched.

Amongst the many types he observed in this way, there was one particular little set of people by whom he was a good deal impressed. The centre of this set, as he saw it, was a dark and extremely attractive girl, with a mass of hair which she always wore uncovered (thus giving the impression that she had just slipped out in a rather slovenly way from somewhere next door to have a drink), and an unsmiling, bored expression which at once repelled and fascinated him. With her there was nearly always to be seen a blond man with a rather savage, pasty face, and a blond "guardsman's" moustache—a little man with a moustache whom they all called Mickey and who was very vol-uble and at times extremely drunk; and an enormous, blue-eyed, tired-looking man, also with a moustache. Quite often there would be others in this circle as well—slightly younger men (and even an occasional woman) who, he gathered, were connected with the theatre.

Young Halliwell was impressed by these people for a num-ber of reasons. In the first place, he was impressed merely by their age and maturity (they were all either a little way above or a little way beneath the thirty level)—by the phase of life they were enjoying—one in which, it seemed, they retained all the appearance, vigour and boisterousness of youth, while obvi-ously having accumulated a stock of worldly wisdom and expe-rience, such as he himself, in the modesty of his eighteen years, doubted whether he would ever acquire. Then he was impressed by the noise they made, and the sophisticated humour and slang they used, and the way they had of making themselves at home, seeming at once to own and despise whatever property they happened to be upon at the moment. Then he was impressed by the amount they drank and the money they spent in conjunction with their seeming total idleness or unemployment. Then he was impressed by their apparent connection with the world of the theatre (the girl, he gathered, was a film actress of some sort). And finally, of course, he was tremendously impressed by the girl herself, whose dark beauty and strange, off-hand manner overwhelmed and haunted his immature imagination, filled him, in point of fact, and although he would not admit it, with a sort of hopeless yet immeasurable longing.

Indeed, if it had not been for the girl he would probably have never thought twice about the set in which she moved, for, though to a certain extent awed by their general swagger and behaviour, he did not altogether like the atmosphere they gave forth. Because of the girl, however, he made a point of visiting the houses he knew they frequented (particularly the "Black Hart") and, standing in a far corner by himself, he would watch all that took place, a certain amount of disdain, but more perhaps of envy, in his heart. He often wondered whether he would live to be old and experienced enough to carry on in public as these people did, and to be on free-and-easy terms with such a girl as that. He felt towards these people, in short, very much the same sensations, half-hating, half-admiring, as a new boy at a public school might feel on observing the antics of the "bloods."

Apart from the girl, there was one character in this crowd in whom he took a slightly greater interest (and towards whom he felt less sensations of awe) than the rest. This was the big, tired-looking man, whose name, he ascertained, was "George." This "George," he noticed, although he drank as much, made considerably less noise than the others, and, in the midst of the revelry or argument, would often sit by himself, staring into space in a lonely, melancholy way. He had also a more simple, kindly expression than the others, with whom, indeed, he seemed at times to be slightly out of the picture.

Towards the end of the summer young Halliwell noticed that this figure seemed to have dropped out of this circle, though remaining in Earl's Court and still drinking.

He would see, for instance, the girl and her friends drinking and making merry in one pub, and then go along to another, and find the big, sad man standing in front of a glass of beer by himself.

It happened that one night he found himself alone in a saloon bar with this "George" and he wondered whether he dared enter into conversation with him. He was eager to do so, not only because he had taken so much interest in this crowd, but because he had at the back of his mind the hope that if he got to know the man he might, in the course of events, get to know the girl, and even establish contact as a whole with this most intriguing senior-form in the school of life.

After pondering various conversational openings, and rejecting them all as too banal or obtrusive, young Halliwell had at last decided that he hadn't the nerve to address the other, when, happening to open a new packet of cigarettes, and to throw its cigarette card (one of a series of "Golfing Hints") on to the counter, to his utmost astonishment and pleasure he found the big man addressing him.

"Excuse me," he said quietly, "do you want that?"

"No. Not a bit," said young Halliwell giving up the card. "Are you interested in golf?"

"Yes. Rather . . ." said George, looking at the card and reading its back. "Not that these hints are any good . . . But I always like to look at them."

"Of course, I could never get on with golf," said young Halliwell, anxious at all costs to keep the conversation going now that it had started. "I've had plenty of tries, but it just beats me. Are you any good?"

"Well, I wasn't bad at one time," said the other. "As a matter of fact, when I was down at Brighton a little while ago, I did a sixty-eight."

"Sixty-eight! That's tremendous, isn't it?"

"Yes. It wasn't bad, was it? It was on a strange course, too."

This little confession of a past triumph was uttered in such a naïve, simple, subdued tone that young Halliwell was quite taken aback. Having seen this man until recently only against the background of the mature, harsh, and aggressive set with whom he mixed, he had got a picture of him as being almost certainly in some measure harsh and aggressive as well. But here he was, like a child, obviously proud of his little feat at Brighton, and anxious to tell a stranger about it. The heart of the younger man from the country, relieved, flattered, and gratified, at once warmed to that of the older man of the town, and before long they were in friendly and easy conversation.

They soon ordered fresh drinks, and the conversation went from golf to games, and from games to books about games, and then to books themselves. Young Halliwell was here again surprised. For he found that the older man, so far from being totally ignorant of such matters, so far from being solely interested in women, and drinking and night-clubs and cars and racing, had, in his quiet, friendly, rather gloomy way, fully as warm an interest in the subject as his junior, and a considerably wider breadth of knowledge. Finally he said that his favourite author had always been Dickens, and that *David Copperfield* was actually the last book he had read.

"I don't know what it is," he added, "but I don't seem to find any time to read nowadays. One's always doing something else. But I mean to try and take it up again now."

Young Halliwell was struck by his use of the word "now" and the oddly wistful and optimistic tone in which it was uttered. It seemed to denote some break in this man's life, some event or tragedy which had brought some sort of release. Young Halliwell wondered, even, whether this could be connected with his no longer being in the company of his usual friends.

They ordered drinks again, and became even more friendly.

They told each other where they lived, and discussed the respective merits and demerits of living in rooms or a hotel. Young Halliwell said that you could get extremely lonely in a room by yourself, and George replied that if it came to that, you could be even more lonely in a hotel.

He went on to say that he had recently had an attack of 'flu (he had caught a chill at Brighton) and that though he had stayed in bed for four or five days, no one in the hotel had taken any interest in him. He said, indeed, that if it had not been for an old friend happening to ring up and coming round to see him, he would have been quite alone. He said, with a smile, that, apart from this friend, his only company had been a white cat, with whom he had made friends.

Young Halliwell asked him if he didn't feel any weakening after-effects of his attack, and George replied that perhaps he did, but that on the whole he believed that the rest had done him good. It was a good thing, he said, to have a complete break sometimes. You could sort of sort things out and start again.

Young Halliwell was by this confirmed in his previous impression that there had lately been some crisis in this strange, likable man's life, and he felt even more curious. But it was, of course, impossible to pursue the matter, and the subject was changed.

It was now nearly closing time, and they ordered one more round of drinks before they were turned out. Time being short, and the succession of small ports he had taken having at last gone slightly to young Halliwell's head, he was emboldened to ask a question he had wanted to ask from the beginning.

"By the way," he said, "I believe I've seen you about before this, haven't I? Haven't I seen you in the Black Hart with a girl, and a man with a moustache?"

"Oh, yes," said George, "that's right. I expect you have." And there was a pause.

"Didn't I hear that she was a film actress or something?" said young Halliwell, disingenuously feigning blithe disinterest and confusion of mind. "Or have I got it all wrong?"

"Oh, yes," said George. "She's been on the films. Yes."

"Yes. I thought she had," said young Halliwell. "She's frightfully attractive, isn't she?"

"Oh, yes, she is. Very. There's no doubt about that. Very," said the big man, looking at his drink, and young Halliwell realized that he should never have mentioned this subject— though he still did not know why. He quickly changed the conversation, and a few minutes later they were out in the air.

They walked down the Earl's Court Road in the glare of the lamps, discussing Poland and the prospects of a war in the near future. They agreed that, in spite of all ominous signs to the contrary, it would probably not take place until next spring.

At the coffee-stall outside the station, they stopped and had tea and a hot pie each. Just before they left the big man asked for two pennyworth of milk, which was given him in a carton.

"This is for my cat," he explained to young Halliwell, again smiling in that peculiarly charming and disarming way, as he stuffed the carton into his shabby raincoat pocket. "I get this every night."

They walked together a little farther, for young Halliwell had expressed a desire to see the outside of George's hotel, and they exchanged views on inclusive terms and bed-and-breakfast problems.

At last, however, the time came to part, and, slightly embarrassed, they shook hands.

"Well, I hope I'll be seeing some more of you," said young Halliwell. "It's been a very nice evening."

"Yes, I hope so," said George, and added, rather awkwardly, and surprisingly, "Though as a matter of fact I shan't be here for long."

"Oh—really?"

"Yes. I'm moving out in about a fortnight's time."

"Oh—really. Where are you going?"

"Well, I don't really know. I haven't fixed yet. But I feel one's got to make a change."

"Yes. I suppose one has." And there, was an embarrassed pause in which neither had anything to say . . .

"Well, I'll run into you before you go, anyway, I hope," said young Halliwell at last. "Well . . . Good night."

"Yes. Rather. I hope so. Good night."

"Good night!"

"Good night!"

And the big man went into his hotel, and the young man walked back along the Earl's Court Road, infected with a sudden feeling of sadness. He had expected to have talked with someone older, harder, more mature than himself, but young as he was, he had a feeling of having talked to someone younger, less hard, and though more knowledgeable even less mature than himself. He also had a feeling of having talked to a ghost. He never saw George Harvey Bone again.

There were others, too, who observed George Harvey Bone from a distance, and indulged in speculation regarding his character and employment. Without knowing it he was something of a character in his hotel. Practically only seen late in the deserted breakfast-room each morning, and then again walking late at night through the lounge to bed, he was yet part and parcel of the small hotel as a whole, and contributed to its atmosphere. The guests would ask each other about "that man." Some would talk of "that funny man," would wink as he passed through—and on the whole he was a somewhat unpopular figure. He seemed to carry his loneliness about him on his person, like someone branded.

Many guests wondered where he worked during the day. Because he was out all day they were certain that he worked at something, and because they could not gain the faintest conception of what this was, they concluded that it was something not altogether reputable. Only the porter, to whom he gave a weekly tip of two shillings, knew of the complete emptiness and unemployment of Mr. Bone's life. Frequenting the public bars of the same houses as Mr. Bone visited in the saloon bar, he knew the Netta gang by sight, and had a pretty accurate picture of Mr. Bone's external life. He liked and respected Mr. Bone, both because he was tipped regularly by him, and because of occasional conversations they had on the subject of professional football and football pools, in which department this unusual hotel guest was both shrewd in his forecasts and impressive in his general knowledge.

The Manageress of the hotel, a thin, affable woman named Miss Mercer, was, on the contrary, of the class which looked upon the unsociable, late and mysterious Mr. Bone with suspicion, if not dislike, and she would have been glad, in her heart, to have got him out of the hotel. There was no means of doing this, however, as he was regular in his payments, and, at least within the walls of the hotel, quiet and impeccable in his behaviour. Indeed, apart from one slight eccentricity—that of having adopted, and of feeding with milk from outside, the hotel cat, whose affections he had completely captured—his normality was nowhere to be questioned. And even this little eccentricity, if such it could be called, was, she had to admit, of the most amiable kind.

One morning, towards the close of the summer of 1939, Mr. Bone came into her "office" to pay his bill. When she had given him his receipt, he surprised her by telling her that he proposed to leave the hotel in a week or so, and that he thought he had better tell her in case she wanted to let his room.

"Oh," she said, easily simulating polite sorrow in an influx of secret pleasure, "I am sorry. Are you going out of London?"

"Well, I don't really know at present," he said, baffling to the end. "I haven't quite fixed up."

"Well," she said, "we'll miss you. You've been here a long time now, haven't you?"

"Yes, I have," he said. "It's well over two years now."

"We'll be quite lost without you," she said smiling. "I hope you come back sometime. I hope you've been happy here."

"Oh, yes, I hope I will," he said, smiling back. "I've been very happy . . . Well . . . Is that all right?"

"Yes," she said. "That's all right . . . Thank you very much for telling me."

"No—not a bit," he said, and, smiling again, walked out of the room.

When he had gone, she remembered his smile, and deciding that she had probably misjudged the man, she was almost sorry he was going. His sad smile, and his big, quiet, morose presence, haunted her on and off all day.

CHAPTER THREE

So that was that, he had done it at last . . .

He walked after breakfast along the Earl's Court Road in the rain, and was astounded by his initiative and audacity. It was all over now; he had taken the final step and given notice.

He couldn't back out of it now, he was through; through with Earl's Court, through with Netta, through with it all.

Earl's Court in the rain . . . The summer had crashed: it had crashed at Brighton: it would never rise again. Only rain now, the grey, wet end of hope and love.

Where was he going? He had a week to decide. Where? Anywhere, Notting Hill, Bayswater, South Ken, Shepherd's Bush, Knightsbridge, but never again Earl's Court. Good-bye to the Squares, the Gardens, the Mansions; the Penywerns and Neverns; the Private Hotels; the Smith's, the Station, the Turkish Baths; the A.B.C. and Express Restaurants; the pubs, the florists and tobacconists, all the bleak scenery of his long disgrace and disaster—good-bye forever. The grey, ending rain was cool and blessed on his face.

He had to thank an attack of 'flu for this—that, and, of course, Johnnie. Johnnie was the only one who came to see him; he came from the other end of London. "They" were nearby; but of course they didn't come near him: they didn't miss him; they wouldn't have missed him if he'd have died. Well, he had died on them, now.

He had thought he was going to honest-to-God die at one

time. He had caught it, of course, at Brighton: all the strain and horror, and walking about in the rain; the bout of "dead" moods, the worst he had ever had.

He had been really frightened one night, but the next morning he had been a bit better, and by staying in bed he had slowly got all right.

Johnnie had been the turning point. The chambermaid had come in and said there was a Mr. Littlejohn on the phone. He had wanted to get up but he was too weak, and he asked her to say he was in bed with a spot of 'flu. Nothing more—but Johnnie was along at seven o'clock in the evening. He put his head round the door, and said "What's all this about, my boy?"

He came every night until he was up again. They drank a little whisky from a half-bottle in a tooth glass and talked. He told Johnnie a lot. Not everything—he didn't mention names —he was somehow ashamed to—and no details. But he hinted a lot, and he believed Johnnie cottoned on.

It was, really, just a talk about women in general. At the end Johnnie had said, "Of course, there's only one thing to do if a woman really gets you down—and that's run away." And at this Johnnie had looked at him rather shyly, and a little while afterwards had left him.

Run away. Somehow the fact that Johnnie had suggested the notion, that Johnnie was secretly behind him, enabled him, for the first time, to think of running away as a serious proposition. He lay awake half the night thinking about it, and took it up again next morning. Then, as he lay in bed and rested, in the peace of his convalescence, the idea slowly grew in strength, itself gave him strength and peace, and at last set into a quiet yet resolute intention. He would leave the neighbourhood and never see Netta again.

He wondered whether, when he actually got up, the thing would be in any way practicable or possible, whether it was within his capacity to walk out of the hotel, to go along the streets and about in the neighbourhood without using the phone, without haunting her haunts, without throwing himself consciously or unconsciously into the way of meeting her, and, having met her once, sinking back into hell. He found, when he at last got out of doors, a little weak and giddy, that he had no sort of desire to see her, that soon he was even taking a sort of pleasure in dodging her.

He believed he had reached the crisis at last: that he had burned his passion out. It was only just in time. His whole health would have been wrecked if he had gone on like that.

But now the climax had come: he had had a rest; the 'flu, and the "dead" moods (both brought on, he believed, by drinking and nervous exhaustion) had receded, and he could start again. He limited himself to two beers in the morning: had lunch at the hotel, slept in the afternoon, had a few more beers in the evening, and went to bed early.

One night he got into conversation with a young man, and talked about games and books and things. It was a great relief, it did his soul a lot of good to meet a fresh face and new personality in a pub, and talk about disinterested things. He could hardly remember a disinterested moment ever since he had met Netta. He told the young man a lot about the books he had read, secretly making up his mind to read them again himself.

The young man, oddly enough, had mentioned Netta: he had seen him about with her. He had said she was "frightfully attractive." That had hurt, but only for a moment. The subject had been changed, and he had found he didn't mind. He knew that Netta was frightfully attractive. He had never denied it. He wasn't going to pretend otherwise. They were welcome to her. It showed, though, that he could never get away from her so long as he was in Earl's Court. Even a stranger talked about her.

Netta was Earl's Court now—he saw that as he walked along this morning in the rain. She was the buildings and the shops and the rain. Now that he no longer phoned her in the morning, now that the centre of his life was no longer her flat, that aura which she once gave forth—that appalling field of magnetic influence—no longer irradiated from her flat (being weakest at the farthest point from and strongest at the nearest point to, her actual bedroom, her being), but was spread out into the entire hateful neighbourhood.

He went into the Express and ordered a small coffee. It was lovely to sit and read a newspaper, without having to look at the clock all the time, arguing with yourself as to what time you should choose to phone her in relation to her bath and Mrs. Chope. He sat over his coffee as long as he liked. This morning he was going to phone Johnnie. He had promised to do that when he was up and well again. Well, now he was up and well.

He went to the line of telephone booths in the station and boxed himself in. He felt a little nervous. By her cruel and arbitrary behaviour she had made this instrument, the telephone, so terrifying and odious that he could no longer use it for any purpose without a feeling of trepidation, without a feeling that the person at the other end of the line was going to hurt him.

He dialled Johnnie's office number, and a girl's voice said, "Fitzgerald, Carstairs and Scott." He said, "Is Mr. Littlejohn there, please?" and the girl said what name please, and he said Mr. Bone, and there was a long pause. He was afraid that he was interrupting Johnnie in mighty theatrical affairs, that Johnnie might be at that moment closeted with the dread Fitzgerald, Carstairs, or Scott, and that he would be embarrassed or angry at being called to the phone by a nonentity who could only claim an old school friendship. Johnnie came to the phone, however, and was most cheerful. "Hullo, old boy," he said. "How are you?"

They had a little conversation, and then he told Johnnie that he had given notice at his hotel, and that he had got to find somewhere to live.

"That's funny," said Johnnie, "my ceiling's fallen in, and I'm homeless at the moment."

"Oh—really?"

"Yes. I'm in an awful mess," said Johnnie, and added, it seemed jokingly, "You'd better come and live with me."

George only laughed at this, but a few moments later Johnnie surprised him by saying, "Well, let's talk about it, anyway. When can we meet?"

They arranged to meet that night, the same place as before, Earl's Court station, and they rang off.

He came out and walked along in the rain.

"You'd better come and live with me." It stuck with him all the morning. It would never come to anything, of course, but he was very proud and happy to have a friend who could say such a thing.

"Well, where are we going?" said Johnnie, as they crossed over the road by the station and he replied, "Oh—we might as well go to the usual." He had thought this out while waiting for Johnnie. To begin with she would probably not be in there. And even if she was, did he care? No—not now—not with Johnnie by his side—an old friend with whom he might be going to stay. Not now that he was clearing out. He wished she *would* come in; he would like her to see him looking well and sober for once, and to learn of his independence and approaching departure.

The Saloon Bar was unusually crowded, but they managed to find seats at a table in a corner. They drank beer and talked about the coming war.

When she came, she was alone, and went and sat on a stool at the bar. He didn't know whether she had seen him, and he went on talking to Johnnie. He didn't know whether Johnnie had seen her, but rather thought he had, because their conversation became a little inattentive, and the atmosphere was curious. They looked rather hard at each other as they talked.

All at once he heard her voice, and she was sitting down beside them, her drink in her hand. "Well, well—how are we all?" she said. "I didn't see you when I came in."

From the beginning she took up the attitude that she was wanted, that nothing could have happened to make her not wanted, and that she expected to revive the atmosphere of the occasion when the three of them had met in here before. She was extremely cordial: he had seldom seen her so cordial: and he had no difficulty in seeing that the cause of this was Johnnie's presence. He knew how much impressed she was by Johnnie because of his connection with Fitzgerald, Carstairs and Scott, and that she hoped somehow to make use of him in that connection. He knew, also, in his heart, that that was one of the reasons why he had brought Johnnie round to the Black Hart to show his friend off, and to spite her.

"Well, what's been happening to you, George?" she said. "I haven't seen you about."

"No," he said, "I've had 'flu."

"'*Flu?* . . ." she said, and asked why she hadn't been told. She gave the impression that if she had known she would have come round with flowers and fruit.

"You are a bloody fool," she ended up by saying. "You never look after yourself." And she appealed to Johnnie to support her in this.

Once or twice before, in his relationship with her, he had known her behave like this. It had taken him in then, but he was too old a hand now. She was very lovely, but he didn't react to her. He didn't like her, and he wanted to get away.

"Well, how are things up at Fitzgerald's?" she asked Johnnie, and soon the two of them were talking about the theatre. It appeared that the firm were again in production with another show—this time a farce—and that it was to be tried out in Brighton shortly.

"And how's Eddie?" she said. "I haven't seen him for ages."

"Oh—he's all right," said Johnnie. "As a matter of fact, I'm staying with him now."

"Oh . . . are you?"

"Yes. My ceiling's fallen in, and he's letting me put up with him for the time being. I've got to find somewhere to live. As a matter of fact, George and I are thinking of setting up together, aren't we, George?" said Johnnie, smiling at him.

"That's right," he said, and smiled back.

He had hoped to spite and snub her, but had never imagined he would do it in this almost spectacular way. That Johnnie should be actually staying at the moment with the famous Eddie Carstairs—whose name was on theatre bills all over London, in whom she took such a peculiar interest, and yet whom she was unable to approach—that he (George) should be Johnnie's friend, and that Johnnie should be avowing in front of her a desire to set up house with him—here was a rich revenge indeed! He might not be such a useless nonentity after all!

He looked at her face to see how she was taking it. She was looking at him.

"Why—are you making a change, George?" she asked.

"Yes," he said. "I've given notice at my place. I'm fed up with Earl's Court."

"Yes," she said. "So am I if it comes to that," and nothing more was said about it.

A little while later he managed to wink at Johnnie as he finished off the remains of his glass, and looking at his watch he said: "Well, Johnnie, we'll have to buck up if we're going to be there on time."

Johnnie, playing up, said, "Yes—we certainly will," and a few moments later they were out in the street.

THE NINTH PART

'FLU

But what availed this temperance, not complete
Against another object more enticing?
What boots it at one gate to make defence,
And at another to let in the foe,
Effeminately vanquished?

J. MILTON, *Samson Agonistes*

e-, pro-voke; raise up, summon up, call up, wake up, blow up, get up, light up; raise; get up the steam, rouse, arouse, stir, fire, kindle, enkindle, apply the torch, set on fire, inflame.

stimulate; ex-, suscitate; inspirit; spirit up, stir up, work up; infuse life into, give new life to; bring -, introduce-new blood; quicken; sharpen, whet; work upon &c. (incite) 615; hurry on, give a fillip, put on one's metal.

fan the—fire,—flame; blow the coals, stir the embers; fan,—into a flame; foster, heat, warm, foment, raise to a fever heat; . . .

Roget's Thesaurus of English Words and Phrases

CHAPTER ONE

It was seven in the evening. He walked round to the chemist's (her breath still on his face, her mouth and cheek still on his lips), to get her medicine and told his heart and senses to be quiet, and not to be beguiled again.

It had all happened so absolutely out of the blue, and such a little while ago, that he was giddy and confused. Never before (save once, when he first knew her, and then she had turned him out of the flat without ceremony) had he felt her face on his. No wonder he was bewildered.

It had been a weird week. She had been ill. She had had 'flu like him, and had phoned him up. Mrs. Chope had deserted her, and he had found her lying in bed, pale, not made up, and plainly fevered. He had got a doctor; he had cleared up the flat; he had found a temporary woman; he had taken the doctor's instructions (he still wondered what the doctor thought) and he had given her her medicine and her orange juice and milk.

Her eyes hurt her and she liked to lie in the dark. She had given him her key, and he had hung about all day. He had had four days of it. One night he had brought Johnnie round and they had had drinks round the bed. Peter and Mickey were away on "holiday." He had told his hotel he would stay on another week and today she had been much better, and talked of getting up tomorrow, and tonight she had made up her face and done her hair. She had put a red ribbon in it.

He still didn't know how it had come about. He had got her

a fresh hot-water bottle and had been walking about her bed-room, talking quite casually, when, apropos of nothing he could remember, she had said (her face sideways on the pillow, and the rest of her body snugly wrapped in the bed-clothes): "But of course you don't love me any more, do you George?"

The remark, presumably a joking one, was so odd, so entirely outside the character of their normal relationship, that he had turned and stared at her. He had said, "What do you mean, Netta?" and there was a pause. And then, something in her silence, something in her expression (she wasn't looking at him), something in her snug attitude in bed, something provocative yet altogether inviting about her generally, made his senses giddy, and the next moment he flung himself down by the bed beside her, and said, "What do you mean, Netta? You know I adore you, don't you? You know I adore you!" And he kissed her face.

Then she had said, "What? . . ." dreamily, as a girl will who is suffering herself to be kissed—who intimates that the situation may remain on its present footing and even be proceeded with—and he said, "Oh, Netta, I do love you so!" and kissed her again.

"Oh, I thought all that was over," she said, still not looking at him. "What with your going away, and all that."

At this, seemingly an invitation from Netta to stay, a soft reproach from a Netta allowing him to kiss her for the first time since he had known and adored and dreamed and schemed all day and night about her—he could hardly believe his ears and completely lost his head, and blurted out, "Oh, Netta, I don't *want* to go away! I love you! Won't you come away with *me*, Netta? Won't you come away with *me*?"

"How do you mean?" she said, "by 'go away'? . . ." But she didn't say she wouldn't.

"Oh, anywhere," he said, "just to get away from this place!

Just to be alone with you, Netta—if only for a little. Do say you'll come away?"

"How can I go away, my dear Bone?" she said, now looking him in the face, and putting her hand on his cheek. "I haven't got any money . . ."

He was for a moment taken aback by this, for a split second entertaining the notion that this was a crude frame-up, that she was letting him kiss her and playing him up simply in order to get more money out of him, but he again dismissed the idea as unthinkable in the case of so proud and aloof a girl, and said:

"Oh, Netta, what does *that* matter? What does money matter, if you'll only come away?"

"But it does matter," she said, "I owe you fifteen pounds already."

"Oh, Netta. It doesn't matter. Forget about the fifteen pounds. *Nothing* matters, if you'll only come away."

There was a pause after this, in which she turned her face sideways again, and he looked at her.

"All right," she said at last, "I'll come away. We'll go to Brighton. I'd like some sea air."

Again he had a feeling of a frame-up. When Johnnie had come round to her flat that night, they had talked about the new farce which was being tried out at Brighton, and they had said that if she had not been ill they might all have gone down there, thus fulfilling the proposal they had made over the other show earlier in the year, but had failed to put into practice. Now that she mentioned Brighton again, he saw that she had some reason for wanting to go there—probably in the hope of getting in thicker with Johnnie, who was staying with Eddie Carstairs, or even with the hope of actually meeting, through Johnnie, Eddie Carstairs himself. No, there was something suspect about Brighton (quite apart from the awful time she had given him there before) and he wasn't going to have any of it.

"No," he said, "not Brighton. I hate the place. Let's go

somewhere fresh. Come away somewhere else, Netta—won't you? Do say you'll come away."

"Why?" she said, again looking at him, and putting her hand back on his cheek. "Aren't all places the same, my dear Bone?"

And at this, what with her hand on his cheek, and a certain enigmatic lock in her eyes, and the sole glorious interpretation he could make of her words (that all places were the same for one purpose), his passion blinded and emboldened him, and he kissed her again and again, her face, her hair, her hands. Then he looked at her, wildly, incredulously, and she murmured, "I think you'd better go and get my medicine now, hadn't you, George?"

He had said, "Yes, I think I had," and here he was walking along the street to the chemist's with her breath still on his face, and her mouth and cheek still on his lips, telling his heart and senses to be quiet and not to be beguiled again.

What had happened? He had got to get it clear and behave sensibly. Had it all started again—was he back on the rack? After getting clear and sane, after all his firm, quiet, healthy resolutions to get away, was he going back to the old torture? Had she only to beckon to him, to be amenable for a minute and condescend to allow him to kiss her face, to have him prostrate before her again?

Or had a change taken place? "Of course, you don't love me any more, do you George?" Was that pique at his recent neglect? Possibly—but he had not known until now that it was within his capacity even to pique her. Was it a desire to have him back—to make some sort of amends to him? Inconceivable! Or was it conceivable? What if she had repented, what if she had been made sorry by his recent neglect and coldness, what if she had been touched by his faithfulness, by his kindness in looking after her when she was ill, in waiting upon her at all hours and looking after her comforts without

any hope or desire of reward? What if a change had come?—
what if he had won her at last!

No. Stop that. Not that again. He knew her now for what
she was. Whatever happened now it could never be the same.
She was entirely promiscuous—a sort of prostitute. Whatever
happened now there was the thought of Peter behind—Peter
and the little school bully at Brighton. If she ever gave herself
to him, she could still never give him what he once desired. He
could only rise to the level of Peter and the others.

But if she was a sort of prostitute, if Peter and strangers
could enjoy her favours in that way—why shouldn't he?
Hadn't that been the whole root of his misery, his idealization
of her, his longing to take her away and have her and cherish
her exclusively forever, to marry her? If he had been a man, if
he had behaved like other men, might he not have succeeded
with her already and got her out of his system? Might he not
try to be a man now?

Had the opportunity now arisen? What was the meaning of
what had just taken place? He remembered her face, her indolent and enigmatic expression, her hand on his cheek, her
amazing acquiescence in his kisses, her consenting to come
away. "Aren't all places the same, my poor Bone?" What
meaning could that remark have save one?

Was she just playing him up because she was short of money
again? She had, he noticed, not failed to mention money. Well,
what if she was? If she was a kind of prostitute, and was willing to give herself in an indirect way for money, was he going
to refuse the offer?

Did he still love her in spite of his knowledge of her? He
looked into his weary soul for the true answer, and found it
soon enough. Yes, he did, God help him. He adored her, and
he would never do otherwise. After all his firmness he had just
blurted out as much to her. Whatever she had done, whatever
he knew about her, she could never be sordid—she was too

beautiful to look at and be with; she was still too incredibly lovely. She just took him that way, and there was no use fighting it. She was not a mercenary slut in Earl's Court. She was violets and primroses in an April rain, and her cheek and lips, the breath of violets and primroses, lingered on his mouth, stupefying him with pleasure and longing.

He knew he was making a fool of himself; he knew he ought to run for his life; but how could he? After an eternity of longing, of hanging outside and beating at her door, it had seemed at last that she was going to let him in. She had put her hand on his cheek and as good as told him that he might, if he was careful, if he was man enough, come in. Not on the terms he had once hoped for—only as a shady equal of Peter and the rest—only, perhaps, because he gave her money—but nevertheless he might be admitted. He was not going to lose the chance.

Life was very exciting. He was going back to see her in a few minutes. He was going to be a man at last. And by the way, if he was going to be a man, he wasn't going to have any nonsense. It was the whole thing or nothing. He wasn't going to be fooled again—and he wasn't going to Brighton. He had got to make that clear.

And it had all happened in a few minutes! Twenty minutes ago he was a beaten dog; now he was a man, and the breath of the goddess was on his face, and her lips and cheeks were on his mouth. He entered the chemist's shop and asked for the medicine, and waited. The bald, grey-haired chemist in the blazing light of the shop, his white-coated assistant, his jars of flaming red and green shining on to the pavement, his bottles and array of patent medicines and lozenges, were all her breath on his face and her lips and cheeks on his mouth, his manhood, his surprise, his sudden bliss.

As he put the key in her door, he heard her voice in the distance. She was on the phone.

He tried to listen, but could hear nothing.

He put the key softly in the door and went in, hoping that she would not know he was in the flat and still trying to hear what she said.

"No, I don't think he even wants to," he heard. "No . . . No, really . . . No, he doesn't seem to like the idea at all." She laughed. "He's off it, apparently . . . Well, you know what a fool he is . . ."

"Hullo—is that you, George!" she shouted through the door, evidently having heard him, or having suddenly suspected his presence.

"Yes," he said. "This is me."

She went on cheerfully: "Look here, I've got to go now. There's somebody in the flat and I've got to go . . . What . . . Yes . . . Well, I'll ring you tomorrow, anyway, and then we can see where we are . . . Right you are . . . Good-bye . . . Oh—*much* better, thanks . . . Good-bye . . . Right. Good-bye!"

She put down the receiver and he went into her room.

"Hullo," he said, smiling. "Here's your medicine." And he put it on the table beside her bed, beside the phone.

"Thank you, George," she said, and she broke the red sealing wax and began to undo the crackling white paper.

"Who was that?" he said, going to the window and drawing the curtains to.

"Oh," she said in her quiet voice, "nobody . . ." And she crunched the chemist's paper into a ball and threw it across the room.

He wondered what she meant by nobody—he tried to think of any of her friends he knew about—but he didn't pursue the matter further. It was not his business.

It did just occur to him that it was his friend Johnnie at the other end of the line, that the "he" referred to was himself, and that the idea that "he" didn't like it at all was that of going to Brighton; but he was easily able to dismiss this notion as another example of his diseased fancy.

Soon enough, at a sign from her (he did not know what sign, but she somehow gave him a sign), he was on his knees before her again, and begging for her love.

"Netta!" he said, "is it true? Are you going to come away with me?"

"Yes . . . I'll come away with you . . ."

"Where shall we go, Netta. Where do you want to go?"

"Well, I wanted to go to Brighton, but you don't seem to like the idea."

He was struck by her use of this phrase "don't seem to like the idea" twice in the space of a few minutes—once to absolutely nobody on the phone, now to him, but again dismissed his thoughts.

"No, not Brighton, Netta," he said. "I had such an awful time there last time. Besides, there'd be people there."

He said "people" as vaguely as possible, but he meant, of course, Johnnie, Eddie Carstairs, the new show. He saw now that she had wanted to be in on the new show, that she had hoped to meet Eddie Carstairs down there with Johnnie, and that in consenting to come away with him (quite apart from any feeling she might now have towards him), she had some idea of killing two birds with one stone—that of getting her fare and hotel paid and of making this contact with the big manager. Knowing her ruthless character he did not blame her, but he was not going to have it that way. He was going to be a man.

"Of course, there'd be people," she said. "That's why I wanted to go. Don't you like people?"

"But I want you alone, Netta. Don't you understand? Do say you'll come away with me alone!"

There was a pause in which he looked at her face turned sideways on the pillow.

"All right," she said. "It's your party."

"Oh, Netta, thank you," he said, and took her hand.

"Where do you want to go then?" she asked.

"Oh, I haven't really thought about it. I thought we might go down the river, right away from where we know. Cookham or Maidenhead, or somewhere like that. What about Maidenhead? I used to love it there a long while ago."

"Very well," she said, the ghost of the ghost of an incomprehensible yet somehow mocking smile on her face. "We'll go to Maidenhead."

"Are you laughing at me, Netta?" he said, referring to the ghost of the ghost of a smile.

"No," she said, "I'm not laughing at you." But the ghost remained.

"When can we go, Netta? When will you be well enough?"

"Oh. Tomorrow."

"Tomorrow? But will you be well enough?"

"Yes, I'm quite well. We'll go tomorrow."

He looked at her. Tomorrow. He thought of all that he had suffered at her hands, and it just didn't make sense.

"You're not fooling me, are you, Netta?"

"No, I'm not fooling you," she said, and added softly, "You know, George, don't you, that you'll have to help me out?"

By a pressure of her hand she seemed to invite him to draw his face nearer to her, and he did so.

"Why yes, Netta. Of course I'll help you out. I've always helped you out, haven't I?"

"Yes," she said. "You've been very nice indeed—all along . . ."

All along. Something in the way she uttered these words, something in her manner, touched and convinced him. He looked at her, and for a space believed that she had a soul: that she was sorry for him, that she appreciated all he had done and suffered, and that she meant to reward him. In fact, he was certain of it.

Well, he wouldn't fail her. He would go on being nice to the end. "What do you want, Netta?" he said. "I'll give it to you now."

"I don't want anything, really," she said. "I'm going to pay you back anyway when I get a job. But I've got to have five pounds just to get out of the flat. Otherwise they simply won't let me leave."

"Very well," he said, "I'll give it to you now." He rose, went into the sitting-room, found her pen and ink, and wrote a cheque for five pounds. His hand trembled with passion and generosity. He returned to her and put the cheque by the telephone.

"There you are, Netta," he said.

"This is very sordid, I'm afraid, my dear Bone," she said.

"What's sordid?"

"Oh—money generally."

Irresistibly moved he flung himself down again and kissed her. "Oh, it's not sordid, Netta," he said, "it's not sordid! Nothing's sordid with you. You're too beautiful. Nothing can be sordid with you!"

"All right, Bone," she said, "keep calm." And she looked at him mockingly, yet kindly. There was a pause.

"Netta," he said.

"Yes."

"Now we're going away together you're going to be nice to me, aren't you? You're going to be really nice?"

He meant, of course, "You're going to give yourself fully to

me, aren't you? You're really going to give yourself to me?"
And he looked wildly into her eyes for her assurance.

She again put her hand on his face, and looked at him.

"Yes," she said, "I'm going to be very nice."

He wanted no more. He believed her. She had repented.
"Oh, Netta," he said, and kissed her hair and laid his head on
her breast.

After a few moments she said, "Listen, Bone . . ."

"Yes."

"I'm tired now, and want to go to sleep. Will you be a nice
Bone, and put out the light and leave me?"

"Yes . . . All right . . . Are you sure you'll be well enough
tomorrow?"

"Yes. I'll be well enough, but now I want to sleep. My eyes
still hurt a bit. You can phone tomorrow."

"Right. What time?"

"Oh—about eleven."

"Right you are. I'll have fixed up where we're going and
everything by then . . . Good night, Netta . . ."

"Good night, Bone."

He kissed her again, trying to remember her kiss—so that he
could carry it on his mouth all night, so that he could savour and
anticipate all the kisses to come—and rose and put out the light.

He heard her turn in the bed in the darkness. "Good night,"
he whispered, and putting out the light in the sitting-room he
went out of the flat.

There was a fresh wind blowing down the Earl's Court Road
and he felt cold. He walked up towards Kensington High
Street with the intention of having a drink.

His passion cooling with his body, he looked strangely, cold-
ly at what had just happened, and even felt for a moment
dejected. Well, that was that. He had got her at last, it seemed.

He was under no delusions as to the nature of the transaction which had taken place. It was half a money transaction

and half something else. He had helped her, had given her money, he had looked after her when she was ill, and she, in return for his help and money, perhaps in gratitude for his faithfulness and perhaps (after seeing that she was going to lose him) in repentance at her long harsh treatment, had intimated that she would give herself to him. She had given herself to Peter and others. She gave herself to men. That wasn't love. She would never love him, and it was all very sad.

Was it sad? Was he not lying to himself? Did he, at this moment, really care a damn in his heart whether she loved him or not? No, he didn't. Just as he didn't mind about Peter and the others, he didn't mind about her not loving him. It might not be love, but it was Netta! That was all he wanted. He was going to get Netta, the object of his desire, Netta whose promising kiss was on his lips, the violets and the primroses in the April rain. Whatever she did, whatever she felt about him, she could not forgo her loveliness or cease to be what she was to him, and no one else.

He saw he could never be happy, that only disaster lay ahead.

But he would have had his moment, a few days, a brief spell of bliss—the fulfilment, the justification of his long trial. He believed on the whole that it had been worth it, and he would not fail to enjoy it.

Why should he worry? She might be ruthless, cold, cruel, a beast—but he had got her. She might be half a prostitute, but he had got her. It might be only by the wild expenditure of his little hoard of money that he was getting her, but he had got her. "Aren't all places the same, my poor Bone?" she had said, and "Yes, I'll be very nice," and her promising kiss was on his mouth. He might only be rising to the squalid level of Peter and the others, but he had risen. (Peter wouldn't like it at all!) He was no longer an outsider, a hanger-on, a stooge. He was a man, a man of the world at last, and he had got her. He might never get her again, he might pay in money, disaster, and misery for getting her, but he had got her, got her, got her!

The big, wretched man had a drink in Kensington (only one—he didn't want to drink) and, walking back down the Earl's Court Road to his hotel, noticed a light shining behind the curtains he had drawn in the bedroom of the unsuccessful and impecunious film actress.

THE TENTH PART

BRIGHTON

*Much more affliction than already felt
They cannot well impose, nor I sustain.*
                                J. MILTON, *Samson Agonistes*

T hough his thoughts kept him awake till three, and he was awake again at seven, he felt calm in the morning, and had his breakfast and went about his business in a methodical way.

After breakfast he went out and bought some shirts and socks and pyjamas. As he walked along he had a funny feeling of the unreality of everything, and felt sadly the need of some-one to talk to. He wanted to confide to someone that he was stronger and wiser at last, that he was going away with the girl he wanted, that he had made good, in a strange way, after all.

After all, when all was said and done, from the world's point of view he was going away with a pretty attractive girl—objec-tively attractive, that was. "She's frightfully attractive, isn't she?" that young man had said. He wondered what the young man would have thought if he knew that he was now going away with her to the country!

He wished he could talk to Johnnie. Johnnie, who had met the girl, and understood roughly (he fancied) the state of affairs hitherto, would be glad to know he had made good, that he was not being made a fool of any longer. He would be impressed, too, by his having established such a relationship with such an attractive and universally desirable girl. In fact, in his heart of hearts he rather wanted to swank to Johnnie, and he wished he could get into touch and tell him before he went.

He thought he would phone Johnnie, anyway, and at least let him know he was going away. Also, there had been that talk of their all going to Brighton, and he had to tell him that that was off.

When he got back to the hotel he phoned Fitzgerald, Carstairs and Scott, and asked the girl for Mr. Littlejohn, Mr. Bone speaking. There was a long silence, and then the girl said that Mr. Littlejohn hadn't arrived yet. This struck him as odd, as he knew Johnnie was very punctual and usually got there at 9.30.

He then looked out trains for Maidenhead, and phoned its leading hotel, and made sure there was plenty of accommodation. He did not book a room or rooms but just made sure there would be room.

He then, because it was eleven o'clock, phoned Netta, who spoke in a rather off-hand way at first, and said she was half asleep. He was made slightly gloomy by her being half asleep, but he realized that this thing did not mean the same to her as it did to him.

He asked her if he might take her out to lunch, and when she would be ready to start. She said she could not lunch with him, because she had to have her hair done, and that she couldn't really conveniently be ready until six. She'd got a funny day, she said.

He had somehow known that she wouldn't meet him until late in the day and had worked out the trains for such a contingency.

"Well, that'll be fine," he said. If I call at six and you're ready, we can take a taxi and get the seven-five from Paddington."

"Right you are," she said, "that'll be very nice indeed."

"Right. Six at your flat . . . Good-bye, Netta dear."

"Good-bye, Bone."

He went and packed, and then went for a walk and had a beer, and then tried to phone Johnnie again. "Fitzgerald, Carstairs and Scott," said the girl (he was getting to know her voice by now), and he said is Mr. Littlejohn there please, and she said what name please, and he said Mr. Bone.

There was another long pause, and then she said, "I'm sorry, Mr. Bone, he's gone out; you phoned before, didn't you. Can I leave any message?"

"No," he said, "it's nothing important—I'll try again later thank you very much." She said, "I'll let him know you've phoned," and he thanked her again and rang off.

He had another beer, and then went to the hotel for lunch. But now he was in a rather excited state, and could hardly eat anything. He thought he had better go up to his room and try and sleep.

The white cat was of course delighted to see him, and weaved itself round his legs. "I'm going away today, pussy," he said. Hope you won't miss me." He did not get into bed, but took off his coat and drew the coverlet over him. The white cat insisted on coming under the coverlet. "You'll spoil my suit, pussy," he said. "You'll spoil my best suit with all your fur."

He dozed on and off, and at four o'clock, moved by some impulse he couldn't quite understand, he got up and went downstairs and phoned Johnnie again.

"Fitzgerald, Carstairs and Scott," said the girl, and he said is Mr. Littlejohn there yet, Mr. Bone speaking? "One moment, Mr. Bone," she said, and a few moments later said, "No, I'm afraid he's not in, Mr. Bone, I'm sorry."

"Oh," he said, "how funny. I've tried him all today—but I don't seem to get him."

"Yes," she said, "I'm afraid you're unlucky. He's been in, but I don't seem to be able to catch him."

He thanked her, and rang off, and strolled round to the Express for some tea. He had two cups of tea, and read the newspaper until twenty-past five. He was very nervous now, but felt he would be all right when he had had a drink. It was weird not getting Johnnie.

He went back to the hotel and tidied himself up under the pink bulb. Then he saw that it was twenty to six, and decided to walk round to Netta's at once. He would pick up his suitcase in the taxi they took to Paddington.

As he climbed up her cold, dark, stone steps, he knew there would be something wrong. Those steps had always been too cold and dark and wrong. And when he saw, pinned to her door, a blue envelope, with "*G. Bone Esq.*" scribbled on it in pencil, he knew his instinct had been right.

He opened the envelope and read:

Dear Bone, Tried to phone you all day. Sorry but our jaunt seems to be off. Have had frantic messages from Chudleigh where they all seem to be dying, and have had to go down at short notice. All well, will be back Sunday.

Gt. haste. Just time catch train. Sorry. Hope later,
Yr.

N. L.

Her mother and aunt lived in Chudleigh, Devon. She went down there for a fortnight every year.

He tore this note fiercely into small shreds, as though tearing her and all her blatant lies into small shreds, and he put the pieces into his pocket.

Then he found in his pocket the key which she had given him while she as ill, and he walked into her flat.

He might have known. She had said she wanted to go to Brighton.

And Netta was used to having her way.

He went straight over to the phone (beside which he had put her cheque last night) and dialled the number of Fitzgerald, Carstairs and Scott. The line went "*brr-brr . . . brr-brr . . . brr-brr . . .*" for a long time (it was after six and perhaps they were closed), but at last there was an answering dick.

"Fitzgerald, Carstairs and Scott," said the amiable girl, his old friend, in a rather tired voice.

"Hullo," he said; "I suppose Mr. Littlejohn isn't there yet, is he? . . ."

"Oh, hullo, Mr. Bone . . . No, I'm afraid he's gone."

"I suppose you can't tell me where I might find him, can you? It's rather urgent now. I suppose you can't tell me where I might get him?"

"Well, yes," she said. "He's gone to Brighton, I think. In fact I know he has."

"Oh . . . Brighton . . . Are you sure?"

"Yes. I heard him talking to Mr. Carstairs." All at once she became more chatty. "It seems everybody in the firm's gone down to Brighton tonight. They've just deserted us."

"Oh—have they?"

"Yes. They're celebrating Mr. Drexel's birthday, and making a big night of it so far as I can see!" Mr. Drexel, he realized, was Albert Drexel, the famous comedian appearing in the new farce.

"Oh, I see," he said . . . "Well. . . Thank you very much . . . Good night."

"Good night, Mr. Bone. Sorry I couldn't help you."

"No—not at all. Thank you very much . . . Good night."

"Good night."

He put down the receiver, and sat on her bed, and looked around her bedroom in the dusk of the rainy evening of the late summer of 1939.

"Making a night of it." No doubt they were making a night of it down there already, while he sat here.

He saw everything. She preferred to go to Brighton. She had said as much. He was not to have her after all. Instead of that she had got his best friend, to whom he had introduced her. She had got Johnnie.

Oh, Johnnie, Johnnie, *Johnnie*! How could you! He gulped down his double whisky and asked for another, and understood—or nearly understood. In regard to her the matter was simple enough. She had made up her mind to go down to Brighton, because, in the vicinity of this new farce, there were famous stars, managers, and general proceedings in which she desired to participate. She had not had the money to go without his help. She had therefore played him up, allowed him a few kisses and hinted at possible favours, in order to get the money out of him. She had given him a chance, perhaps, of going to Brighton with her (in a crowd and on a purely "innocent" basis, of course), but directly he had demurred she had decided to deceive him instead. In fact she had almost certainly meant to deceive him from the beginning, because in order to further her schemes in Brighton she would certainly want him out of the way—she wouldn't want an oaf and nonentity hanging around and cramping her style with distinguished people. And so she had invented this fiction about going away with him purely in order to let him down by a trick at the last moment and keep him in London while she went to Brighton unhampered. It was in some ways very clever, in some ways very crude, in all ways cold and merciless, and in all ways characteristic.

In regard to himself he was quite clear, too. Blinded and maddened by his love for this girl, he had just played his usual role of hysterical dupe: that was routine by now. But in regard to Johnnie—there it was not all entirely clear, and that was where his deep, aching grief lay.

He saw a lot, though he could not see it all. He remembered the telephone call he overheard last night. That was obviously Johnnie: he had known it at the time, though in his infatuation he had dismissed the idea as fantastic. So Johnnie phoned her up and held conversations behind his back!

"No, he doesn't seem to like the idea at all . . ." he remembered her saying, and he remembered her laugh. "He's off it, apparently!" That was obviously a reference to himself and the Brighton project. So Johnnie was scheming with her, laughing with her, behind his back, about a trip from which he was to be excluded. Oh, Johnnie, Johnnie, how could you! He couldn't believe it of him. He couldn't!

He couldn't believe it of him, and yet now everything fitted in. He remembered how well those two had always got on together, how they had talked above his head about the theatre, left him out of it. He remembered how he had sometimes seen Johnnie looking at her, in a funny, thoughtful way. He remembered how he had seen her looking at Johnnie, shyly yet boldly, in the same way that she had looked at him when he had first met her. He remembered how shy, evasive, Johnnie had been whenever her name was mentioned. He had thought at the time it was unexpressed sympathy on his behalf, but now he could interpret it quite differently. He remembered how, when he had winked and dragged Johnnie away from her that night, Johnnie, when they had got outside in the street, had seemed embarrassed, almost displeased. He remembered how, when he had phoned Johnnie and asked him to come round to her flat during her illness, Johnnie had made no demur, had taken it wonderfully for granted, almost as though he had been in her flat before. He probably had. He had probably been in touch with her behind his back all along.

Johnnie a traitor! . . . No, he couldn't believe it! It wasn't

Johnnie's fault! He knew his Johnnie, Johnnie was his friend, he had known him all his life. It was *her* fault, not his. She had twisted things somehow. She was fooling Johnnie, just as she was fooling him. Johnnie, no doubt, was crazy about her. Everybody was. He couldn't blame him for that. Johnnie, no doubt, could not stop himself where she was concerned— nobody could if that was her desire—but Johnnie was not a traitor to his friend in his heart.

And yet Johnnie had told him nothing of his intentions of going to Brighton, had evaded him on the phone all day, and was now in Brighton with her.

So he was not to have her. He had built up his pride, his manhood; he had bought new shirts and socks and ties; he had looked up trains; he had swaggered all day mentally like a cox-comb; but he was not to have her. Here he was in London, in the wet cold, alone—while she and Johnnie moved in the lights, flashed among the stars at Brighton. He was not fit for such society. They had got rid of him. He was not to have her. Instead, she was to have his friend.

There was the grief—the aching grief he could never wipe out—she had got his only friend. He had introduced her to Johnnie; he had shown Johnnie off; he had played Johnnie proudly as a trump card; he had looked upon Johnnie as his one resource against her—his one resource in life. And now she had taken him as well. She could take no more. She had won. It was all over now.

Annexed him without an effort! There was the last blow to his pride, his hope, his resistance, his belief in himself or anything.

He wondered whether they were talking and laughing about him at this moment. Probably Johnnie was an absolute beast, after all. He expected so. There was, of course, no friendship in life as he understood it.

And yet he couldn't see it! A sudden wave of feeling came over him and he couldn't believe that Johnnie was in on this.

Johnnie could never be cruel and treacherous; it just wasn't in his character. She had twisted things somehow: she was playing Johnnie up as she played up him and everybody. They ought to get together against her. He believed, if he appealed to Johnnie, Johnnie would be on his side. They could talk it out man to man.

Was Johnnie madly in love with her? Yes, probably. Had she encouraged Johnnie, given promise of herself, as she had to him? Probably. But what did Johnnie know about her, about her dark ways? Ought he not to warn Johnnie? Ought he not to tell Johnnie about what he knew?

Poor Johnnie!—poor, that was, if he was crazy about her and thought he had any chance—if he, too, was toying with the idea of getting divine happiness from her. She wasn't after Johnnie: she was after much bigger fish; she was after Eddie Carstairs. Did Johnnie know that? And if he didn't know it, ought he not to be warned? He could give him a lot of inside information!

What if all this was pure imagination? What if Johnnie was at Brighton, and Netta was with her mother and aunt at Devon? What if all this was a mad, bad dream on his part, the creation of his overwrought imagination?

Well, he could soon find out. He could go down to Brighton and find them—catch them at it. What about that, as an idea? No—that would be spying—undignified. Let him, at least, be dignified.

But why not go? The drink was going to his head, and he had half a mind to. He ordered another large whisky, and proposed it to himself. He could easily find them, if he went to the theatre. They would be seeing the show, and then, no doubt, going out to celebrate the birthday of the famous Albert Drexel afterwards. He could hang about the stage door. He would only have to see them together once, from a distance, to see all he wanted to see. Why not go and make sure?

What could he do if he stayed here? Drink and torture himself into a frenzy, alone in London on this wet, appalling night? Go home to bed, not knowing? Wake up in the blackness of tomorrow—not knowing? Perhaps never knowing? Sit in distraction and misery here, while they, together, the lovely girl who had been promised him tonight, the man who had been his only friend, enjoyed the warmth, the company, the high lights at the seaside? No—why should he be left out of the fun? He would go down to Brighton too. He was a free agent. They couldn't stop him.

He wondered whether any man, in the history of the world, had been treated as this girl, Netta, had treated him. Did other women say they would go away with men, take money from them and promise themselves, and then coolly leave notes on doors and go away with their best friends instead? Were there other men in London tonight, left stone cold, desolate, with their hope of love and friendship wiped out at one stroke?

There might be, but he wasn't going to be one of them. You could still get drunk; you could still enjoy drink, and nothing could stop you going to Brighton, and having a good time.

He had another large whisky, and looked at his watch. It was a quarter to seven. If he took a taxi now he could get the 7.5 from Victoria. But he didn't want to take a taxi. He wanted to go on drinking. He drank down his whisky, walked round to another pub (because he was ashamed to order any more at that one) and ordered another large one. They could wait.

A sort of elation came over him—the elation of whisky, the elation of a journey to be taken, the arrogant elation, even, of the eavesdropper or spy. Did they think they could fool him? He knew he was a fool, but he wasn't quite such a fool as that. He was going to fool them, actually.

The time crept on to a quarter-past seven. He drank down his whisky, and went out into the street. He caught a taxi at once. "Victoria Station, please," he said.

He noticed that he stumbled as he got into the taxi. That meant that he was drunk already.

That was bad. He saw what a fool he was making of himself: he saw how absurd this trip was, leading to nothing, doing no good. He saw how he would repent it in the morning. But what did he care?

It was all over now. Everything was over. He had a curious feeling that this was the last night of his life. He might as well enjoy himself, get drunk and do what he wanted to do, on his last night.

Approaching Brighton in the darkness, the train slowed down, hesitated, seemed to be feeling its way before risking itself in a dangerous area, and then lolloped oilily and methodically forward.

The raindrops spat feebly on the Pullman window in which he could see himself. He realized, for the first time, that he had forgotten to bring any luggage. He had never thought of that. Never mind. It didn't matter. Nothing mattered now.

He gave up his ticket and smelt the sea. So here he was in Brighton again!

Almost the first thing he saw—as though it were a reminder of what he had come for, or a portent of what he was to find—was a huge poster advertising the show. "Fitzgerald, Carstairs & Scott—present BY YOUR LEAVE—a new Farce by Leonard Golding—with ALBERT DREXEL and CORNFORD HOBBS." And then again, a moment later, "ALBERT DREXEL and CORNFORD HOBBS in 'By Your Leave,' etc., presented by Fitzgerald, Carstairs and Scott." It was as though the two famous comedians had seized the town, were in complete dominance and occupation of it under the orders and generalship of Fitzgerald, Carstairs and Scott. And they were going to celebrate Albert Drexel's birthday, and Netta was after Carstairs. He was profoundly impressed. They were all very famous. He didn't wonder she had wanted to get rid of him.

He walked down Queen's Road towards the sea, and more of these posters hit him in the face. What was he doing here?

What had he come for? He didn't know. Just to make sure, he supposed. Just to know for certain that everything was over for all time. It would be funny if she wasn't here—if he had made a fool of himself the other way this time. But he wouldn't mind making a fool of himself that way.

Where was he going to stay? At the Little Castle again, he supposed. At the Clock Tower it began to rain quite hard. He didn't want to spoil his best suit (and his best overcoat and hat which he had put on for Netta) and he managed to jump on a bus going down to Castle Square.

Outside the Little Castle he funked it. He just couldn't face the manageress and the porter again, after all his disgrace last time. There was a little street near by where he could remember having seen "Apartments" signs, and he decided to try one of them.

The woman who came to the door was scared out of her wits, particularly when he said he had no luggage. But when he said he would leave a deposit and produced a pound note, she became affable, indeed obsequious, and showed him her wretched little room, which he said was very nice.

He went and had a drink in East Street at once, and then walked down to the front and had one at the old place where he had warmed his wet trousers and been so miserable about Netta after she had gone away that morning. Then he walked round to the theatre.

The whole narrow street was ablaze and electrically twinkling with "ALBERT DREXEL AND CORNFORD HOBBS," and as he approached the front of the theatre he saw notices: "Stalls full," "Gallery full." It was a great occasion all right.

He went into the terrible plushed quiet of the foyer—the terrible plushed quiet of a foyer of a show upon which the curtain has gone up and is doing enormous business—and he asked, or rather murmured conspiratorially, for a seat. Yes, they had one in the circle at the side. They made stamping noises and gave him his ticket. He took his change, and was told by an awed attendant to go to another attendant, who, in low frightened tones, told him how to go upstairs.

Another attendant opened the door for him at the top of the stairs, and a huge roar of smoke-hazed, lime-lit laughter, coming out of the door like blast from a bomb, hit him in the face. It was like the world's laugh in his face, Netta's laugh, the last laugh of everybody at his failure and isolation, his banishment from the world of virile people who were happy and made love and had friends.

He was shown shamefacedly to a gangway seat at the side, and amidst another ear-splitting roar, like a breaker of the sea crashing over one's head, given a programme, and left. The laughter went on, and he looked at the stage. There, in the brilliantly lit, almost blinding set, was the famous Albert Drexel in person—arguing irascibly and inimitably with the famous and inimitable Cornford Hobbs, whom he had seen so many times on the films. But he couldn't make out what they were saying, or what everybody was laughing about, because he wasn't listening to what they were saying, but just looking at them. Everybody else's laughter shook through him, and he just stared. It was funny that, on this night of all nights, he should be watching a farce . . .

The first act came to an end, and the lights went up. People began to move out to the bars and the foyer. What was he doing here? He wished he hadn't come. He was drunk, among other things. He might be seen. He had better go home. They probably weren't here. They probably weren't in Brighton at all. Well, he might as well have a look, now he had come. He went down to the edge of the circle and looked down at the stalls.

Yes, there she was . . . Yes, there they were . . . He was glad to have seen them. It was what he'd come down for. She was walking up the gangway with Eddie Carstairs (of Fitzgerald, Carstairs and Scott), who was making her laugh with something he said, and who was carrying her coat.

Johnnie was bending over and talking to someone seated in a gangway seat. Soon Johnnie followed the others out, looking about the theatre with a cheerful, satisfied expression . . .

He had better have a drink and go home. It was all over now.

He went and sat down in his seat for a little, and looked at the programme. He was pretty sure they were coming up to the big circle bar, and he wanted to give them time to do so before he dodged out of the theatre. He looked at a picture of Albert Drexel, whose birthday they were going to celebrate.

As he passed, he looked through the glass door of the circle bar, and saw them again. They were at the bar. Eddie Carstairs had his back to him, but he could see her full-face. Eddie Carstairs was talking, and she was looking up at him and listening, and occasionally smiling. It was funny that she should be doing this, now, tonight, instead of being in Maidenhead with him, as she had promised she would be. She was a bitch, all right.

A man, wanting to get into the bar, said "Excuse me," and he fled down the stairs through the crowd into the street, and got into a pub over the way, and ordered a large whisky.

He felt he had seen her for the last time. He felt he no longer had anything to do with her. She was a success now—he was sure of that. She had got her Eddie Carstairs at last—her Eddie Carstairs to carry her coat. She was way up with the big people. She was going to be a film star. She would never look back now.

He ought always to have thought of it like that. He ought always to have known he wasn't in her class. He began to tremble violently, and he ordered another whisky. He caught sight of himself in the glass.

He could hardly blame her for shaking him off. He wouldn't look well with people like that. Apart from his looks, he couldn't even talk. The Eddie Carstairs, the Nettas, the Johnnies, were in one level of life—he in another. They were "successful" people, people of the smart world, of the theatre, he was a battered boozer from Earl's Court—now a lonely eavesdropper, a spy. And yet Johnnie had been his *friend*!—had known him all his life—had known him in the old Bob Barton days, the wonderful days—had laughed and joked with him—had come to see him when he was ill—*that* was what he couldn't get over. Why should *Johnnie* leave him out of it? Why should *Johnnie* join the others and go behind his back?

And if he himself had never introduced her to Johnnie, she wouldn't be here now, wouldn't be in with the great Eddie Carstairs, wouldn't be going ahead to success. And it was he who had given her the money to come down here!—paid her fare, paid for her hair being done, for Eddie Carstairs to look at!

Oh, well—what did it matter? It was all over now, and the drink had stopped his trembling, and he was going to get a good deal drunker yet, and he didn't care a damn. About an hour later he noticed the people were flowing into the pub, and gathered the show was over. He decided to go on somewhere else.

Passing the yard in which the stage door lay he saw a great bloody Rolls, and realized that this belonged to Eddie Carstairs. He had heard of Eddie Carstairs' Rolls—Netta had talked about it with Johnnie. He had no doubt Netta would be enthroned in it on her way to the birthday party in a little while. They would go on to the Palatial. He had heard they all went there when they were down in Brighton. It was wonderful how the Eddie Carstairs of life got everything, while others got nothing at all. He could hate Eddie Carstairs if he thought about it, but he wasn't going to think about it because it was all over now.

He had another drink, and bought a half-bottle of Haig, and went down to the sea and walked towards Hove.

He walked the length of the lawns and then turned back again. The sea crashed in a rising wind, and it rained slightly. He began to tremble all over again, and sat down in a shelter, and opened the bottle, and took a pull at the whisky, and then walked on. He had got to keep walking: bed was out of the question and it was early yet, not twelve o'clock. He would walk to Black Rock now.

It was all over now. He didn't know what he was going to do or where he was going tomorrow, but it was all over, and he knew he would never see her or Johnnie again. When he had run down the stairs of the theatre he had run out of their lives. He had run away, though there was nowhere to run to, and no one to whom he could run. Never mind, somehow it would solve itself—tomorrow—black tomorrow would look after itself. He passed the Palatial Hotel.

He saw the great bloody Rolls again, and realized that she was inside. He wondered whether she was staying there, and what time she would get to bed. He had heard about these parties, and knew they went on till three or four. Well, good-bye, Netta. Good-bye, Johnnie. That was that.

Oh, Johnnie, *Johnnie!*—and the old Bob Barton days!—that was what hurt! They had all been such *friends!*

He began trembling again, and felt so cold that he thought he had better turn away from the sea, get out of the wind up a side street.

As he turned the corner, under the white-blue light of a lamp, he bumped straight into Johnnie, who was walking by himself.

He simply stopped and stared at him, and Johnnie stopped and stared back.

"Good God!" said Johnnie, affably. "What are you doing here, old boy?"

He couldn't answer, he simply stared.

Johnnie came up to him, a look of concern on his face. "What's the matter, old boy?" he said. "Is anything the matter?"

And Johnnie put out his hands, and touched him, held him. "What's the matter, old boy?" he said.

He knew at once he was going to cry. It was the firm touch of his old friend's hand, the sincere, concerned face, the old voice, calling him "old boy" in the old way.

"Oh, Johnnie, *Johnnie!*" he said, and began to cry. "Johnnie . . ."

Johnnie held him closer, drew him into the wall, hid him, like a mother with a child, from passers-by. "What's the matter, old boy?" he said. "You're all worked up. What are you crying about? Take it easy now, and tell me."

"I'm sorry . . ." he said, "I'll be all right . . ."

"But what's the matter, old boy?" said Johnnie. "What've you been doing with yourself?"

"I'm sorry," he said, "I'm sorry . . . I'll be all right . . . I thought she'd got you, you see. I thought she'd got you! . . ."

CHAPTER FOUR

"Who? What? Who's got me?" said Johnnie. "What are you talking about?"

"But you came *away* with her, Johnnie, and didn't tell me . . . I thought she'd got you, too."

Light dawned on Johnnie. "Oh, Lord—*that* bitch . . ." he said, "I begin to see . . ."

"Yes, she *is* a bitch, Johnnie, too. That's the truth . . . If you only knew . . . And then I thought she'd got you, too . . ."

He was staring miserably in front of him, and Johnnie still held him.

"Listen, George, my boy," said Johnnie, "I didn't come away with her. She rang me up last night and suggested coming, and said you didn't want to come. And she rang me up again today, and said if I was coming she was, and that she'd meet me at the theatre. I had to be polite to your friend, and that's all there is to it, George. She's not after me, you know. She's after someone else . . ."

"Yes, I know," said George. "She's after Eddie Carstairs, isn't she?"

"Oh," said Johnnie, smiling, "you know that, do you?" And George smiled faintly back.

"Oh, yes. I know that. I'm sorry, Johnnie. I thought she'd got you. I'm so happy she hasn't."

"You believe me, don't you, George?"

"Of course I do, Johnnie. I've been a fool."

And he looked at Johnnie and believed him utterly, and saw what a fool he'd been.

"You've got all worked up, George, my boy," said Johnnie. "You've got into a state. You musn't let a woman get you down, you know. There are plenty of others, and *she's* not worth it."

"No, I know she isn't. I'm afraid she's got me down."

All at once he began to shake and tremble again and to breathe in a hissing way between his teeth.

"Come on," said Johnnie, "what you want is a drink."

"But I've had a lot to drink," he said.

"Never mind. You come and have another. I'll look after you now."

"But how can we have a drink? All the pubs are closed."

"Oh, we'll get a drink," said Johnnie, and taking his arm, led him back along the front in the direction from which he had come.

"Oh, by the way," said Johnnie, as they walked along, "there's one thing, while I remember it."

"Yes?"

"She asked me tonight not to tell you she had been down here. She said you'd had a sort of row and you'd be hurt. Does that fit in?"

"Yes. I suppose she was afraid you'd tell me. Yes. That fits in."

"Good. Here we are," said Johnnie, and led him up the steps of the Palatial.

"But we can't go here," he said. "Isn't she in here? Isn't she in here?"

"No," said Johnnie. "She's not. You'll be surprised."

As he entered into the bright lights, he had an awful feeling of faintness, and his trembling simply would not stop. "All right, old boy," said Johnnie, "you'll be all right. Take it easy."

He took him through the huge lounge, and along to the left through corridors into a large smoking-room, and put him down at a table. He was aware that, in one corner of this room, a lot of men were making a lot of noise, but he was so faint and giddy that that was all he knew. "Are you all right?" said Johnnie. "I'm going to hunt up the waiter. Are you all right?" "Yes," he said, "I'm all right." And Johnnie vanished.

There was a great roar of laughter, and he looked up at the men in the corner. He at once saw Eddie Carstairs, and a moment later, Albert Drexel and Cornford Hobbs. He had never seen a famous film star up close in a room before, and he was so surprised, intrigued and pleased to do so now, that he forgot about his faintness, and stared at them. Then Johnnie came back with the waiter, and there was a large brandy in front of him.

"Come on, drink up," said Johnnie. "You'll soon be better."

He drank, and began to feel better, and the trembling became less uncontrolled.

"That's Cornford Hobbs, isn't it?" he said, "over there?"

"Yes, that's right," said Johnnie. "Go on, drink up."

Suddenly he heard a quiet voice which he knew.

"Well, Johnnie," he said. "What are you up to?"

And he looked up and saw Eddie Carstairs standing over them.

"Oh, hullo Eddie," said Johnnie. "Can I introduce Mr. Bone (Mr. Carstairs—Mr. Bone)? . . ."

"Hullo," said Eddie Carstairs, smiling and shaking hands. "How do you do?"

"How do you do?" he said, and smiled back.

"Mr. Bone's a very old friend of mine, Eddie," said Johnnie. "And he's having a fainting attack or something. So I brought him in for a stiff brandy."

"Oh, I'm sorry," said Eddie. "Are you all right? Is there anything I can do?"

He looked up at his rival, the almost legendary Eddie Carstairs, the terrible man, the owner of the great bloody Rolls, Netta's ambition, the manager and maker of stars about whom he had heard so much, and he saw the friendly face of a slim, brown-eyed man of about forty, and he smiled back.

"No, thanks," he said. "Thank you very much. I think I'll be all right."

"Mr. Bone," said Johnnie, "is yet *another* acquaintance of Miss Netta Longdon's, Eddie."

"Oh, my God," said Eddie, suddenly taking a chair and sitting down beside them. "*That* bitch . . . is he?"

Then, having looked at George again he said to George, "I'm terribly sorry. Is she a friend of yours? . . ."

"No," he said, and smiled again. "She's no friend of mine."

"No!" said Eddie, protestingly and looking and talking at them both. "She really is a bitch. She absolutely chases *me*—doesn't she, Johnnie?"

"She certainly does."

"No. It's true," said Eddie. "Wherever I go she turns up. The bloody woman absolutely haunts me. I only escaped tonight by the skin of my teeth. I said the play wasn't any good, and we'd got to have a script conference! They're having a lovely script conference," he added, nodding over his shoulder at the men in the corner. "Aren't they?"

Johnnie laughed, Eddie laughed, he laughed.

"No," said Eddie. "I don't know what it is but there's something absolutely sinister about that woman. She's sort of scheming. Don't you agree? . . . Well, I'm going to the bathroom." He rose. "Why don't you come and join us?"

"Thanks, Eddie," said Johnnie, "we will."

"How are you feeling, George, old boy?" murmured Johnnie. "You see what *he* feels about her—don't you?"

"Oh, Johnnie," he said, "what a fool I've been. I've got all worked up about nothing."

His terrible trouble was that he was afraid that he was going to cry. To have got Johnnie back, the old Bob Barton Johnnie, to realize that he had never really lost him—that Johnnie valued their friendship as he did—it was all too much.

"I think you'd better leave Earl's Court for good, old boy," said Johnnie, "hadn't you?"

"Oh, yes," he said. "I'll never go back now."

"A thoroughly bad lot if you ask me," said Johnnie, "though it's not my business."

"No, you're right. She is a bad lot."

"Feeling better? You're looking better."

"Yes, much." He had stopped trembling now. It was only that he wanted to cry.

A few moments later Eddie Carstairs came back, said, in passing, "Come along you two," and joined the others.

"Come on," said Johnnie, "let's go over."

"But I can't, can I! I don't know them," he said. "They won't want me."

"Come on," said Johnnie, and they rose.

They were all hooting with laughter about something (he was strangely sober now, and he could see, actually, that they had had quite a lot to drink) and there was a gusty welcome for

Johnnie. "Well, if it's not our little Johnnie! . . ." Then "Mr. Drexel—Mr. Bone; Mr. Bone—Mr. Hobbs." "How do you do, Mr. Bone?" "How do you do?" There were six of them altogether: he didn't catch the names of the others, but they were friendly men who looked him in the face and smiled, and made him feel at home. He was put next to Mr. Hobbs, and the question of drinks arose at once.

"And what's yours, Mr. Bone?" asked Mr. Hobbs, having asked the others.

"Oh," he said, "I don't know. I don't really think I want any more."

"Now then, now then, none of this," said Mr. Hobbs, in the rich, inimitable voice, which brought houses down with laughter. "This is a birthday party, you know. You can't start that sort of thing here."

"I know what he wants," said Eddie Carstairs, who was lying back in his chair. "He wants an *extremely* large, *extremely* expensive brandy, because he's been feeling faint, and don't let him do you out of it," he added, looking at George. "He'll twist you if he can."

There was more laughter at this, as it was evidently a followup of some other joke. "Very well," said Mr. Hobbs to the waiter, who had now appeared. "A beaker of brandy for Mr. Bone, and the same again all round."

"A beaker of your most *expensive* brandy," said Eddie Carstairs, and they all laughed again.

It was like a dream. It was too good to be true. This was where *she* had wanted to be tonight—cheating him and leaving him out in the cold—but it was he who was inside, who had come to the wonderful birthday party instead! It was fairy-like. A battered failure, a stray Earl's Court boozer, but he was good enough for Johnnie, and it seemed he was good enough for them. They made him welcome, these strong and powerful ones with whom she had schemed to insinuate herself: they made him welcome, and gave him brandy and liked him, and thought she was a bitch!

His brandy came, and he felt better still, and he sat there, listening to their noisy talk and not talking. Among other things he was so profoundly impressed by the mere fact that he was looking at Cornford Hobbs's face a few feet away in the flesh, that he could hardly open his mouth.

He had seen the man so many times on the films, he admired him as a comedian so much, that he was almost stupefied with delight and interest to see him and talk with him in person.

"Did you see the show tonight, Mr. Bone?" said Mr. Hobbs, suddenly breaking away from the general conversation, and speaking in a confidential tone.

"Oh, yes," he said, "I did."

"What did you think of it?"

"Oh, I thought it was wonderful," he said. He was lying, of course, but he knew it must have been wonderful because of all the laughter he had heard, and he was so taken aback by the honour of having his opinion asked that he could think of nothing else to say.

"Yes," said Mr. Hobbs. "I think we got away with it—if it only wasn't for this ghastly war."

"Yes," he said, and then, because he just couldn't help it, because even if it was the wrong and silly and dumb thing to say, it was sincere, he said, "I've seen you such a lot on the films, Mr. Hobbs. It's wonderful to meet you here like this."

"Well, I don't know about that," said Mr. Hobbs. "It's extremely nice to meet you!" And they both laughed as though they were old friends.

A fresh round of drinks was brought, and the conversation became general again, and he sat listening. Soon the talk got right above his head, but he was still fascinated to listen. But all at once he began trembling again, and Johnnie, coming and sitting next to him, said, "How do you feel, George? Do you want to go home? You look rather pale."

"Yes," he said. "I think I'd better go." And the trembling came on more violently.

Eddie Carstairs had observed what was going on. "Is he all right?" he said.

"Yes. He'll be all right," said Johnnie. "I'll see him home in a taxi."

"I'll be all right," he said. "It'll soon stop. It's only this trembling."

"Well, you'd better go home," said Eddie Carstairs. "I've got the car outside. You can come in that."

"No—don't bother, Eddie," said Johnnie. "I can easily take him in a taxi."

"No—the car's outside. Come on. We'll see him home together."

"What's all this about going home?" said Mr. Hobbs. "Who's going home?"

"We're seeing Mr. Bone home," said Eddie Carstairs, "he's not feeling too good."

"Seeing Mr. Bone home. Fine! Can we come too?"

"Yes. You can come," and all at once the thing to do was to see Mr. Bone home. Nothing else would do. "I'm sorry you've got to go," said Mr. Hobbs in his ear. "I expect you've got a chill or something?"

"Yes, I think I must have," he said. "I'm all right, but it's just this trembling."

There were a lot of cracks as they got out their hats and coats from the cloakroom, and then decided they didn't want them and put them back, and they all flowed out of the revolving doors into the night, where they found themselves, as people will coming out into the night, decidedly drunker than they had been previously.

There was a lot of argument as to who should sit where, but

at last they had all, except him, crowded into the back, and Eddie Carstairs went to the driver's seat, and said, "You come and sit here, Mr. Bone—don't bother about them." And George Harvey Bone—the guest of honour—climbed into the great bloody Rolls and sat beside its owner.

B ut it wasn't a great bloody Rolls any more, because he was inside it at its owner's invitation: it was a warm, infinitely fascinating and voluptuous piece of mechanism which backed quietly and slid forth like a liner.

"Where are you staying, George?" said Johnnie from behind, and he said he didn't know exactly; but he could find it: it was a room in a little street near the Little Castle Hotel.

There was a great deal of argument behind as to where the Little Castle Hotel lay, some saying it was in Kemp Town, others saying it was in Hove, and one jovially dissentient voice hotly declaring it was in Edinburgh, but Johnnie said he knew it: it was just off Castle Square, and Eddie Carstairs drove ahead in silence.

His trembling had stopped again, and he felt weak and happy and dazed. He watched Eddie Carstairs using the gears, and marvelled at their quietness and precision; and he said, not seeking to please, not even conscious of himself: "What a wonderful car—isn't it?"

"Yes, it is nice, isn't it?" said Eddie Carstairs. "I've had it three years now and I'm still crazy about it."

"Yes," he said, "it's wonderful."

He sat there, this enormous, ill, simple-minded man who had suffered so much mentally—he sat there, in the late lights of Brighton chasing through the darkness of the car, looking now at the driver's steering, now at the street, weak, happy, and at peace, his blue unhappy hunted eyes staring out, harmless, bewildered, hopeful, grateful. All the years and sorrow seemed to slip away from those eyes, and there was the little boy again, the little boy who had been hurt, and was being given a treat. He was unaware of his pathos, his simplicity, the fact that he had a charm—a charm which made him entirely acceptable to all who valued such things. He was only infinitely grateful to Johnnie, and to this once dreaded and hated man who had come out of a hotel to see him home, and to the friendly accepting men behind.

They were still making a great deal of noise behind, but Eddie Carstairs remained quiet. All at once, however, he broke the silence.

"Well, George," he said, not looking at him, for he was taking a corner with care, "I suppose you've been having a lot of thick nights lately, haven't you?"

He was so amazed and flattered to hear himself called "George" in that offhand yet friendly way, that he hardly knew how to answer.

"Yes, I have," he said. "I have really."

"One has to stop sometimes, doesn't one?" said Eddie, "or it gets one down."

"Yes, one has," he said. "Though it's not really late nights so much with me. I just seem to have got into a state . . ."

"What sort of a state? . . ." said Eddie Carstairs after another pause, in his quiet voice . . .

"Oh—just a state . . ."

"Not a woman, I hope," said this remarkable man . . . And there was another pause

"Oh, well . . . perhaps . . . sort of . . ."

"Because that's not worth it. You take my word for it," said Eddie Carstairs, and from behind, Johnnie's voice suddenly said, "Yes, he's right there, George. He's certainly right there, you know."

And he saw in a flash of perception and gratitude that Johnnie had somehow told Eddie Carstairs something of the truth, and that not only Johnnie, but Eddie Carstairs himself, was trying to help him out, trying to console him and make him feel better, trying to be kind. And he couldn't bear it, because it made him want to cry.

"There's only one thing that's any good with a certain type of woman, you know," went on Eddie. "Ask her for what you want, ask her whether she means to give it to you, and if she doesn't, throw her out of the window."

They all three laughed at this, because, among other things, he did not use those exact words, but more vulgar, vivid and racy ones. Johnnie laughed shyly, George holding back his tears.

"No," said Eddie. "That may sound hard, but that's all there is to it, and all there ever will be . . . You remember that, and you won't go wrong."

There was a pause, and then Eddie said, "Well, here's the Little Castle, where do we go from here?"

"Just round there," he said, but he could hardly speak.

They found the house, and the car stopped. "Shall I see you up?" said Johnnie, and he said, "No, no—no, thanks!" And Cornford Hobbs shook hands and said, "Well, goodbye, Mr. Bone. I'm very sorry you're going. Hope you'll be better in the morning." And all he wanted to do was to get away, so that he didn't cry.

"Well, good-bye Mr. Carstairs," he said. "Thank you so much. Thank you *really*?"

"Good-bye, George," said Mr. Carstairs, smiling at him in a peculiarly amiable and knowing way.

"Sure you wouldn't like me to see you up?" said Johnnie— and he said "Yes! . . . Yes! . . . Thank you, Johnnie . . . Thank you very much."—"See you soon," said Johnnie. "I'll phone you tomorrow when I get back?"—"Yes! Yes!" he said. "Well, goodbye and thank you. Thank you *all* very much. Good-bye!" "Goodbye!" they all yelled, and they all waved and the car moved off.

He reached his wretched little room, by lighting matches, and found the gas and lit it. He stood there, holding on to the brass bedstead, the hot tears pouring down his cheeks. He had won at last! He had had the birthday party—not she. *He* had had the ride in the Rolls—not she. They liked *him*—not her! Johnnie was *his* friend not hers, and Eddie Carstairs, the famous Eddie Carstairs of Fitzgerald, Carstairs and Scott, had given him some advice! Oh, God—they were so *kind*—they weren't like Netta and Peter—they were *kind*!

They were the high-ups, they were the stars (whom Netta and Peter envied and schemed to meet), and they were *kind*! Netta and Peter were not kind: they were the low-downs and harsh and cruel. But he had won after all, and he was right after all, and Johnnie had done it for him—old Bob Barton Johnnie!—and Johnnie was his friend! Oh, God—they had been kind at last to him: at last they had been kind!

He flung himself on the bed, and hid his face in his arms, incontrollably, vastly sobbing, incontrollably, vastly happy.

And then, of course, a little later, something snapped in his head.

THE LAST PART

MAIDENHEAD

. . . what your commands imposed
I have performed, as reason was, obeying,
Not without wonder or delight beheld;
Now, of my own accord, such other trial
I mean to show you of my strength yet greater
As with amaze shall strike all who behold.
          J. MILTON, *Samson Agonistes*

CHAPTER ONE

C lick! . . .

He lay on the bed in the dull green gaslight of a little room in Brighton, and it had happened again.

It was an extraordinary sensation, but he was used to it. It was as though a shutter had rolled down on his brain, and clicked tight. It was as though the soundtrack in a talkie had broken down and the still-proceeding picture on the screen of existence had an utterly different character, mysterious, silent, indescribably eerie.

It was as though he had dived into a swimming-bath and hit his head on the bottom, and was floating about, bewildered and inaudible to himself, in hushed green depths.

He had never known it click so tight. He felt as though it was locked for good this time, as though it would never click back. He was so confused by it, when it happened, lying with his head buried on his bed, that he couldn't think where he was or what he was doing.

He was aware of being in his best suit, of feeling cold and trembly, and of his face being wet, evidently with tears. But what it was all about, he couldn't, for the moment, make out. No doubt he was doing something, had been doing something, and he would find out soon what it was. No doubt he had something to do . . . Yes, that was it, he had something to do. He had come to wherever he was to do something. He had got to find out what it was. If he didn't nag at it, if he didn't "press," as they said in golf, if he just lay peacefully and relaxed, it would come . . .

He lay and relaxed, wet-faced and weak, in the light of the gas, and soon enough it came quite easily. He had to kill Netta Longdon, and then get to Maidenhead . . .

Who was Netta Longdon? He couldn't for the life of him remember. It was a familiar name, but he couldn't place it . . .

Oh, yes, of course, "Netta Longdon" meant Netta, the Netta he knew and there was such a lot of fuss about . . . Oh, dear—hadn't he killed her *yet*?

He sat up on the bed in the ghastly light. This was awful. He had meant to kill her weeks ago. What had he been doing in the meanwhile? What had stopped him?

Oh, yes—and he had to kill Peter too. He had been just going to kill Peter when something happened. What had happened? What had he been doing all this time?

He was in Brighton—he realized that. Had he been in Brighton all the time? Had he dreamed that he had gone to London and nearly killed Peter? No—there was more to it than that. This was a separate trip. It would all come back soon . . .

He was trembling, and he had been crying. She had made him tremble and cry. It had all been going on too long—it had all been going on *again*—and still he hadn't killed her, and still he hadn't gone to Maidenhead. What had he been thinking all this time; had he been making more excuses, or had he forgotten about it, or what? It didn't matter. He must kill her now. He must go to London and kill her at once.

He rose from the bed and stared at the light of the dull, green, midnight, nightmare gas. He must go to London and kill her at once.

He looked at his watch. It was five and twenty past twelve. Could he get a train now? Probably not. Very well then, he would walk. He would walk to London and kill her at once.

What a good idea. He would like a walk, it would clear his head. He would walk the whole way back to London and kill her, and then walk on to Maidenhead. He couldn't sleep again until he had killed her, and so he had to keep walking, anyway. He was a great walker. And he was able to walk, because he had no luggage. It all fitted in—it was like fate. And he could go now, because he could remember paying a deposit—he had given the woman a pound.

He could go just as he was, unencumbered. It was all arranged.

He put out the gas, and lit a match, and groped his way down the stairs, and let himself out of the little house in the little Brighton street. The rain had stopped, and it was a fair, breezy night.

There was nobody about, except an occasional policeman, and the echoing streets were so cool and fresh that he wondered more people didn't walk to London like him, instead of stuffing in trains. They had lost the use of their legs.

He passed Brighton Pavilion, and then the big church, and was soon well on the London road going under the vast Roman-aqueducty bridge. Then along by Preston Park and Withdean Nurseries, and out to Patcham with its petrol pumps and church. Then out on the great motor road, with its two white pillars, saying you were in Brighton, and on to Pyecombe. He meant to go via Hassocks and Burgess Hill. Occasionally a motor-car or lorry blinded and flashed by him.

Dawn was in the sky as he climbed the long, slow slope of Clayton Hill, with its windmills and strange little forts—funnels from the great black dreadnought which was the tunnel beneath—and when he reached the top the sun had risen and he could see the whole shire stretched out and gleaming in mauve, rook-calling mist below. He did not feel weary, but it occurred to him that he had a long way to go.

Then it occurred to him that he had made a mistake. He was supposed to be walking to London to kill Netta, but actually Netta was in Brighton. Also, he had forgotten—he kept on forgetting things, it was getting bad—that he had to kill Peter too.

Oh, well—it didn't matter. She would be going back to London today, and they would both be ready for him.

Half an hour later he was so tired and weak that he realized he would have to rest. He sat down by the roadside, and lit a cigarette, and dozed off as he sat, the swish of a passing car every now and again interrupting his heart-beat and disturbing his reverie . . .

It was broad daylight when he went on again, and he realized he would have to give in and go to bed somewhere. He couldn't remember quite why it was that he had to walk to London instead of taking a train, but he was sure that was how the thing stood.

He branched off to Hassocks, and found a pub opposite the station, where they stared at him, but, on his producing money, gave him breakfast and a room. He drew the curtains to, and undressed and slept in his shirt.

He did not wake till half past five in the evening. He went out in a dazed way and bought a paper at the station to see what day it was, and saw they had gone into Poland. He supposed that meant war.

He didn't go back to the hotel, but began to walk on again to London. He now saw that there was no need to walk to London at all: he could easily take a train, and he didn't know how the idea had got into his head. Muddle again. But he knew this part of the country, and he had a fancy to see Apple Lodge, a little farmhouse, with cows and a donkey and ducks, where he had stayed as a child and been happy, before they sent him to school and made him miserable. It was on the way to Burgess Hill, and he would like to have a look at it, as when he had got to Maidenhead there would be no coming away and looking at anything like that again.

He passed it in the dusk, and said good-bye, and walked on to Burgess Hill, where he found himself exhausted again, and where they seemed to have no street lighting. He found another pub near the station. He had some beers in the saloon bar, and they were all talking about Poland and the war. It bored him stiff, though he realized that it was rather useful actually, that they should be having their war while he was killing Netta and going to Maidenhead, because that way he would get out of the war too. Netta and Peter!—he mustn't forget Peter! It kept on slipping from his mind.

He went to bed early and slept long and late. He was not up till half past ten, but they gave him some breakfast in a parlour. After this he found a barber's and had a shave. It was all war, war, everywhere. The barber went on about it all the time. He supposed it interested people in a small place like Burgess Hill, because they had nothing else to think about.

He had quite a few beers after that, and worked out exactly how he would do Netta in. He had a longing for some yellow pickles he saw on the bar, and ate them ravenously with an arrowroot biscuit.

He looked out trains and there wasn't a decent one till after four o'clock, and as he wasn't at all impatient now, he went to the local picture theatre and saw "Tarzan Finds a Son," with Johnnie Weissmuller and Maureen O'Sullivan.

He didn't get into London until nearly six o'clock, and when he came out at Victoria Station he thought he was having a liver attack because the sky was full of distant gnats. These were barrage balloons. They were getting down to it now all right. He was only just in time.

He had some drinks at the "Shakespeare" opposite Victoria, and everybody was very excited. There was a strange atmosphere altogether. Then he went back to the station and tried to phone Netta to make sure she'd be there tomorrow, but he couldn't get her. Then he went into a draper's shop to buy some thread, because he had decided at Burgess Hill that that would be necessary, so that nothing was disturbed.

The girl asked him what colour thread he wanted and what

it was for. He couldn't explain, of course, and he said any colour would do. He came out with four reels of grey thread. Then he went to a shop he knew in Victoria Street which provided things for dogs, and bought a basket for a cat. He had decided to take pussy with him. He put the reels of thread into the basket and carried them into another pub, feeling rather like a fisherman.

He had a lot of whisky to drink because he had a lot to think about, and because this was his last night on whisky and he might as well enjoy it. When he got to Maidenhead he would only be having an occasional beer. He went from pub to pub and the wirelesses were going in all of them, and people were listening, but he couldn't be bothered. The streets were pitch black because they had put all the lights out. At eleven o'clock he got a taxi to his hotel.

He found the white cat in the bathroom and brought it into his bedroom, and put it into the basket to see if it would fit. It fitted all right, but the cat didn't like it, and sprang out. He undressed and got into bed. The cat came in with him, and they both slept.

He woke up at about three o'clock in the morning of Sunday, September the third, nineteen hundred and thirty-nine, with the cat still beside him, and realized that he would be unable to take the cat to Maidenhead after all, because the cat was a bit of Earl's Court, and if a bit of Earl's Court, however small, got into Maidenhead, it would upset Maidenhead completely. This made him miserable, because he loved the cat, and saw that this was the last time they would ever be together. "I'm sorry, pussy," he said, "but you can't come with me after all." And he hugged the cat closely, and even kissed it, and went to sleep again, while it purred.

CHAPTER TWO

H e awoke at seven and had a bath and dressed. At eight o'clock he went down to the hotel phone, and phoned Netta.

She was, of course, angry at being phoned at such an hour, but he couldn't bother about things like that.

"What? . . ." she said. "It's only eight o'clock. What's the matter?"

"Nothing," he said, "I only just wanted to know if you were there—whether I could come round and see you this morning."

"No," she said in her old bad-tempered way. "I'm afraid you can't. I'm going out."

"When will you be going out?"

"*I* don't know," she said rudely. "When I get up . . . It's eight o'clock now."

"Did you get back from Devon all right?"

"Yes."

"Right you are, Netta," he said, "sorry. I'll phone you some other time . . . Good-bye."

"Good-bye."

He didn't mind about her saying she was going out and not wanting to see him. He just wanted to know she was there. He could get in with the key she had given him when she was ill.

Next he phoned Peter, who was almost equally rude. "Sorry," he said, "I just thought I'd phone you to see if you'd got back."

"Yes. I'm back," said Peter. "What do you want? What's the matter?"

"Oh, I just wondered whether I'd be seeing you about. It's a long time since we met."

"Look here, I'm in bed," said Peter, and a few moments later they rang off. He only wanted to know that Peter was there.

He then had breakfast alone (the first in the dining-room instead of the last as usual), and then went for a walk to the top of the Earl's Court Road and back again to his hotel.

He went up to his untidy, slept-in room, meaning to pack a bag, but found one already packed for the journey he had meant to take with Netta a few days ago. It was odd how always everything fitted in. He took the reels of thread from the basket he had bought for the cat, and put them into his pockets. Until this moment he had had no feeling of nervousness, but when he came to say good-bye to the cat, which still lay asleep on the dishevelled bedclothes, he had a slight feeling of not being altogether calm—a feeling like the feeling you got just before you went on the stage in the plays they did at the end of term at school, or before you had an important interview to get a job. This was really final. "Good-bye, pussy," he said, and kissed it again. It blinked its eyes lazily, but did not open them, and, not daring to look at it again, he walked out of the room.

He walked out into the Earl's Court Road, and by the time he had reached her house he had lost his nervousness completely. It was five and twenty to eleven. He walked up the bleak stone stairs and let himself in with the key she had given him when she was ill.

He walked into the sitting-room, and heard her call out from the bedroom, "Hullo—who's that?"

"It's all right," he called back. "It's only me."

There was no answer, and he heard her geyser bath-water running into the bath in the bathroom off the little hall. A few moments later she came out from her bedroom, and looking at him irritably yet curiously, said, "How did *you* get in here? What do you want? I'm going out." She was dressed in pyjamas and dressing-gown.

"It's all right," he said. "I only came to give you back your key." And he showed it to her and put it on the mantelpiece.

"Oh . . ." she said, and went back into her bedroom.

A few moments later she came out of her bedroom, with a sponge-bag and a bottle of nail varnish in her hands, and, passing through on her way to the bathroom, stopped to take a cigarette from a box on the table, and to light it.

"Do you mind if I stay a bit," he said, "while you have your bath?"

"No," she said, without looking at him. "But I'm going out afterwards. I've got a date." And she went into the bathroom.

She didn't properly close the door of the bathroom (she never did) and he heard the water still running in. He knew that she wouldn't be able to hear him because of the running water, and he at once went into her bedroom, to her phone, and dialled Peter.

"Yes!" said Peter, angrily.

"Look here, Peter," he said, "I'm at Netta's. She wants you to come round as soon as you can. Can you manage it?"

"Yes, I think so. What's the matter?"

"I can't tell you over the phone. It's all rather weird. Can you come round straight away . . ."

"Yes, I think so. What's the matter?"

"Can you come round in about ten minutes?"

"All right. I'll be round." And they rang off.

He came back into the sitting-room and took off his overcoat.

The water had now stopped running. He hesitated as to whether he should take off his ordinary coat or not, and then decided to do so. Then he walked into the bathroom. She was sitting up in the full, already soapy bath, facing him.

"All right," he said, trying to speak in a matter-of-fact tone. "Don't bother—don't bother. Don't be frightened. Don't bother."

He saw her staring at him, first in surprise, then in terror: he saw that she was trying to speak, but that nothing would come from her throat: he saw that she was trying to scream, but that nothing would come out.

"Don't bother!" he said. "It's all right. Don't be frightened! Don't bother! *Don't bother!*"

He seized hold of her ankles firmly and hauled them up in the air with his great strength, his great golfer's wrists. Then he grasped both her legs in one arm, and with the other held her, unstruggling, under the water.

His shirt and waistcoat were soaking wet when he came out; he hadn't allowed for that. He lit her gas-fire and tried to dry them off on his body. Poor Netta—he had made a good job of it and hadn't hurt her—he was sure of that. That was the one things he had sworn—that he wouldn't hurt anybody.

Soon he heard Peter coming up the stairs. He put on his coat quickly and looked about the room. Peter rang the bell, and he went to the door and let him in.

The blond fascist was dressed in his high-necked grey

sweater and grey trousers. "Well, what's all this about," he said, in his pasty, moustached, nasty way.

"It's all right," he said. "Netta's out for the moment. I'll tell you in a moment. Come in."

Peter went in, and he picked up the golf club—the number seven—which he had already put carefully in the little hall, and he got behind Peter, and with all his strength swung at his head just behind his ear where he understood it would kill instantly. Then he went in front of Peter and said, "Are you all right, old boy? I'm sorry. I didn't hurt you, did I? Are you all right?"

Peter, still standing, looked at him with complete serious-ness and interest, as though entertaining a rather good new idea, for four or five seconds, and then slumped down, bring-ing down the table and the cigarettes and the ash-tray and the lamp with him.

That was all right. It was all right now, and he hadn't hurt either of them. Now for the thread, the thread so that nothing should be disturbed, so that there should be no intruders, and it was all over.

He got the reels out of his pocket and wondered where he should start. He chose the leg of the upset table. He tied the thread round that in a knot, and then, unwinding it from the reel, took it over to the latch of the window, and twisting it round it, came right back over the room again to the nail of the picture over the fireplace, and twisted it round that. Then to the electric-light switch, and then to another picture. Then to the table again, and then to the door-handle of her bedroom, and then round the chair and back to the electric-light switch, and then criss-cross to this and then criss-cross to that. He had to be careful not to fall over it and break it, he had to be cautious and patient and climb through. He heard a door open in the flat below, and he thought he heard footsteps coming up. He paused. Then the door banged, and the footsteps receded down the stairs. It occurred to him that someone might hear the obscure process in which he was engaged, and he put on the wireless so that no one could hear him.

"... *prepared at once to withdraw their troops from Poland,*" he heard, "*a state of war would exist between us* ..."

That was old Neville: he knew that voice anywhere.

"*I have to tell you now* ... *that no such undertaking has been received* ... *and that consequently this country is at war with Germany* ..."

Oh, so they were at it, were they, at last! Well, let them get on with it—he was too busy.

"*You can imagine what a bitter blow this is to me* ..."

He had exhausted two reels and done all he could in here; now he must go into the bathroom.

"*But Hitler would not have it* ..."

He started on the pipe of the geyser, and over to the cold tap of the basin, and then to the window, and then round the leg of the bath.

"*We and France are today* ... *in fulfilment of our obligations going to the aid of Poland* ... *who is so bravely resisting this wicked and unprovoked attack on her people* ..."

Round the hot tap, round the electric-light switch, back and forth, and across. A real net. Netta. Poor Netta—don't worry, nothing should be disturbed: nothing should be disturbed until the police came. It must all be in order for her. He must see to that: he owed her that much. He got tired of climbing in and out, but he meant to be conscientious to the last.

At last the thread was exhausted. There!—he would like to see anybody interfere now, anybody disturb anything before the police came. He had done his duty to them: his duty to the police, and his duty to himself. It was all threaded together. All the threads were gathered up. The net was complete.

The net, Netta. Netta—the net—all complete and fitting in at last.

"Now may God bless you all. May He defend the right. It is the evil things that we shall be fighting against, brute force, bad faith, injustice, oppression and persecution—and against them I am certain that the right will prevail."

He turned off that nonsense, and put on his coat. Then he took it off again because his shirt was so wet. He got close to the fire to dry himself off. As he knelt there, drying himself, he heard the gloomy sirens rising, wailing and answering each other, rising and falling, across the sky. He heard whistles in the street . . .

At last he was dry and ready to go to Maidenhead. Only one thing more—the note on the door for the police. The note to keep people out. He found an envelope in Netta's desk, and a pencil in the pocket of his overcoat, which he put on.

PRIVATE

FOR THE POLICE ONLY

DO NOT DISTURB

he wrote on the envelope.

There. He had done all he could now. He went out of the flat. He shut the door, and stuck the envelope to its outside with the weight of the knocker.

CHAPTER FOUR

He went down the stone stairs. It was all plain sailing now.

Half-way down he realized that he mustn't go to Maidenhead till after dark because that was part of the Maidenhead thing. This was a nuisance and he wondered what he was going to do all day.

At the front door he met Mickey, who was coming up the steps. He stopped and looked at him.

"Hullo," he said, "how are you, Mickey?"

"Hullo," said Mickey, "how are you? Where have you been lately?"

"Oh—nowhere much. Where are you going?" he asked.

"I was going up to see Netta," said Mickey. "Is she in?"

"No," he said, "she's not. She's out. I've tried. Let's go and have a drink?"

"Right," said Mickey, and they walked along together. "Well, this is all very exciting, isn't it?" said Mickey. "Are you staying on in London?"

"No," he said, "I'm not. I'm going to Maidenhead."

"A very good spot I should think," said Mickey, and went on talking about the war and his own plans.

They went into the pub, and he ordered a double whisky. He had only taken one sip at this, when he began to tremble violently and to feel everything swimming around him. He had to go to a chair.

"All right, take it easy, old boy," said Mickey, "drink up, and you'll soon be all right . . . What's the matter—our old friend Hangover Square?"

"Yes," he said, "I'm afraid it must be."

He hadn't known his body would do this. His mind was all right; he had done everything as it should be done; he had nothing on his conscience; he was quite safe, and he was going to Maidenhead; but his body was letting him down; his body had a feeling of disgust and it made him tremble.

Mickey plied him with drink, and he soon felt better again. Soon he saw that Mickey wanted to get drunk about the war, and he decided to join him and get a bit drunk too. He had all the day to waste and it was the last time he would get drunk, because at Maidenhead there would only be an occasional beer.

They stayed on and on and at last were turned out when the pub closed in the afternoon. He asked Mickey where he was going and Mickey said he thought he'd have another shot at Netta, and asked George to come up with him.

"I don't think you'll find her there," he said, but Mickey said, "Well, I'll have a try anyway. Come on. Come with me."

"No," he said, "I think I'll get off now. I've got a lot of things to do. Well, so long, old boy." And he left Mickey looking rather surprised and funny in the street . . . (Mickey had already said, in the course of their drinking, "You're having one of your dumb moods, aren't you, George, old boy?")

It was a nuisance about Mickey wanting to go up. He would find the note and tell the police. And then they would start meddling with him. He wanted to help them all he could, but they musn't start meddling until he was in Maidenhead.

He walked up the Earl's Court Road. This was bad. Mickey might phone the police at once, and then they would be looking for him to meddle. He couldn't even go back to his hotel now because they might be looking for him. He had timed this very badly.

In fact, although he had thought he had worked it out, he hadn't worked it out at all.

If he could only get to Maidenhead straight away it would be fine: but he couldn't: he had to wait till it was dark or it didn't work. And by the time it was time to take the train they would be guarding all the stations. They needn't think they could be cleverer than he was, because they couldn't.

Well, the only thing was to walk, it would fill in the time and keep them from meddling; and he was aware that they couldn't get him while he was walking any more than they could get him while he was in Maidenhead—that was part of the thing, too.

He went out by Hammersmith and Chiswick and Gunnersbury—into the late afternoon of the late summer's day.

He branched off into the Great West Road, and walked on and on to the incessant roar of following cars speeding from the town, with refugee luggage and bedding and perambulators stuffing their insides and tied on to their backs. He followed the signposts and did not tire—neither did the cars with their incessant passing noise. It had been cars, cars, cars all his life . . .

At six o'clock he stopped at a lorry drivers' place for some tea, and then went on again, completely bewildered; and then, at sunset, he became melancholy and filled with foreboding.

He looked back on the great deed of the day, and although it made him feel sick and repelled, it did not make much sense— not the same sense as it made in the morning. Even Maidenhead didn't make much sense. He supposed Maidenhead was going to come up to scratch? How was Maidenhead going to solve things exactly? He couldn't quite see. Perhaps he was tired, but he couldn't see it now.

Of course, if Maidenhead let him down there was only one thing he could do, because that would be the end of all things.

He had a peculiar feeling of being in a dream—unable to focus his mind. He felt he had been in a dream for days now.

And yet something told him now that he must not wake from this dream—that only in this dream state could he understand and see in their true perspective the now haunting and repellent events in which he had participated this morning. If he woke up now, if anything happened to change his dream state of mind, he felt that he might be faced with some inconceivable horror of the mind such as he could not bear.

As it grew dark, and he passed out of Slough, he began to hurry his pace, and his melancholy changed to fright. The indescribable misery of the idea of Maidenhead not working had seemed to break his spirit. Keep asleep, his whole being cried out, keep asleep! He didn't believe Maidenhead was going to work, and he had to keep asleep! He entered a pub on the high-way, and ordered a large whisky. They were all talking about the war and did not notice him. He had three more large whiskies and then bought a bottle. He felt better. There. That would keep you asleep—if nothing else did.

A little further along he found another pub, and had two more large ones. He noticed that he had only eleven shillings and sevenpence left. How was he going to live if Maidenhead didn't work? Never mind—keep asleep till you get there, keep asleep till you had made sure! Maidenhead would work yet. It must work: he had worked it all out.

When he got outside it was quite dark, and there were no lights to guide him because of the bloody war, and he was drunk. Soon he took the wrong direction, and though he bumped into people who said he wasn't far from Maidenhead, they weren't interested, and he couldn't find his way at all. He kept on swilling at his whisky to keep his mind asleep.

At last he found a gate near a hedge: he went through the gate, and lay down under the hedge and swilled some more whisky and fell asleep.

At dawn he arose, blue and stiff with cold, and saw he was in a field only a little way from the highway.

"Maidenhead 3/4" he read on a signpost, and he walked into the town by Skindles over the bridge.

He had very little idea of what he was doing now, but he was utterly resigned, and he appreciated at once the fact that Maidenhead was no good at all.

It was just a town with shops, and newsagents, and pubs and cinemas. It wasn't, and never could be, the peace, Ellen, the river, the quiet glass of beer, the white flannels, the ripples of the water reflected quaveringly on the side of the boat, the tea in the basket, the gramophone, the dank smell at evening, the red sunset, sleep . . .

It ought to have been, but it wasn't. He had made a mistake. In fact he could hardly recognize it. It had let him down, like Netta.

But as there was no Maidenhead, there was no anywhere, and he had got rid of Netta and Peter, and now of course he must get rid of himself. He had worked that out last night.

As long as his brain stayed where it was, as long as he remained dead, numb, asleep, he would be all right. But he had to get through the day.

He went into the High Street and asked a policeman where he might find rooms, and the policeman directed him to a mean street where he found an "apartments" sign and got a room with a gas-ring on the top floor front after giving up his last ten shillings as deposit. He had now only one and seven-pence left. He slept on the bed in his shirt till two o'clock in the afternoon, missing the cat. "I'd have brought you here, pussy," he whispered to the sheets, "if only I'd known it was no good."

He went out and had coffee and a bun at The Olde Tea Shoppe in the High Street, which cost him fivepence. He then bought a packet of writing paper and envelopes from Smith's, a pencil and five newspapers. They were all about the sinking of the *Athenia*. He was sorry for everybody. Then he took a long walk along the river, returning at about six, and having a cup of tea at the same place. Then, completely penniless, he went back to his room and slept until it was dark.

Then he rose and lit the gas, and sat down in its dim light to write a note. As he wrote it, he drank, with the aid of a tooth-glass and water-bottle, the remains of his bottle of whisky, which was still three-quarters full. He wrote:

Dear Sir, I am taking my life, as coming to Maidenhead was not of any use. I thought it would be all right if I came here, but I am wrong. No doubt you will have found my friends by now. I left all in order with nothing disturbed. This will help you. I am so tired I cannot write clearly. I realize I am not well. I feel in a dream.

Please order that they look after my white cat which I left behind. He belongs to the hotel, but I gave him milk nightly and it was my custom to let him into the room in the morning. I do not know its name. I know that I have done wrong, but I am not well. I do not really know what I am doing. I thought I was right, but now I am wrong about Maidenhead. I may be wrong. Please remember my cat.

Yours faithfully, GEORGE HARVEY BONE.

He put this in an envelope and addressed it to "THE CORO-NER, MAIDENHEAD."

Then he got the newspapers and stuffed the crevices in the door and windows with them, as well as he could. Then he put out the gas and crawled down in the darkness and turned on the gas-ring.

He pulled it near to his face, and it made a dreadful roaring noise, and it smelt acrid and choking. But he was so full of whisky and tiredness he felt he could stand it—he didn't mind.

Before his eyes, great coloured whorls of whisky and gas spread out and closed in again, and spread out and closed.

Then he began to go down a dark tunnel—then he began to go up a dark shaft. He realized he was having an operation. He was under gas.

He was under chloroform. It was like that time, years and years ago, when he was a little boy before he went to school, when he had that operation for adenoids, and his sister Ellen was allowed in to hold his hand . . .

He put out his hand to see if Ellen's hand was still there. Yes, he felt it there—amidst all the whorls and tunnels and shafts. "All right," she said, as she said in those old days. "It's all right. Don't be frightened, George. It's all right."

He died in the early morning, and, because of the interest then prevailing in the war, was given very little publicity by the press. Indeed only one newspaper, a sensational picture daily, gave the matter any space or prominence—bringing out (his crude epitaph) the headlines:

SLAYS TWO

FOUND GASSED

THINKS OF CAT